ENDLESS SKIES

Jane Cable

SAPERE
BOOKS

ENDLESS SKIES

Published by Sapere Books.

20 Windermere Drive, Leeds, England, LS17 7UZ,
United Kingdom

saperebooks.com

ISBN: 978-1-80055-013-1

'Up, up the long, delirious burning blue'

For Jim, from a place we love, and in memory of John Reeve, whose passion for aviation history was an inspiration.

ACKNOWLEDGEMENTS

Oddly enough I am writing this shortly after *Another You*'s publication day and still feeling rather overwhelmed by the warm-hearted generosity of spirit of the writing community. For a solitary occupation it's an amazingly collaborative and supportive place to work, particularly as part of author organisations, in my case the Romantic Novelists' Association. Joining it was one of the best things I ever did. Friendships with individual authors are important too. My daily check in buddy (just to make sure we're working rather than slacking) is Kitty Wilson and without her to lick me into shape I probably wouldn't be half so productive. I probably wouldn't laugh so much either. Also very important to me are Angela Petch, Carol Thomas, Cass Grafton, Claire Dyer, Jen Gilroy, Kirsten Hesketh and Susanna Bavin.

In particular for *Endless Skies* I need to thank my husband Jim, who not only took me to Winteringham in the first place, but for the wartime parts of the book became my willing research assistant. And I mustn't forget my good friend and patient beta reader Sally Thomas, who is a total godsend in every area of my life. I have used real locations I know around Lincolnshire, including Winteringham Fields restaurant with rooms, The Pyewipe Inn and Hemswell Antique Centres. All are definitely worth a visit, but Winteringham Fields in particular is a really special place and my thanks go to Colin and Bex McGurran and their team for making it so. Talking of teams, Sapere Books have one of the best, and I'm indebted to them for their expertise in making their authors' books as good as they possibly can be and their skill in bringing them to the attention of as many readers as possible.

PROLOGUE

On the long journey home he searches the sky for her face in the stars. It's a game he plays, to keep himself alert as the adrenalin drains from his body. The job may be done, but the danger isn't over.

The roar of the engines surrounds him as he scans the darkness from his Perspex bubble. Most likely they'd come from below, but you can never be sure. Before, he didn't mind, but now he has so much to live for. And he will marry her. He has to.

As the miles go by, he uncurls his fingers from the triggers and stretches them within their layers of gloves. He wriggles his toes but the cold has eaten so far into his boots it's pointless to expect any feeling, even the soft wool of the socks she knitted him. He longs to feel its caress on his toes; it reminds him of lying in the cornfields with the endless blue above, her fingers trailing over his skin.

He snatches his mind back to now. Vigilance. Dawn streaks the far horizon behind him, a scattered line of orange-pink as the night clouds chase the Wellington westwards. Some tiny variation in the rocking turbulence tells him they are over the sea. Exhaustion begins to claim him as the hiss of the oxygen line stutters and fades.

In his mind's eye he sees the airfield, dew glistening in the first rays of the sun. She waits beside the hangar, a lone figure searching the sky, his flying jacket wrapped tightly around her. She believes her vigil keeps him safe. His guardian angel. He is coming to believe in angels.

For some reason the plane is circling. Below him is a field. Two people digging strange square holes. His bubble floats lower and lower. There's danger in the earth, on the breeze — he isn't sure, but he has to warn them. His fists hammer against the Perspex, useless in their gloves. He's screaming at them now, fighting for air to force the words out…

The intercom crackles his name. Again and again. Someone swears. They're low now, flying over the wolds. He shakes himself and finds he can breathe. One gulp after another, and finally he can find the words to reply.

Cornfields ripening below them, endless skies above, they come in to land. The banns will be read for the third time on Sunday. In less than a fortnight, he will claim his bride.

CHAPTER 1

I stand for a moment in the entrance hall, my back pressed against the smoothness of the wall. Outside, under the endless blue of an early September day, the parade ground reverberates beneath booted feet as airmen in navy serge uniforms march and wheel in front of the cheering crowds. Inside the barracks it's cool, calm, with just the faintest strain of 'I Remember You' drifting from the heart of the building.

"Can I help you?"

The woman behind the reception desk must have finished with her customer. I rearrange my face into a smile and shake my head before walking past the vintage suitcases and trunks piled at the bottom of the staircase. Ahead of me is a corridor, one side lined with glass cases, and I dawdle along it as the stamping footsteps fade and the crooning becomes louder, accompanied by the muted clatter of crockery. A 1930s hatpin catches my eye, topped with an elegant twist of silver and an amber bead. I stop, rest my hand on the cabinet, picturing the pin on the vintage glass dish on my washstand at home in Southampton. No use buying it now.

At the end of the passageway is another staircase, identical to the first. Sunshine from the metal-framed window half way up sparkles on the brass handrail and floods the dark green lino with light. If I close my eyes I can almost hear the airmen running up and down. Not anymore. Today Hemswell's heady labyrinth of rooms is given over to antiques' traders. That's why I came — I adore antiques.

My love of such things comes from my grandmother. On wet Saturdays we'd amble around Leominster, in and out of shops, taking all day to choose just one new piece to add to her collection. Very often we'd simply pontificate. 'Only buy it if it catches at your heart, Rachel.' That's what she used to say.

But what's catching at my heart now is grief. Three long years without her and look how I've managed to screw things up. I shudder. At least she isn't alive to see it — although I'd have probably covered my tracks in my usual polished manner and she'd have politely ignored the obvious lies.

At the back of the building is a run of box-like rooms. The first is packed with small items of furniture; side tables, bookcases, a teak chest with brass corners; the scent of beeswax permeating the air as the wood gleams under the spotlights. The next room is filled to the brim with watercolours; a few on the walls but mostly stacked against them in untidy piles. Far too much effort to plough through them.

Sunlight streams into the room opposite and sitting behind the table is a woman, her dark wavy hair swept back from her oval face and held in place with a tortoiseshell comb. In her hand is a vintage powder compact with a pink rose in the centre of its enamelled lid, and she's using the mirror to apply the last of a stub of lipstick from a gold-coloured metal tube. Her dress is beautifully tailored in navy polka dot fabric with a run of pearl buttons from navel to breast.

There is little for sale in the room. Next to her, on the table, is a scant display of jewellery and to one side a rail of vintage clothing. I flick through the items, mainly dresses, and I never wear a dress if I can help it, but there is a beautiful tablecloth edged with a chain of bright blue forget-me-nots linked with tiny green leaves. The fabric is cheap but the stitching exquisite, each individual flower identical to the last.

I turn around to ask the woman if she made it, but she has gone, leaving nothing but the faint scent of lily-of-the-valley. Motes of dust dance in the sunlight from the high window. As I return the tablecloth to the rail a brass band strikes up on the parade ground. Time for me to leave.

Memories of Gran follow me all the way back to my new flat in Lincoln. My horrid, soulless modern flat. She would have hated it as much as I do. For so long she was my rock, my anchor, the only person I really needed. The only one who *knew*. Although to be fair she was old school least-said-soonest-mended and that always seemed like a good idea to me.

We became close when I was a teenager at boarding school, my mother following my father's army postings around the world. So it was entirely logical when said mother finally washed her hands of me I would go to live with Gran. And she was amazing; convincing me I hadn't really messed up my life and chivvying me to apply for a university place through clearing. All right, it wouldn't be Oxford, but it would be somewhere and I could set about rebuilding my future.

We shared a passion for history and a love of beautiful things. That first summer we walked Hadrian's Wall and later, when I spent my holidays volunteering on archaeological digs, she would always take a cottage nearby for a week. She relished cooking huge pots of food for unwashed diggers and allowing them free run of the bathrooms and fluffy white towels. She lent me money, she bought my tools and books, she argued every premise of my thesis through with me. My first class honours was as much hers as mine, and the same could be said for my Masters degree. Sadly she never lived to see me become

Doctor Rachel Ward but I know no-one could have been prouder than she was.

I need something tangible of Gran with me now but the minute I unwrap her Royal Albert Festival tea service and spread it along the breakfast bar I can see it was a mistake. The achingly stylish cups with their clambering bluebells wilt in the face of the lime green kettle and toaster. Grudgingly, I repack each delicate item in tissue paper and relegate the box to the cupboard in the hall, along with her Murano glass animals.

I sink onto the cream leather sofa. The wall in front of me is decorated with an ugly triptych of botanical prints in bright green mounts. Which match the cushions. Which match the stripes in the curtains. Which almost match the toaster.

At least there are shelves I can fill with books, but perhaps that's a job for tomorrow. I close my eyes and inhale — air freshener and new carpets. When I accepted the post as Visiting Lecturer in Archaeology at the University of Lincoln, they agreed to provide me with somewhere to live. It was the show flat, they said, you'll love it. Well, all I can say is — they don't know me.

But how could they? It happened so fast I hardly know myself. In retrospect, it might have been an error of judgment, sleeping with my head of department. Hardly worth the effort, to be honest, but there was a certain thrill … half hidden smiles across the table at meetings, quickies against his office door with students' feet clattering outside. And a good mind — lord, he had a good mind — and the intellectual jousting was a massive turn on. Just a shame he couldn't cover his tracks with his wife.

I can see him now, clasping and unclasping his hands in front of the tiled fireplace in my living room in Southampton. Muttering. Mumbling. *Great opportunity — visiting lectureship in*

Lincoln — standard-bearer for archaeology at this wonderfully thrusting university…

I'd folded my arms. "I'm not going."

"Come on, Rach, I've already teed it up for you."

"I'm not going. I don't have to. If it's over between us then OK — no broken hearts either way. We'll just forget it."

"But you don't understand…"

"Try me."

"It'll be good for you, Rach … for your career … it's only a year…"

"I make the decisions about my career — not you." I jabbed his chest and he shrunk back, his shoulder rattling a brass candlestick on the mantelpiece. "And don't call me Rach."

"Can't you see it from my point of view? My wife —"

"Oh, so now we're getting to the bottom of it. Told you to get rid of me, has she?" I turned away in disgust. "Just get out."

He slid past me towards the door. "Well, don't say I didn't try. I've got to lose some headcount — thought this was a civilised way to do it."

My half-finished mug of tea crashed against the woodwork. It took me ages to get the stain out of my Wilton carpet.

One good thing about this apartment is the wine glasses are a decent size. I fumble my way through a drawer full of kitchen utensils I'll never use, but I can't find a corkscrew. Frustrated, I stand in the square bay window looking out over the canal.

Across the narrow strip of water is a series of moorings. Three tatty houseboats and a brightly coloured holiday barge. One of the houseboats is chunkier than the others and painted a dull black. I almost expect to see a skull-and-crossbones, but instead the flag curling damply around its pole is a white cross against a black background.

A middle-aged man with unruly salt-and-pepper hair half trapped in a bandana sits on the deck, smoking a cigarette and drinking from an over-sized mug. A wire-haired terrier stretches out next to him, head on paws, watching the ducks as they drift past on the current.

Below me on the towpath a woman is walking a red setter. It stays impressively to heel, tail sweeping behind them. They glide along, serene as the family of swans which has appeared from the reeds to enjoy the evening sun. The man on the barge has finished his cigarette and picked up a guitar. Head bent, he twists a peg to tune it. People everywhere, getting on with their lives.

Sod the corkscrew — I'm going out for a drink.

CHAPTER 2

There are a few tables outside Ask on Brayford Wharf so I settle down to people-watch with a glass of Pinot Grigio.

My attention cannot fail to be drawn to the couple on the other side of an oversized turquoise planter. Her blonde hair is swept back under a pair of sunglasses and her coral lipstick matches her nail varnish and clinging top. A fine-looking man with a straight nose and incredibly sexy cleft in his chin is altogether less obvious in a pale blue shirt, but his gold cufflinks glint in the sunlight and even I can recognise his shades as Oakleys.

There is a sharp undertone to his teasing as she sloshes champagne into her glass. "Look on the bright side — you wouldn't be able to do that if you were pregnant."

"You bastard." It is somewhere between a hiccup and a sob.

"I know you've had a difficult twenty-four hours, Denise, but you could say I've had something of a shock too, so don't take your temper out on me."

"But I want a baby."

"Well, I don't."

"Oh, Jonny, please…"

"For god's sake — a baby isn't like a Chanel handbag or a pair of your Jimmy Choos — it's not a fashion accessory."

I find myself nodding in agreement. Then praying neither of them is looking in my direction. I needn't have worried.

"I know that — it's not just any baby I want — it's *your* baby. Can't you understand?"

A waiter drifts by and the man raises his finger to order an espresso. There are two empty cups in front of him already.

Out of the corner of my eye I see her reach to stroke the back of his hand. He snatches it away.

"You're not getting around me like that — this is much too important. It's a new human life we're talking about and fond of you as I am, if you want a baby then you need to find someone else to father it."

"But what if … what if I had been p-pregnant?"

He looks away from her. "Let's not go there, Denise. Because you wouldn't like my answer."

"You bastard." She is sobbing again and I find myself switching allegiance; it may be no light matter having a baby, but taking active steps to not have one… I down a large gulp of wine.

The man says nothing, offers not so much as a paper serviette to blow her nose. The waiter puts the espresso in front of him and he asks for the bill. Somehow their silence embarrasses me in a way their argument didn't and I reach into my handbag for my phone, pretending an interest in my emails. The waiter returns, the credit card machine changes hands. The woman moves to pour herself some more champagne.

When the man finally speaks, his voice is more gentle. "Best not, Denise. Come on — I'll take you home so you can sleep it off. Tomorrow's another day, huh?" And I watch as she staggers down the wharf in her ridiculously high heels, clinging to his arm as though her very life depends on it.

I drain my wine and fumble in my purse for some cash. I leave it tucked under my glass then make my way back along the canal towards the flat. I stop to watch the swans, but the warmth of the sun on my shoulders just adds to the heaviness of a memory I can't push away.

I may have been seventeen when we met but Tommy was my first proper boyfriend. When I started to feel sick just before my A-levels I put it down to nerves. But after it kept happening, eventually I plucked up the courage to buy a pregnancy test. I stared at the blue line for hours, agonising over what I should do.

I was too young and too green to know that with my body awash with hormones rational thought would be difficult. Before royally screwing my A-levels because I kept throwing up I'd been heading for a glittering academic career and it had always been my focus. But even that certainty seemed fuzzy and remote.

If I didn't know whether or not I wanted the baby I knew absolutely I didn't want its father. Tommy and I had met at the tennis club at the base in Cyprus where our fathers were posted. He was already at university and initially I thought he was sophisticated and hot — probably because of his impressively tattooed biceps — but as time progressed the only thing binding us together was sex. Good sex admittedly, but otherwise he was a bit of a jerk.

My mother, of course, wanted me to keep the baby. She saw Tommy as the perfect match; his dad was my father's commanding officer and for her plain, academic daughter to catch him would be quite a coup. Never mind what said daughter actually wanted.

So when Tommy was due home to Cyprus for the summer she made me up and dressed me up and I was so exhausted by it all I let her. A floaty pink top, cheek skimming cut offs and sequinned flipflops. Well, we were going to the beach. When we were on the island we always went to the beach, to sit in the bar and get drunk until it was dark enough to screw in the back of his jeep.

I figured a little Dutch courage wouldn't hurt so we'd been in the bar almost an hour before I told him I was pregnant. It had taken me most of that time to get him away from his friends and although I hadn't expected him to be exactly delighted his reaction rocked me to my core. First he asked whose baby it was and then he said he'd met someone else, his voice increasingly desperate. So I told him he was welcome to her, that I didn't want to spend my life chained to him and his child anyway so he could sodding well 'f' off.

I remember the blinding heat of that anger. I remember stumbling down the steps, and laughter as I picked myself up from the sand. But after that...

It's only when a woman with a pushchair politely asks if she can pass I realise I'm standing in the middle of the tow path. The intensity of the memory drains away and the breeze brings up goosebumps on my arm. The swans I stopped to watch are nowhere to be seen.

Normally I try not to remember and this hasn't happened for the longest time. I'm unbalanced, out of kilter. I need to bring myself back to now.

There's a bench a little further along and I sink onto it and call the first number on my speed dial. Jessie. My best friend since day one at Southampton University. I need to hear her cheery voice.

"Rachel! How it's going?"

"Pretty rubbish, actually."

"Hey, what's up?"

"The flat is an affront to good taste. There's a leatherette headboard on the bed, the carpets stink of cleaning fluid and the toaster's bright green."

Even all the way from Manchester her giggles make my shoulders drop. "Are you sure you're not just being a teeny bit grumpy about it?"

"You would be if you had to live in it."

"But I thought it had a view of the canal?"

I hesitate, looking around me. "That's the only good thing about it. There are some houseboats moored opposite and I'm wondering if they'd let me sublet it and rent one of those."

"You could always ask. But maybe not straight away, you don't want to go in all guns blazing upsetting them before you've even started. You've got a whole year there, remember."

I groan. "And don't I know it."

"It can't be that bad — you've only been there two days. Anything else eating you?"

"No. I just wanted a moan really. But I guess it's almost teatime in your fully domesticated household so I'll leave you to it."

"Call me again tomorrow — let me know how you're getting on."

"Yes, that would be good."

"I'll look forward to my daily dose of Dr Grumps."

"Oh, piss off." But I'm smiling. What on earth would I do without Jessie?

CHAPTER 3

After a week in Lincoln, twiddling my thumbs and waiting for term to start, boredom has become my enemy and I'm in danger of the wine bottle becoming my only friend. As ever, running is my saviour, my sanity check. Pounding the pavements and towpaths in the autumn sunlight lifts my spirits and makes me feel rather less alone.

This afternoon I decide to try the other side of the canal. My route crosses the road bridge that cuts the university campus in two, separating the student union and lecture blocks from the serried ranks of identical halls of residence. Within a couple of weeks the place will be teeming with students and at least some of my days will be governed by timetables, thank the lord.

The road loops around the back of the buildings to the towpath. I pound alongside the water, my steps in time with the lap of the swell against the holiday barges. Then my route swerves behind a boatyard I hadn't noticed from the other bank and I'm briefly shaded by trees. Out in the open again a car creeps along behind me so I divert onto the grass to let it pass.

The big black houseboat is impossible to miss, its flag fluttering in the breeze. The guitar player is flicking ash from his cigarette into the water. I look away, towards the makeshift allotments squeezed between the towpath and the railway, so I don't see the terrier trotting alongside me until I have almost fallen over it.

I stop and gaze at the bright little eyes staring up at me and the wagging tail.

"Don't mind him," the guitarist calls. "He likes a run. He'll go with you if I don't call him back."

"Doesn't bother me."

The man laughs. "Me neither. Don't worry if you lose him — he knows his way home."

The terrier is undemanding company as he scampers along, claws clicking on the concrete. Sometimes he races into the undergrowth and once he stops to bark at a train. The towpath on this side of the canal is quiet; most of the boats deserted, already shut up for winter perhaps, canvas stretched tightly over their decks. Eventually the road becomes a grassy track before petering out at a low industrial building with an elongated pond behind it. I watch a family of swans feed in front of the sluice gates before retracing my steps, the terrier once again at my heels.

Now there are two men sitting on the deck at the back of the barge, the other bloke much younger than the guitarist.

"Brought Toast back then?" the older man calls.

I stop to draw breath before answering. "You were right — he's no trouble — quite good company, in fact."

"You can take him any time you're passing — just give him a shout."

The younger man is leaning against the rail and I am acutely conscious of my none too clean leggings and the sweat-marks on my lycra top.

"Well, Jem," he says, "perhaps we should offer our new friend a beer for her trouble."

"Another time — right now I need a shower. I … I live opposite … not far…" I feel myself crumble beneath those black, black eyes.

"I know," he says. "I've seen you."

I try to recover myself. "Yes ... well ... you'll see me again." And I take off down the path at what I hope looks like an untroubled pace.

I am surprised when there is a knock on the door of my flat just as I am finishing towelling my hair after my shower and sheer curiosity makes me rush to open it.

"Hello, I was in the building checking the communal lights and I thought I'd drop by to see how you're settling in." In front of me is a dark haired woman in her late forties with improbably large bright pink framed glasses. She holds out her hand to shake mine. "I'm Caroline Barnes, PA to the directors of DSD." I frown. The name sounds vaguely familiar. "We own your flat."

"Oh, I see. You want to check I'm not trashing it?"

Her cheeks almost match the colour of her glasses. "Not at all. I was just…"

I hate to see her discomfort and I grin. "I'm joking. Would you like to come in? I was about to put the kettle on."

She follows me through to the kitchen. "So, what do you think of it?"

I remember Jessie's words about not going on the offensive. "It's… it's very well equipped."

"Oh, I'm so pleased. Of course all the show items were here anyway, the kettle and suchlike, but I went around myself and bought everything else. But it was hard to fathom how much of a cook you were so I hope I got it right."

"It's fine. So do you manage the building as well? I thought DSD were builders."

"Only temporarily and we're property developers, not builders; you know, buy the land, get planning permission and then employ someone else to do the spadework — literally.

But you must know about that if you're an archaeologist — we have to use them quite a lot in our line of work."

"I'm afraid I'm more of an academic. It's a long time since I've been involved with a pre-development dig."

She takes her mug of coffee from me. "So it's not something you'd consider?"

"What?"

"A bit of consultancy on the side. Jonathan — he's the managing director — wondered if you might like some freelance work."

Ah, so that's the real reason she's here, but it's something to think about. My teaching timetable doesn't exactly look full and it's not as though I have anything else to do. "I'd need to know a bit more about it."

"That's brilliant. I can fix for you to meet up with Jonathan if you like. Maybe over dinner?"

An added incentive. I smile at her. "That's one night I won't have to avail myself of your perfectly equipped kitchen."

CHAPTER 4

However transparent Caroline's excuse for visiting me, her natural enthusiasm is surpassed only by her efficiency and one brief telephone call later I find myself agreeing to meet her boss the next evening at The Electric Bar in town.

When I walk in, the Maître D' asks if I have a booking.

"I assume so — I'm meeting a Jonathan Daubney for dinner."

"Yes of course. He's waiting for you in the bar."

There aren't many people about. A couple perch on stools in front of the champagne cabinet and a grey-haired man has his back to me, newspaper spread on the marble surface of the counter. The only other person is sitting at a low table next to the windows, spinning a pair of Oakleys around in his fingers.

I barely have time to register he's the man I saw outside Ask before he is on his feet and walking towards me with his hand outstretched. "Rachel?"

"Yes. You must be Jonathan."

He nods. "What would you like to drink?"

While he goes to the bar I pretend to admire the view. Just my bloody luck. Right now I'd do anything to unhear his argument with his girlfriend, to unknow the cruel streak he hides behind those over-priced shades. Because whatever I might think of him, if I take the job, I'm going to have to be civil to him at very least.

Jonathan makes small talk as we browse the menu. I choose a tiger prawn starter then pavé of beef; I just know when it comes it will be lost in a jungle of pea shoots on a huge plate, surrounded by multi-coloured blobs of sauce and — if I'm lucky — a neat cube of half a dozen chips.

Moving to the restaurant is the signal for business to begin. Jonathan's long fingers break into a bread roll and I ask exactly what he wants me to work on.

"Initially I'll need appraisals on the pieces of land we're actively considering. After that it depends if the planners insist on a dig. But, tell me a bit about yourself. You're currently working at the university here?"

"Yes. I've always been at Southampton before that; my degree, my PhD and then lecturing."

The waiter appears and pours more wine. I gaze past Jonathan's shoulder at the twinkling lights to the south of the city.

"So, how would you propose to conduct a survey of a piece of land?"

"It would depend on the land — brownfield or greenfield. I assume you develop both?"

"Brownfield, infill. I rather like the countryside as it is."

"Then desk research mainly — local history, the archaeological record — published and unpublished reports. I'd need to get up to speed with the area. That should give me an idea of what might be underneath. Walk the ground, get a feel for it — take a metal detector along, even. Then if there is a risk, dig a few test pits if that's permitted. Sometimes aerial photographs help, but if they don't already exist they can be expensive." Just talking about it I find I'm warming to the task.

He nods. "And what would you say is your particular area of expertise?"

"My PhD's related to fieldwalking. Not much use to you by the sound of things."

He shrugs. "If it doesn't bother you then it doesn't bother me. Although one of the sites we're looking at is at an old RAF base so it's little more than a field these days. Anyway," he continues, "it sounds as though you're organised and you've got a bit of commercial nous. Proof of the pudding to come. Talking of which, would you like dessert?"

I shake my head. I'd rather go home and eat the chocolate in my fridge.

"Coffee?"

"No, thanks."

"Well, I'll just have a quick one while they sort out the bill. If you are interested in taking the job, I'd also like you to give some thought to putting together a talk you could give for PR purposes. Just general stuff about archaeology."

"Give to who?"

"Local WIs, Rotary, community groups. It all helps; property developers aren't always the most popular people on the planet." Do I detect a sparkle behind those glasses? I'm not sure, and he continues, "My mother runs a retirement home — you could use her residents as guinea pigs. Half of them will fall asleep but Mum will give you honest feedback."

"Wouldn't it be more interesting for them if I talked about something relevant? Something local, perhaps?"

"Well, you could, but I suggest at least 80% of the talk is boilerplate and you just tailor a small part for your audience. More efficient that way if you end up giving a lot of them. And quite a bit dumbed down from your normal lectures I would imagine. Talk for about thirty minutes, with some pictures and time for questions. All right?"

"And would you like to check my notes?" I find it hard to keep the sarcasm from my voice but it shoots straight over Jonathan's head.

"Good lord, no. What would I know about archaeology? That's what I need you for."

But do I need him? Apart from his appalling behaviour towards his girlfriend there's something about his whole attitude that irritates me. But on the other hand this work could lead to being involved with a real live dig for the first time in years.

I push back my chair and he stands with me. I hold out my hand. "Thank you for dinner. It's been most instructive. I would be delighted to work with your company."

I turn off the lights in my bedroom before settling into the chair by the window. This is a spying mission — although why I am watching Jem and his companion from the safety of my room when I could be over there having that beer they mentioned…

Come on, Rachel, you know the score. That man — with eyes like Jonny Depp in *Chocolat* — he even lives on a bloody barge — spells trouble. Exciting, sexy trouble. And you promised yourself you wouldn't be going there again for a long, long time.

I watch as he stretches his arm, the glow of his phone lighting Jem's face as they laugh at whatever's on the screen. And I imagine those arms around me, strong and muscular, that torso firm beneath my touch.

I am saved from myself by a Facebook message alert flicking across the screen of my phone. *Jessie.* I smile. Paul must be putting the kids to bed. She probably has a deadline — always mistress of displacement activity it's a wonder she ever finished her degree. But she's also mistress of knowing when I need taking out of myself. Even across the miles from Manchester.

How's it going, honey? Followed by Jessie's trademark seven winking emojis.

Still hanging around waiting for term to start. Bored, bored, bored.

Want to write this article for me? Right up your street — best Roman villas to visit this weekend for The Times.

Ha! Could've guessed you wanted something from me.

You know me too well. More winking emojis.

I'm considering my reply when I see she's typing.

Still in a sulk about going to Lincoln?

I'm not sulking… and I don't need you to tell me… AGAIN… that it's my own fault.

She's never pulled her punches about my boyfriends — she's never liked any of them. But then if I'm completely honest with myself, neither have I.

Sorry xx, I add.

It's OK … really. Look, why don't you come to see us this weekend? Cheer you up?

But the last thing I need is her cosy domesticity rubbed in my face.

I'll think about it. Now go and finish that article!

CHAPTER 5

Once again I find myself impressed by DSD's efficiency when the next morning Jonathan emails me the details of a site he wants surveyed in Burton Road. As it's quite close to the centre of Lincoln and I could do with a few things from town, I decide to head out to look at it for myself.

Even from a distance I can see the plot Jonathan has in mind. Two properties on the corner are a charred mess, a huge tarpaulin making a valiant effort to keep out the worst of the weather. To what end, I don't know — this lot is clearly coming down.

An elderly woman pushing a wheeled walker with a shopping bag over the handles stops beside me.

"If you're looking for the Post Office, love, it's gone."

I nod. "I can see that. When did it happen?"

"Must have been about three weeks ago. Those bloody squatters next door. Thankfully Miss Khan wasn't there — it was her nephew's birthday so she was at her sister's. Lost everything, though. Tragic."

"How awful."

The woman is warming to her tale of woe. "Terrible… terrible, it was. All her lovely saris, her photographs of her parents, her beautiful wooden carvings. She can't face coming back, poor duck. Not that I blame her, but we're without a Post Office now. I have to get the bus to town to draw my pension. And it's miles to walk if I need some milk — all the way to the petrol station — and then they rip you off something chronic. It's not the same."

"Do you think they'll build another shop?"

"Not when some developer gets his filthy hands on it. We'll fight it around here, of course we will — Khan's was a real hub for the community — but what chance do we have? Flats, it'll be. And then where will we go for a chat and a loaf of bread when we're too ancient to hop on a bus?"

"So what you need is a developer who'll put a shop into their plans."

"Dream on, love. They don't care about people, only profits."

I stride towards the town centre and walk into a pub called The Brewster's Tap. It's an unprepossessing sort of place, its redeeming features being some original Victorian tiles in the porch and a poster advertising live music. But on a weekday lunchtime the bar is almost empty and the atmosphere redolent with slightly stale beer.

The moment the barman turns I recognise him as the younger man on the boat. Today he's wearing a short-sleeved white shirt with the brewery's logo, but it still seems a size too small as his biceps bulge from under it.

"Hey, it's you," he says. "How did you find me?"

"That rather implies I was looking for you."

"You weren't? Why else would you rock up in a pub on the other side of town. You must have walked past a dozen places to get here."

"Because I've been to Burton Road and now I want some lunch?"

"Kitchen's closed but I can sweet-talk the landlady into making you a sarnie. Cheese or ham?"

Neither sounds particularly appealing but I don't want him to think I'm a raging alcoholic. "Cheese, please." I figure it's less likely to kill me. "And a half of bitter."

He winks at me while he pours. "Cheap date, then?"

"Oh no — on dates I am very expensive, but I assure you I'm worth it."

He stares at my tits. "I bet you are. You've got that look about you."

As has he. I can just imagine how good he'd be in the sack but then I remember myself. No more disasters. Not for a while, anyway. And this guy is definitely a bed-hopper. But it takes one to know one so maybe we're well matched.

Before I am tempted any further I pick up my drink and slide off my stool. "Give me a yell when my sandwich is ready," I tell him and retreat towards a table near the door.

"You haven't told me your name," he calls after me.

I turn and smile over my shoulder. "No, I don't suppose I have."

I decide to visit DSD's offices to deliver my bank details so they can pay me. Of course I could have done it by email but I'm curious to see what sort of company I'm working for.

The answer is one that does modern pretty well. In this case anyway. While the flats where I'm living are dull in the extreme their offices are an impressive patchwork of red and cream bricks, with huge tinted windows. I gaze at it from the car park. I don't know why, but it really works.

Inside the glass doors is a spacious reception with two rows of touch screens, each bearing a different company's logo. I tap the highly stylised bright blue DSD and Caroline's voice materialises from nowhere.

"Rachel — hang on a tic — I'll come and get you."

I follow her through more sets of doors into a smaller reception area beyond. As well as a desk this one boasts a squashy blue sofa and a coffee machine. To one side of it is a boardroom with an oval table, at the centre of which is the latest video-conferencing kit, and at the other an office space with three desks and a workstation next to the window with a drawing board angled towards the light.

"Welcome to DSD," Caroline says. "I'm so pleased you decided to work for us — it'll be nice to have another woman around."

"Well I won't actually be around very much…"

"No-one ever is. They all work from home most of the time. Except Jonathan of course."

"What about the other directors?"

She perches on the edge of her desk and I take it as my cue to sink into the sofa. "There is only one other. DSD — Daubney Sinclair Developments. Jonathan's the business brains and Christopher's the architect."

"Did he design this building?"

"Yes. Smashing, isn't it?"

"Very different to the flats." It's out before I can say it.

"Oh, he didn't do those. Willow Gardens was our first development without him and Jonathan sweated blood to get it right. Chris is…" she bites her lip, "he's on a sabbatical, you see."

I smile at her, "Well, without wishing to cause offense, the sooner he's back the better."

She fiddles with her cuff. "I'm not sure he will be coming back." Her voice is shaking with emotion.

"What happened?"

She sighs. "He got divorced and it was long, drawn out and nasty. With his five year old daughter Charlotte in the middle of it. His wife went off with someone else and he wanted custody but couldn't get it. Every other weekend, that was all. And Charlotte was the centre of his world. It just kept eating away at him and in the end he had some sort of breakdown and his ex wouldn't let him see her at all. He was totally shattered and however hard Jonathan tried to support him it just wasn't working, so in the end they decided he'd take some time out.

"Chris decided to get right away — as far as he could — so he went to New Zealand. At first he kept in touch regularly but then he said he was going off grid, walking in the national parks, and that was the last we heard of him. Jonathan and his brother even went over there to try to get them to open a missing person enquiry but I don't think anyone's actually looked for him that hard. I just keep hoping he's out there, healing, and one day…" Her eyes are filled with tears and I reach forward and squeeze her hand.

"I expect he is, you know. You have to have faith."

"Thank you, Rachel. Sorry for welling up like that. It's just he was such a nice man, so kind and always had time for everyone, and it's ages since I've talked about him."

Yes, I guess she must miss him. Especially as she's only working for Jonathan Daubney now. Not much humanity there. "Well any time you want to talk, I'll listen. Remember that."

She smiles. "You know what, Rachel? I think we're going to be friends."

CHAPTER 6

There's something about the clatter and clamour of a new term that gets me every time. Empty corridors fill with footsteps, ringtones and laughter, the vague smell of cleaning fluid masked by an endless variety of perfume and hair gel.

I share an office with Davina Short, a silversmith turned lecturer, and Andrew Pleat who oversees the history modules. He is intense, grey-jumpered and preoccupied with his research, which seems to be something to do with social class and dinner plates. She is a fish out of water in an academic world with dirt under her fingernails and a bouncing enthusiasm for life which belies her fifty-nine years.

She boils the kettle which sits on top of the filing cabinet and makes three mugs of strong black coffee. Andrew nods his acceptance then goes back to slowly turning the pages of the papers on his desk, scribbling the occasional note.

"So," asks Davina, "what was your first group like?"

"Split more or less down the middle between nervous and hungover. I always think freshers' week should be before term actually starts — then they could enjoy it and buckle down to work once they sober up."

"Some of them never sober up."

"I can remember going through a phase like that." I take a sip of coffee so bitter I almost gag.

"So did I. Quite a long one, in fact. I read law at LSE but I just wasn't interested," Davina tells me. "Scraped a 2:2 then took the first flight to New York and found a job selling high-end jewellery on 5th Avenue. Partied until I realised how vacuous it all was then came home to London and got my apprenticeship."

"What made you come back to the academic world?"

"Partly arthritis in my fingers — I just couldn't do the very intricate stuff anymore. But partly wanting to give something back — help the kids with a brain and a practical bent do something useful with their lives. In my day it was a choice between one or the other and I always thought that was wrong."

Andrew coughs. "Excuse me, ladies, but I really am trying do some work."

Before Davina can open her mouth I ask if she'll show me the conservation labs. She stands, shaking crumbs from her kaftan-like dress. "Of course — but you're not going to be able to keep the peace in here so easily every time."

The workshop is on the floor below our office and stretches along a whole side of the corridor. At one end the room is furnished with large tables, scrubbed bare and waiting for the new term, and at the other it is divided into individual workspaces, each one flooded with pure white light from an LED above. A good number are occupied by students and there is a convivial buzz about the place.

"It's the final years," Davina explains. "Gearing up for their dissertation projects. They did their placements last term and most are building on what they learnt."

"I didn't know they went out into the big wide world."

"Oh yes — some even get to work at the most prestigious museums and the like. Tori — that girl with the unlikely shade of red hair — went to Cairo to work on jewellery from the Twenty-first Dynasty. Imagine…"

But that isn't where my imagination is taking me. Ahead of me is a dark-haired figure in black jeans and a matching T-shirt which barely stretches over his muscular back. The familiarity of it pumps a rush of guilt through my body. *Oh god, don't let the barman from the barge be a student…*

As he turns I can see the celestial powers are not on my side. His lips curl into a knowing smile the moment he sees me and his 'well, hello' is almost a whisper.

Thankfully, Davina is oblivious. "Morning, Ben — ready to start the new term?"

He lounges against the partition, thumbs looped through the belt of his jeans. He's older than the other students, set a little apart… The brunette he was talking to is looking at him like a lovelorn sheep.

He shrugs. "As I'll ever be. Aren't you going to introduce us?"

"Sorry. Ben, Suki, this is Rachel Ward, visiting lecturer in archaeology."

"And how long are you visiting for?" Ben asks.

"A year."

"I'm interested in archaeology myself," he continues. "Perhaps you could help me find some pieces to work on for my final project."

"You mean you don't have anything lined up yet?" Davina sounds incredulous. "What have you been doing all summer?"

"Working. Some of us don't have rich mummies and daddies to pay the bills."

Davina shakes her head and we move on, but Ben calls me back. "Miss Ward?"

"It's Dr Ward, actually."

He lowers his voice to a whisper. "I don't care what you call yourself — your arse looks just as good in those trousers as it does in running pants."

I shake my head but the struggle to keep the smile from my face is just too much.

All day I think about Ben's comment. Inappropriate as it was, it's nice to be fancied — probably too nice. Even so, I'm disappointed there's no light shining from the barge opposite. No clink of beer bottles, no Jem strumming his guitar. Not even Toast waiting to pounce on a passing runner. Jessie would say it's a good thing, but perhaps there's no harm in fancying a bloke from a safe distance.

Is any distance safe? It's been a while now, since I've had sex. The tantalising waltz of a new hand on my skin; slipping and sliding over sweat and more to a crescendo of oblivion. But this man, this is one I really can't have. Not even once for the hell of it. Bad enough screwing another lecturer but you never, ever sleep with a student. This is a temptation I have to resist — for the sake of my career, for everything I've worked for, everything I care about. I sit in the chair in my bedroom, gazing out over the darkened canal for quite a long time. *No Ben. No men. Come on Rachel, you can do it. For a while, anyway.*

The moment I close my eyes that night something's wrong. Ahead of me specks rise; harsh, black, disappearing into forever. For never. Not this again — I can't bear it — the waiting — always waiting, but I'm waving, smiling. Everyone's waving — like a flying circus. While all the time the dread inside is pressing my body down, a crushing weight on top of my baby.

I come to with a start, heart pounding as my hand cups my stomach. The glow of the street lamps filters between the curtains, a yellow streak across the carpet towards the foot of the bed. Normal. Hold it. Breathe. Relax my muscles, one at a time. Listen for the city sounds; a car door slamming, music a long way off.

Engines again. Full throttle. Screaming. Straining. Rattling on the endless runway. In the distance a sliver of moon but then comes the flash. Blinded by whiteness I start to run, jagged breaths sinking my feet into treacle. I. Have. To. Get. To. Him. But arms are grabbing me, pulling me back as the smoke claws my throat, tighter and tighter until…

For a moment I am pinned to the bed but then I can take no more and leap out, pulling my fleece around my shoulders. Get up. Make a cup of tea. Do something — anything — to stop my head from thumping. The clock on the oven tells me it's 3.55. I flick on the kettle, shivering as I wait for it to boil.

Oh, I have slipped the surly bonds of earth. I frown. Where the hell did that come from? It sounds familiar, but however hard I try I can't place it. Forget it, Rachel, do something else for a while to chase the dream away. Mug in hand I curl my feet onto the sofa and start to flick through *British Archaeology*.

And then it hits me — the line's from a poem. Something about a wartime pilot. And the nightmare fits too. I have absolutely no idea what's been nestling in my subconscious this time. Shaking my head, I open the magazine properly, finding an article about Must Farm. That's better. Stuff I need to know. But holding an artefact for the camera is a man I recognise; Charlie Manford, dark curls escaping from a beanie hat. Still just a digger by the look of it. Nothing's changed.

Charlie was the first after Tommy. He was sexy and bright and we wanted the same thing — a no-strings screw. We met on a dig on Anglesey at the end of my second year at Southampton University. I didn't know I'd missed sex until he ran his hands over my T-shirt when we were walking back to the hostel after a drunken night in the pub.

He pressed me against a wall, rough stonework digging into my back, and kissed me. My heart thudded against his chest. I had to take control; it was that or nothing. I ran my tongue around his teeth then pushed him away. "Come to my room in an hour. And don't bring any baggage."

It was good while it lasted. Our paths crossed on a number of digs that summer and the next. But when he turned up in Southampton just as I was starting my Masters I knew it was time to say goodbye. My work was more important than any man.

I fold the magazine and return to the article but my concentration's broken. What would it feel like to find something like Must Farm, something important? That's what made my heart beat faster when I was a student but somehow I've lost it along the way and I don't really know how that happened. The wave of emotion accompanying the thought is surprising and I find myself wiping away a tear.

CHAPTER 7

Over the first weekends of term I've got into the habit of an early morning run. Apart from the steady thud of my training shoes along the pavement all I can hear is birdsong. And not very much of that. They're probably waiting for their little bodies to be warmed by the feeble ray of sun struggling through the greyness of the dawn. The cob swan glides down the centre of the canal but he and I are the only things moving.

Well, not quite. When I draw level with Jem's barge, Toast appears and his welcoming barks split the morning. As he scrambles down the ramp onto the towpath I spy Jem leaning against the door having a fag. He raises his hand. "You walk Toast — I'll put the kettle on."

I grin up at him. "It's a deal."

I focus on the path — that's what running's all about: the steadiness of breath, the first glint of sunlight, the rabbits scattering as we approach. The gentle exertion and the here and now. *Release. Breathe. Will Ben be up? Heart thuds. Breathe.*

Back at the barge, I follow Toast up the ramp. The only sign of Jem is the acrid tang of cigarette smoke but he must have heard us because he calls to come in. The interior is brighter than I expected, the living space wider. The windows may look black from the outside but from here there is a perfect view of both towpaths and my block of flats at Willow Gardens beyond. Along the first half of the canal side is a kitchen area and a battered metal kettle whistles on a gas ring. Reclaimed pine benches covered with an eclectic mix of rugs line the rest of the walls and Jem's guitar is propped in a corner. At the far end the wall becomes a bookcase, split down the centre by a bamboo curtain which must lead to the sleeping area.

"Wow — it's bigger than I thought."

"Most people say that but it's an industrial barge so there's more space. In the days it was in use there would have been an outdoor deck piled with coal or suchlike with the family living in a tiny cabin around the wheelhouse."

"Does it still go?"

Jem shakes his head, his salt-and-pepper hair escaping from his bandana. "Haven't got the money to do the engine. Or the knowledge. Ben says he'll help me but somehow he never gets around to it." He laughs.

I settle on a bench with a view of the canal while he pours water from the screaming kettle into an enamel teapot. He turns to me. "Fancy some t-o-a-s-t? Can't say the actual word or he thinks it's his breakfast time too." All the same, the little dog is wagging his tail.

"I think he can spell."

"Yeah — better than me probably."

As Jem cuts two enormous wedges of bread from a wholemeal loaf I ask him how the dog got his name.

"Bit of a joke, really. I'd had a few drinks when I stole him."

"You stole him?"

"It's not what you think. We were doing a gig in a pub and these guys brought him in. Cowering under their table, he was — just a little scrap of a puppy — and one bloke kept tugging on his lead and saying, 'you move and you're toast'. I was watching all the time we were playing and getting madder and madder, but in the end two of them left and the other one went to chat up the barmaid. He was still there while we were packing up so I just slipped Toast's lead and popped him in the van with our gear. I reckon we were miles away before he even noticed he was missing."

"He's a friendly little chap given what he's been through."

"I think that was his problem — he's always been so trusting. But you're all right with me, aren't you, buddy?" Jem ruffles his ears as he bends to take the milk and butter from the fridge.

"So do you make your living from music?"

"That and taking in lodgers. I'd prefer my own space but needs must and Ben's no trouble. Spends more time in the pub than he does here. But I don't suppose I should be saying that to one of his teachers."

I shrug. "He's an adult — it's up to him. But he must be bright enough to get as far as his final year."

"I don't know about that but he's good at the practical stuff — really gifted with his hands. Probably sweet-talks his way through the academic side."

"Well he's not going to be able to sweet-talk me."

Jem raises an eyebrow. "He'll probably try. He's taken quite a shine to you, but on the other hand it might actually motivate him to get off his arse and do some work."

"He's chosen an ambitious project so he's going to have to pull his finger out. And he was late starting."

Jem reaches under the grill and starts to butter the toast. "Kids, huh."

I smile. "Yeah. Kids."

"I wouldn't go back, you know. Couldn't keep up with the pace. We did a gig at the Tap last night — one drink to wind down and I was in bed by midnight. Still no sign of Ben. Not that that's unusual."

"Is he in the band too?"

Jem snorts. "He's tone deaf. He worked behind the bar there over the summer but now he's back to just roadying for us. We pay him money which helps him pay me rent. Bizarre."

"That's capitalism for you."

"Guess so."

The tea is scalding hot and bitter strong. I look over Jem's head and find I am gazing up into my bedroom window, so close I can make out the leather chair, which has yesterday's bra slung over the back of it.

I'll have to be more careful with my curtains.

And my underwear.

CHAPTER 8

I had almost forgotten I'm meant to be preparing a PR talk for DSD, but then Jonathan emails me the address of The Firs, his mother's retirement home. It's in a village called Winteringham on the banks of the Humber. The name rings a vague bell and after a while I remember it's right at the very end of Roman Ermine Street and there's always been something of a conundrum about how — and where — they crossed the river. Inspiration strikes — the topic for my talk has just presented itself — but it would be good to see the lie of the land first.

I text Jonathan to tell him and feel slightly awkward when he asks me for lunch at a restaurant in the village. As much as I don't want to see him, I don't really have a reason to refuse.

The further north I drive from Lincoln the wider the skies become. Up old Ermine Street, past the turn off to Hemswell Antique Centres, and after a while I glimpse the Humber for myself. Fields roll away on either side but ahead is a glistening expanse of water with hills rising beyond. Although I've never been here before, the openness of the countryside has a familiarity that all but takes my breath away.

In Winteringham, I leave my car below a terrace of impressively well-kept Georgian and Jacobean cottages, some red-brick warm and others whitewashed. A late flowering pink rose rambles across one of them, its last blooms fading gracefully, making the whole image picture-perfect.

In front of me an untidily shaped crossroads is watched over by a double-fronted post office and general store. The road to the right slopes gently downhill towards the river and is lined with houses just as well kept as the ones where I parked my car. The nearest are older properties fronting the road, but as I approach the edge of the village gardens appear and the buildings are more well-spaced, suburban almost. To my left is a farm and the vista opens with fields on either side, a tractor making slow progress down one of them, the plough behind it churning stubble into the rich brown earth.

The road veers to the left but a track carries on towards a muddy creek. To my astonishment a yacht club lies at the end of it, some boats askew where the receding tide abandoned them and others with masts upright, neatly parked on trailers on the grass.

I take the isolated footpath which runs along the top of a dyke. From this height I can see the creek wriggling its way to the river proper, a dark gash in the marshy land. Above me the silence is broken by the growing thrum of engines and I look up to see half a dozen aircraft heading out over the North Sea, light glinting from their glass noses and cockpits.

The sun is flitting from cloud to cloud and as I stand in awe of the broadness of the sky a breeze springs up and ruffles my hair. The footpath could take me as far as the next village but to the south west the horizon is turning an ominous grey. This is a sky which goes on forever, echoing the flatness of the land, the faded gold of stubble sliced by the squareness of ditch cuts and dykes against the rolling mass of cumulus above.

And ahead of me is the Humber in all its majesty. Sluggish and brown on the receding tide but consulting my Ordnance Survey map the number of sandbanks in this stretch make it the most likely place for a ford across the river. The only other option for the Roman crossing is a mile or so downstream — right at the end of Ermine Street — where perhaps a harbour could have been built.

I scramble down the bank onto a metalled track that doubles back towards the village. From this angle I can see Winteringham is built on a gentle rise, the pastures around it oases of green in the midst of the ploughed fields closest to the river. After half a mile or so the track gives way to a footpath which runs alongside a drainage ditch slashed deep into the earth.

I am two thirds of the way to the village when I hear it; the steady patter of a million footsteps chasing across the stubble behind me. It's impossible not to swivel around, heart in my mouth, but as I do so the first drops reach me, the advance guard not of a cohort of Roman soldiers, but of a curtain of rain. I take to my heels and escape over a wooden footbridge into the thicket beyond, the droplets of water running off my anorak and soaking into my trousers. As I catch my breath I can hear more planes overhead but when I look up they're obscured by branches and cloud.

Although I am ten minutes early for lunch I find Jonathan sitting under an enormous garden umbrella in the courtyard of a restaurant near the crossroads called Winteringham Fields. As I approach he stands to greet me, putting his newspaper down next to an empty espresso cup.

"Hello, Rachel — I managed to dodge that shower effectively, but we can go inside now if you prefer."

"No — it's fine here."

He hands me a dry cushion and almost before I've made myself comfortable in the rattan cube chair a waiter appears to take our drinks order.

"It's a set *menu du jour*," Jonathan explains with impeccable French pronunciation. "Six courses might seem a lot at lunchtime but none of them are very big and the food here is an absolute experience. Exquisite in fact."

"Well, that's OK — I won't have to cook tonight."

"Me neither — Mum said she'd eat at work when she heard I was going out."

"You live with your mother?" I try to take the surprise out of my voice.

"She lives at The Firs but she does like to escape sometimes." He winks. "Now tell me, Rachel, how are you settling into Willow Gardens?"

The waiter brings our drinks; a tall glass of mineral water and another espresso. I am just about to curse that my moment has passed when Jonathan repeats his question.

"Look … I don't mean to sound ungrateful, but is there any chance I could sublet it and find somewhere else?"

Jonathan's eyebrows furrow above his Oakleys. "You don't like it?"

I shake my head. "It's just not what I'm used to."

"But it's so convenient for the university. What's wrong with it?"

"It's a bit … square."

"It's meant to be. It's space efficient." He folds his arms.

This could be a long lunch if I'm not careful. "Look, I'm sorry. I didn't mean to cause offence."

"None taken." But he isn't smiling. "Come on — it's getting a bit chilly — let's finish our drinks inside."

We manage to negotiate lunch around safer conversational territory until the dessert arrives. Neat cubes of richly coloured autumn fruit jelly, a perfect quenelle of ice cream and a scattering of crushed hazelnuts which work together so well my taste buds are almost screaming with ecstasy.

Jonathan arranges his spoon and fork in a straight line down the middle of his plate. "I really don't know how they do it. Every ingredient perfect and put together in such a way ... attention to detail, I guess. And huge skill."

"And knowing what people like to eat."

He swirls the last of his wine around in his glass. "Know your customer — it's vital."

"Is that how you decide what to build on a plot of land? Knowing your customer?"

"Pretty much. For me it's largely dictated by where the land is. I mean, there's no point building to the same spec as Willow Gardens in Burton Road — you'd never get the money for it."

"Does the finished spec make that much difference to the cost?"

"It can do. And sometimes we're working with pretty tight margins. Take Burton Road, for example; I can get six one-bedroomed flats onto that site — I'll need to sell four of them to break even — five if something goes wrong along the way. So all six before I see a profit."

"So you wouldn't think of putting a Post Office back there?"

He shakes his head. "It isn't needed."

"Yes, it is."

"Oh come on, Rachel — nobody uses local Post Offices anymore — up and down the country they're having to close. I expect the owner's glad to take the insurance money and run."

"How can you say that? She lost everything in the fire — all her family pictures — everything."

He folds his arms. "How do you know?"

"I went up there to see the site and I got talking to this lady and she told me. And she used the Post Office — it was the heart of their little community — so it seems I know more about it than you. The residents will fight you and..."

"I do not pay you to gossip on street corners." He stands up, startling the waitress who has come to clear the plates. "Wait here — I'll get the bill."

Instead I choose to wait outside. Not that I have to wait at all, but good manners dictate I should thank Jonathan for lunch. And graciously accept the apology he owes me. I hear footsteps behind me and I turn. "Thank you for the meal — you were right, the food here is something special."

He inclines his head in my direction. "Indeed. Email me to let me know when I can expect your factual report on Burton Road."

Rather than trail after him I watch as he strides up the drive and disappears in the direction of the crossroads. *Arrogant shit.*

His words prompt me to finish my report so as soon as I get home I add the final touches and email it to Jonathan. Then I message Jessie: *I need someone to pat me on the head and tell me I've been a good girl.*

But it's her children's bedtime and there's no reply. As I wait I put a carton of soup in the microwave and pull some cheese from the fridge to make a sandwich. I'm just contemplating adding a rasher or two of bacon when my phone rings. I tuck it under my chin and answer.

"Couldn't wait to find out why my halo's shining?"

There is a short silence. "Rachel? Is that you?"

Shit. "Sorry, Jonathan, I was expecting someone else."

He laughs. "Yes, it sounded like it. Look — I won't keep you — just wanted to thank you for such an excellent report on Burton Road; well researched, sound conclusions. Well done."

"It's kind of you to say so, but that is rather how I work."

"I'd hoped so, despite your comments at lunchtime, but proof of the pudding and all that. Very pleased to have you as part of the team, Rachel. You're going to be a huge asset."

I brush his condescending remark aside. "Having walked the ground, I'm about to start on my presentation for your mother's residents too; if it rains again tomorrow I might have chance to finish it." I don't want it to sound as though I have nothing better to do.

"Don't forget what I said about making it transferable to other audiences."

I try not to sound too scathing. "Would you like me to send it to you to check?"

"No point. The whole idea is to trial-run it with my mother and some of her residents. Sometime in the next week or so, preferably."

"I don't have any teaching commitments on Tuesdays."

"Brilliant. Well, I won't keep you now — you're expecting another call if I remember rightly."

He hangs up without another word and I pull a bottle of Pinot Grigio from the fridge and attack it with my new corkscrew. What is it with that man? Already he's testing my patience to the limits and I wonder whether working for him is really such a good idea.

CHAPTER 9

When I arrive at The Firs the entrance hall is impressive to say the least. A wide staircase with a dark oak banister sweeps a rich navy carpet upwards and the scent of hothouse hyacinths drifting from a blue and yellow porcelain jardinière tickles my nose. The carer who answered the door ushers me to one of a pair of high-backed armchairs, which stand either side of a table covered with glossy magazines.

I hardly have time to study the baronial shields decorating the glass panels which give onto the porch when a tall woman with dark hair pulled back into a bun bounds down the stairs.

Her handshake is firm and dry. "Hello Rachel, I'm Pat — Jonathan's mum. Thanks so much for offering to talk to our residents, it's really good of you."

I can't help but smile at her. "It's my pleasure, and I think Jonathan's hoping you'll give me some feedback on my presentation."

She laughs. "Oh, he can be such a bossy-boots — as if I could teach a lecturer anything about public speaking."

"Lecturers can always learn, you know." I cast around for something to say. "For example, I don't think I've seen that crest before."

"Oh, you probably wouldn't have. This place was built by my late husband's great great uncle so it's only really of interest to our family. Come on — would you like a cuppa while you set up?"

Pat hands me a tea and then gathers a few of the residents to listen to me. Swanky coat of arms or not, Jonathan was right about one thing — most of them struggle to stay awake for even a twenty-minute talk. But not a lady with a platinum bob who approaches me afterwards, making her way across the room on a stick with a pearl handle.

"That was so interesting, Dr Ward. But there is one thing I should put you right on and that's Read's Island. It simply wasn't there in Roman times."

"Really?"

"The Humber's a powerful river — constantly evolving. As you said, it would have been different in Roman times to how we see it today. And there's a wonderful map from 1734 with no trace of an island near Old Winteringham."

Pat swoops in. "I wondered how long it would take you two to meet." She grins. "I should have warned you, Rachel, there's not much Esther doesn't know about the history of Winteringham."

"I'm beginning to realise that. She's already put me right over Read's Island."

"I was going to ask if you wanted a bit of lunch," Pat says.

"Oh, I couldn't put you to any trouble…"

Esther turns and smiles. "The food's not bad, you know."

"And you could sit with Esther and continue your conversation."

"I would like that, if you can spare the time." Esther's voice is light, but there is a catch of something in her milky eyes I recognise from my own lonely reflection. It makes up my mind and I nod.

"Then I'd love to stay — I have a feeling I'm going to learn quite a lot."

Over an excellent lunch of chicken breast wrapped in pancetta accompanied by sauté potatoes and crisp broccoli, Esther warms to her task. From her I discover the existence of some antiquarian reports from the early eighteenth century, which mention fast disappearing evidence of a harbour close to where the Roman settlement was found at about the same time.

"That's fascinating," I tell her. "Rather puts the ford theory to bed once and for all."

"Oh no — I wouldn't say that. In fact, some say it's been proved possible although goodness knows how when we've agreed the river's so changeable. But in the early fifties a local landowner decided he'd try to walk across at low tide. He almost did it too — needed a boat for a bit on the Yorkshire side but other than that he reckoned he was no more than knee deep in water at any point."

"Where did he start from?"

"A little upstream from the village — not down towards Read's Island."

"You know, when you look at the modern Ordnance Survey maps that does seem to be the easiest route — the one with the most sandbanks."

Her eyes gleam behind her glasses. "So the case isn't closed."

"It seems not. I guess it's of particular interest if you've lived in the village for a long time, which you sound as though you have."

She nods. "I was born in Hemswell but came here as a new bride. When my daughter was young I didn't have much time for history — it was rather a full-time job being a housewife back then. But as you get older... I don't know ... space seems to open up around you. People move away, die ... and you have time to fill. If only I understood how to work the internet..."

"I can show you. Perhaps not now — I need to be getting back. But I'll come another time if you'd like me to."

"Rachel — I would love you to."

"Then how about at the weekend? I'll come on Saturday afternoon if you're free."

"Free? Sadly, my dear, I'm almost always free. Just phone Pat and let her know if you change your mind."

I stand up and shake her hand. "Don't worry, Esther — I won't."

CHAPTER 10

As it happens, by the time Saturday comes I have more than one reason to head north up Ermine Street. There are hardly any cars on the old parade ground at Hemswell so I park as close as I can to the antiques' centre and hurry through the drizzle into the entrance hall.

The square space at the bottom of the back staircase is now filled with bookshelves and I'm distracted when I see a signed first edition of Guy de la Bedoyere's *Eagles Over Britannia*. I met the author when he came to speak to our students; such a kind and interesting man and of course we had a passion for the Romans in common. When I was a teenager, in the early days of Time Team, I used to fancy him something rotten and I always thought I'd end up with someone like him. But that was before I discovered what men are really like.

My train of thought is interrupted by the public address system announcing it's almost eleven o'clock and inviting shoppers to join in a two minute silence. The eleventh hour of the eleventh day of the eleventh month. Motes of dust dance down the stairwell and in a distant room someone coughs. I gaze through the window at the leaden skies, the heaviness of the morning settling around me.

At the end of the silence 'The Last Post' rings out. I tuck the book under my arm and turn towards the vintage dress-seller's room but I can't find it. I suppose traders come and go; the books certainly weren't here before. I return to the front desk to pay for my find then follow my nose to the cafeteria.

With a latte and a piece of walnut cake in front of me I set about my real task for the morning. Opening my emails on my phone, I click on one from Jonathan attaching the munitions report on the site on the other side of the airfield. I couldn't believe it when I saw the old RAF base he talked about at our first meeting was here. Coffee, cakes and antiques on tap, it's beginning to sound like my perfect job. As long as I can avoid the boss as much as possible.

I run my finger along the map forming part of the report. There are metalled roads through the industrial buildings which will take me most of the way, then a footpath skirts the straightest edge of the roughly triangular field.

It's ages since I've been involved with a real dig. I gaze at my fingernails; manicured and varnished pearly pink. That won't last if I actually have to take up my trowel. But will I? Or will I just be supervising a team?

One thing's for sure, I couldn't bear the ignominy of stuffing up in front of Jonathan. I need to be ahead of the game and a little bit of fieldwalking isn't going to do any harm. He doesn't even need to know about it.

I go back to my car and change into my wellingtons then head north from the parade ground. To my right is another building, identical to the antiques' centre, even down to the blue and gold sign above the pillared porch. Glancing over my shoulder I notice there are at least three others evenly spaced around the square, which confirms my suspicion they must have been barrack blocks.

I turn left, and then right, up a wide metalled road with a muddy wasteland on one side and a thick hedge shielding a tangle of industrial buildings on the other. Further on the road kinks around a vast circle of concrete that must have been there since the airfield was operational, but I have no idea what it is. I can already see Tuesday being taken up by desk research. I know nothing about the Second World War and the thought of diving into a completely new period both terrifies and excites me.

I stop and look up at the sky; the clouds are racing east towards the distant wolds. I'm only thirty-one, for god's sake, and already I've sunk into an intellectual rut inhabited by Romans. The sort of dried up old academic Jessie and I despised. But now I have the opportunity to change that. I wrap my anorak more closely around me as the rain starts to spit.

Past the remnants of another concrete circle, past more industrial buildings and a mass of shiny grain silos, eventually I reach the field. Frost comes early to this part of the world and the grass is dying back, just a few straggly thistles standing proud. Even the wooden footpath sign looks abandoned but I climb over the stile and skirt the hedge along the eastern side.

The strip of land narrows towards the far end. At best the field's about three times longer than it's broad, the boundary opposite curving away then in again, reminding me of the shoulder of an hour glass. I know from the plan I'll lose the footpath at the northern end of the field but if I follow the hedge line I should be able to see the target area from all angles.

The gusts of rain come and go, and it's for this reason more than any scientific fieldwalking purpose my head is down. As the field arcs back to abut its much larger neighbour I spot a curve of metal in the ground; something which looks like the edge of a coin. I bend and prise it from the sodden earth but it's so covered in mud it's hard to see exactly what it is. I brush it gently with the tip of my finger but it's no use; it's not only dirt — there's corrosion too, and a greenish tint which indicates brass.

I wrap the coin in a clean tissue and put it in my pocket, casting around for something to mark the spot. It is then I notice a man watching me from the larger field. He's some distance away but all the same I feel uncomfortable; he's probably the farmer and I could be on his land. Jonathan hasn't even started the purchase yet. I take a quick photo of the hedge behind where I found the coin and scurry back to the footpath.

CHAPTER 11

I arrive at The Firs just before two but even so Esther is making her way down the stairs to welcome me.

"I saw you from my window," she explains. "I'm so glad you didn't change your mind."

"I've been looking forward to it — but first I have something to show you."

The dayroom is all but deserted and we settle ourselves in a pair of armchairs next to one of the huge sash windows.

"The light's better here," Esther tells me, "even on a grey old day like today. I struggle so hard to see sometimes but I've got my magnifying glass in my handbag — you never know when you might need it."

"I think now might be the moment. I've been at Hemswell this morning — Jonathan Daubney's looking at some land there so I bought a book at the antiques' centre then wandered up the road to take a look. And I found a coin, just at the edge of the path."

"It always amazes me how there's archaeology just lying around and people never notice."

"Today I realised how much I miss actually getting my hands dirty."

"It must be quite a thrill when you find something."

I take the hint and unfold the coin from the tissue before passing the bundle to Esther. First she holds it under her nose then lifts it to the light. Her eyes are filled with excitement behind her thick glasses as she asks, "How old do you think it is?"

"I can't tell when it's in this state — it could even be fairly modern but it's not a size I recognise. It's just a little too small to be a pre-decimal half penny, although that's the closest. I'll need to get it cleaned up first."

"How on earth did you spot it?"

"Experience, I guess. Something about the shape, the angle it was lying in the grass. Instinct as much as anything, I suppose."

She sighs. "I'd love to know how you do it."

"I'll take you when we get properly started on the dig. We could go for a coffee at the antiques' centre too."

Esther looks away. "Oh, I..."

"Well, well, well — this is something of a surprise." Jonathan is inches behind Esther's chair when he speaks and I didn't even notice him come into the room.

"I... I came back to see Esther..."

"Rachel has rather rashly promised to teach me how to use the internet. Very courageous of her — and extremely kind."

"Knowing you, Esther, you'll pick it up in about five minutes." Jonathan laughs.

"I very much doubt that. She's going to need the patience of a saint. Talking of which, how did the gentlemen's lunch go?"

Jonathan draws up a chair between us and hangs his sports jacket over the back before sitting down. "That new chap Graeme isn't doing too well. He's all right for a while when you start him talking about the RAF, but then he gets panicky and asks where his wife is. Ted calmed him down by telling him it was a gentlemen's lunch so ladies weren't allowed but this happened three times. I'm going to talk to Mum about getting him some specialist help. He can't live the rest of his life looking for her, poor bloke."

Esther smiles at him. "That's why you're so good with us oldies, Jonathan, you never write us off to the scrap heap, never assume we're just waiting to die. Although lord knows on some days… But not when I have young friends come to visit me."

"I can't believe you'd ever give up, Esther." Jonathan pats her hand.

"That's because we don't have a choice. Our time is our time — whether it's much too soon or much too late. You just make the best of it. I mean, look at your mum after she lost your dad — she ploughed every ounce of energy into this place and made it somewhere really special."

"She is pretty amazing — but not everyone has her strength of will."

Esther turns to me. "He's being tactful now. My daughter… my daughter… didn't always cope too well… Drank herself into an early grave. I don't think I've ever felt so helpless in my life, one way or the other."

"I'm sorry…" There doesn't seem to be anything else to say.

It is Jonathan who breaks the silence, pricking a tiny hole of gratitude in my resentment. "What's that on the table?"

Esther's bright tone rings slightly false. "Rachel tells me you're buying some land at Hemswell and she did a bit of fieldwalking there this morning. She thinks it's a coin."

"Yes. I was just showing Esther before her lesson."

Jonathan's 'really' is accompanied by a lift of his eyebrow.

"Rachel, my dear," Esther continues, "I'm afraid my sight isn't up to much this afternoon and I'm not sure I could peer at a screen for very long. I think I might have wasted your time."

"You haven't wasted it at all — shall we try again next Saturday?"

"You wouldn't mind coming again? It's a long way from Lincoln…"

"It isn't, not really. I'd be happy to."

"Well, in which case I'll just go and rest my eyes. Thank you so much for coming." She grips both arms of the chair and pushes herself out of her seat. Jonathan hands her her walking stick and we watch her slow but purposeful progress across the room.

I gather the coin and shrug my waterproof over my shoulders. "I'd better be going."

"Me too."

We walk in silence across the hall and Jonathan opens the door for me. The rain is teeming down and his Jaguar is nowhere to be seen.

"Can I give you a lift?" I ask.

"No — it isn't far. Look, Rachel, while I appreciate your enthusiasm, you really shouldn't be poking around at Hemswell until we get much further into the process. It isn't very professional on your part and I'm surprised at you."

"For your information I was taking a walk along a public footpath, in my own time. Nothing to do with the work I'm doing for you."

"Yes, but…"

"And also for your information, there is nothing — and I repeat *nothing* — unprofessional — about what I've done. Should there be any value in the coin I will of course return it to the land owner. The current land owner; not the prospective one."

"All right, all right. There's no need to get worked up about it." He opens his umbrella with a shake and sets off across the gravel, the only sound the rain on the car roofs and the scrunching of his feet.

CHAPTER 12

Davina looks up as I walk into the office. "Ben's been asking for you again."

"Again?" I consult my watch. "I'd imagine it's unlike him to be in so early."

"Just as well you only have a tutor group of one," Andrew mutters as he gathers his lecture notes and sweeps out of the room.

"Not that you're bitter and twisted..." Davina flings after him, but he doesn't even bother to slam the door.

I turn to the kettle on top of the filing cabinet. "Coffee?"

"Yes, please. There's a new packet of bourbons in the top drawer."

"Brilliant — I'm starving. I didn't have time for breakfast after I came back from my run."

"You're nuts, running in this weather."

"I assure you I'd be even more nuts if I didn't." She laughs, but I'm not kidding. Sundays are fast becoming the longest day of the week. "To be honest, I think Ben's struggling — bitten off more than he can chew."

Davina folds her arms. "To be honest, I think he fancies you."

"Rubbish. If that was the case most of the female students would hate me."

"And half the female staff. I can name three or four who wouldn't mind a bit of the old conservation treatment from him."

"You're kidding! Abusive relationship guidance and all that."

"Doesn't stop it happening though, does it? And anyway, if it's a mature student… I mean, Ben's closer to your age than he is to the other undergrads."

Come on, Davina, don't give me an excuse. That's the last thing I need. I fumble with the biscuit packet. "I have to admit he's extremely decorative but rather too full of himself for my liking. Although I do need to ask him a favour — if he has the time."

"Oh?"

I put the bourbons down and take the coin, now in a proper finds bag, out of my trouser pocket and hand it to her.

"Where did this come from?"

"A field near Hemswell Antique Centres that DSD are looking to buy. It's probably quite modern but it would be interesting to know. Always assuming there's anything left to date under that lot."

"God, I wish my hands were steady enough to do it but the cold plays havoc with my arthritis. If Ben really is struggling I'll ask one of my group to have a go, although I suspect he'll jump at the chance to impress you."

I shake my head. "He needs my help, that's all. Look — he can have the pick of any student here, why would he even think of me that way?"

Davina rocks back in her chair. "Cut the false modesty, Dr Ward — have you looked in a mirror recently?"

I scoop the finds bag from her desk. "Not if I can help it. Anyway, I'm off to find Ben."

"What about your coffee?"

"I'll be back before it's cold."

Ben is in the conservation lab, head bent over a substantial piece of pottery. The cotton-wool bud in his long fingers strokes the clay and scraps of glaze are beginning to show.

"That's looking very good, Ben."

He looks up and grins. "Thanks. I reckon when I put the bits together I'll have close to eighty per cent of it. It's so cool."

"Ms Short said you wanted to see me?"

"Yes." He glances around at the other students working nearby. "Fancy a coffee?"

"If you want to talk confidentially we could go back to my room. Davi… Ms Short's there but…"

"No, no — it's OK. I'll grab another chair so you can sit down."

It's a tight squeeze in front of his workspace and I'm all too conscious of the warmth of his body. His smile is inches away when he breathes, "That's better — much more private."

I try to lean away but my shoulder is already rammed against the partition. "So what's the problem? It looks as though it's going very well to me."

"The practical side is and I'm making notes of everything I do — see." He holds up a digital voice recorder. "But it's the archaeological bits I'm struggling with — things like the damage — whether it was caused in the ground or by excavation — how things perish over time and what can slow the process or speed it up. You know the sort of thing."

"I can certainly point you towards some reading which should help. Or you could sit in on some of the lectures I'm doing with the first years if your timetable permits."

"I was hoping for something more in the way of personal tuition." His knee presses against mine under the table. I can't even stare him down for fear of what might show in my eyes. *Get a bloody grip, Rachel.*

"OK — there are a couple of lectures you'd benefit from — one on Friday and the other in two weeks' time. And rather than whole books I'll select some chapters and published papers for you to read. Then when you've grasped the basics we can have a meaningful conversation. I'll block out a couple of hours in my diary the week before the end of term and we can plan the most relevant points for you to write up over Christmas."

"That's brilliant, thank you. I certainly owe you one now. That drink, perhaps?"

"There is something you can do for me if you have the time." I take the finds bag from my pocket. "Have a go at cleaning this up?"

Ben's black eyes are shining inches away from mine. "Anything for you, Ra... Dr Ward."

CHAPTER 13

The car park in front of The Firs is full so I leave mine in the road. The sunlight is glistening on the Humber beyond the rich soil of the ploughed fields and the clock on my dashboard tells me I'm early so I decide to go for a walk.

I'm locking my door when I hear Jonathan behind me. "Hello, Rachel — come to give Esther her computer lesson?"

I turn around to see he's dressed in a thick navy jumper with a crew neck and leather patches at the elbows. It suits his colouring and his smile makes the cleft in his chin more pronounced.

"Yes, but I'm a bit early so I thought I'd go for a stroll."

"Do you mind if I join you? I'm grabbing a bit of fresh air before I get back to work."

I set off and he falls into step beside me. "So what's so urgent it needs doing on a rare sunny Saturday?" I ask.

"There's always something when you have your own business."

"What sort of something?"

He tucks his chin into his jumper. "Everything. It's all down to me with Chris away. Not that I'm grumbling, of course," he adds.

"I never really thought… it must be quite lonely running a place like DSD on your own. I mean, whatever happens the buck stops with you."

He turns to look at me. "Not many people understand that. It's one hell of a responsibility. But the pressure on Chris was worse — if an architect messes up, people's lives can be at stake."

"How do you mean?"

"Not enough sprinklers if there's a fire; calculating loads wrong and a wall falls down."

"I suppose I took that sort of thing for granted."

Jonathan turns to me and smiles, but there's a shadow behind his Oakleys. "People do take a job well done for granted. I suspect your students assume you get everything right, but nobody thanks you when you do."

For a while our footsteps on the tarmac are the only sound and I search the corners of my brain for something to say. And then I remember — I saw the plans for Burton Road on Thursday and had something of a surprise. "So is putting a Post Office in Burton Road part of a job well done too?"

He shrugs. "Could be. It's planning gain. I'll price it at more than a flat and if it doesn't sell convert it back again. Might be a cashflow disadvantage but it will pacify the residents' group and they might even get what they want. If you're right, that is."

"And is that … ethical?"

His eyebrows shoot over his glasses. "It's common practice. Commercial sense." He quickens his pace for a moment then stops. "Rachel, we're both plain speaking people and that means we are going to have our differences, but I don't want to feel there's any … unpleasantness … between us. OK?" For a moment I think he's going to say sorry for jumping down my throat last Saturday, but he just looks at me, head on one side. But all the same this is an olive branch so I nod and he smiles.

We are almost at the point where the road curves in front of the sailing club. "I'm planning on quite a large loop along the dyke," Jonathan tells me. "Your shoes…"

I laugh. "No, they're not really suitable for a hike and I need to be getting back soon, but I'll just come a little further to get a better view of the river."

"It is stunning. I can always treat you to a polystyrene cup of coffee at the club house."

"You make it sound so tempting but I wouldn't want to keep Esther waiting."

"You're getting on well with her, aren't you?"

"Yes."

"I'm glad. She went through some really tough times with Sally but she's always been so brave."

"Her daughter?"

"Yes. From what I understand she was quite a tearaway when she was younger and even when she married Donald she never really settled. He works on oil rigs and she had affairs, so not unreasonably he said he'd leave her, then she turned badly to drink. Such a waste."

"Poor Esther. If I'd had a mum like her…" But that's sharing far too much. I pull my phone from my pocket. "My goodness — is that the time? I'd better run."

Esther is waiting for me in the hall, wearing smart dog-tooth checked trousers and a cream cardigan with brass buttons.

"Pat's switched the computer on for us," she explains as she leads me past the lounge into a small, book-lined room. "I didn't realise they took so long to warm up, but she showed me how to do it and I took notes." She points to a pad, the top sheet of paper covered in large, bold capitals written in navy blue ink.

I smile at her as we sit down. "My gran always used a fountain pen. Seeing one brings back such lovely memories."

"The way you said 'used' makes me think she's no longer with us."

"She died three years ago — just before I got my doctorate. She'd have been so proud, but she knew I was well on my way."

"Who wouldn't be proud to have a granddaughter like you?"

"I don't think that was always the case. I went to live with her when I was eighteen and it can't have been easy having an hormonal teenager around."

"So what happened to your parents, if you don't mind me asking?"

"Nothing. They're fit and well and living in Cyprus. But Mum and I don't get on. We have nothing in common whereas Gran and I did. She loved history too — and she was a great walker. That first summer we hiked from one end of Hadrian's Wall to the other — it was amazing."

"How wonderful. For both of you." Esther's voice is full of warmth but all the same she looks away.

I wriggle the mouse and the screen springs to life. "OK, Esther. What do you want to know?"

"I'm not sure what you mean."

"Well, how do you plan to use the computer? To write letters, send emails, do online shopping?"

"Most of all, I want to be able to look things up. And perhaps read the news — especially if it's in large print somewhere. I struggle with the paper when my eyes aren't very good."

By the time Pat comes in with a tray of tea we are crying with laughter at the antics of some penguins on YouTube. Esther adores them and, it turns out, has an encyclopaedic knowledge of their behaviours and habitats. I am amazed to glance at the clock and see we've been here well over an hour.

"I thought it was time you had a break," Pat says, "but it doesn't sound too much like hard work to me."

"Esther's picking it up very quickly," I tell her.

"Rachel's an excellent teacher and very patient," Esther says. "But that isn't surprising given it's her job."

"It's always a pleasure teaching someone who wants to learn."

"Aren't your students keen?" Pat asks.

"Some of them. And others are there just because they don't know what else to do, or because it's expected of them. It's sad because they're burdening themselves with debt for no real reason."

"I always hoped Jonathan might go to university one day," Pat says. "But he wanted to work with his father and it wasn't very many years before he got the property development bug, met Christopher and they set up on their own."

"Then he probably did the right thing not wasting three years studying. Of course, there are some mature students…" I'm thinking of one in particular, but now isn't the moment to unleash a lustful fantasy so I slap the thought back down and turn to Esther. "Time for a tea break?"

"My poor old eyes have had enough for today, Rachel. But I think, with my notes, I can find my way around a bit and I'll keep practising so I don't forget."

"It's honestly the best way to learn. Just remember you can't break the computer, can she, Pat?"

"Jonathan can always set it up again if she does," Pat replies. "Now if you'll excuse me, I must be off. I promised poor old Graeme I'd drop in for a chat. It takes all my patience to listen yet again about the bombing raid over Nuremburg when he had to bail out, but he's so lonely without his wife."

I pick up my cup and saucer and Esther passes me the plate of biscuits Pat left on the tray. "I suppose the war was so awful it sticks in people's minds," I say.

"Yes. It seems the older we get, the more we talk about it. As if it was the only thing of any importance our generation achieved. I don't know, maybe it was."

"I guess you were still at school?"

She shakes her head. "For a while. But I had to get from Hemswell to Lincoln Grammar and transport became so difficult it just wasn't possible. I got a job in the laundry at the airfield."

"What, in the WAAFs?"

"Goodness me, no. I was only fourteen. And by 1942 they needed them to do more important work. Even my supervisor was a civilian."

"So what was it like?"

"Honestly, Rachel, you don't have to ask. Thankfully the war wasn't the only memorable part of my life. Shall we see if we can find some more penguins to watch? They were rather good fun."

CHAPTER 14

Shopping is not my favourite pastime, especially for clothes, but I can't put off my trip to town any longer because we have a faculty drinks reception on Wednesday and I need a dress. At least I can recycle it for the DSD Christmas party next month.

My mother being so clothes obsessed is probably why I loathe them. I gaze into the window of House of Fraser, trying to summon the enthusiasm to go in, but there's nothing remotely enticing about the mannequins in their little black frocks, standing around a fake mantelpiece decked in tinsel. It's like a seasonal uniform for corporate wives. The DSD Christmas party will probably be like that. And I'll be on my own, despite Caroline's insistence I can bring a guest. The fact I can't makes it a whole lot worse.

The last time I let my mother dress me like a doll I was too drained by morning sickness to care. Of course for Tommy's homecoming everything had to be right; haircut, facial, pedicure (I drew the line at a manicure because my nails were bitten to shreds), and of course, the outfit. I sat on an overstuffed chair in her favourite boutique, air conditioning and ceiling fan competing to cool me, protesting feebly we were only going to the beach.

It was the shop owner who brokered a compromise; a pink floaty top that would sit well over denim cut-offs, and a pair of sequined flip-flops to match. I actually liked the flip-flops. Until they started to cut into my feet on the long walk home after I'd told Tommy what I thought of him. I never wore them again, although they were a dark enough colour not to show the blood. Unlike the shorts. I stuffed them into a plastic bag with my knickers and that god-awful top, ramming it as far into the bin outside my parents' garage door as I could manage with the pain ripping my stomach in half and the stench of synthetic lemon loo cleaner making me retch.

"Penny for them? You look miles away."

I spin around, lurching back to now. "Jem!"

"Well that's a smile to brighten a filthy morning. Are you busy or do you fancy a cuppa?"

"A cuppa would be magic, better than looking for a dress."

He grins at me then winks. "Then follow me."

Jem takes me to a café with formica tables and picture windows looking over the canal and the back of the shopping centre. The tang of bacon sizzling on a hotplate behind the till permeates the warm air, making my mouth water.

"Oh, wow, it smells amazing in here," I tell him.

"Temptation at its worst," he replies and orders tea and two bacon butties.

He carries the tray with its generous metal pot and thick white mugs to a table by the window. As I shrug out of my anorak and hang it on the back of my chair he releases two ibuprofen from their blister pack.

"Headache?" I ask as I sit down.

"Everything ache. We did a gig last night and I got rather over enthusiastic with the leaping around. I'm fifty-five, for god's sake; my body's much too knackered to pogo. And it wasn't helped by our roadie being too busy chatting up the barmaid to carry the gear. We ended up doing most of it ourselves."

"Ben? That must be an occupational hazard…"

"I blame you."

"Me?"

He opens the lid of the pot and gives the bags inside a prod with a spoon. "He said she had eyes like yours."

"Oh, for god's sake." I fold my arms as the waitress brings our bacon butties. "What's that got to do with anything?"

Jem pours the tea, strong and black. "I think he's just a little bit obsessed with you, you know."

"Only because I'm unobtainable. Normally he can have the pick of any woman and this time he can't. It's the challenge." I bite my sandwich, butter oozing into my mouth. "This is delicious."

"I don't know. He'll probably sulk all afternoon when I tell him we had a bit of breakfast together."

"Then he needs to get over it. If I agreed to go out with him, which isn't going to happen, by the way, he'd be fed up and moving on in about five minutes. I know his type." But all the same there's a tingle deep in my stomach that the spark is mutual.

Jem puts his sandwich back on his plate. "You're probably right. There was this girl last year — Russian, she was, over here studying economics. He was the same with her but when she finally gave in it was over in a couple of weeks. He said it was because she was frigid — charming." He rolls his eyes. "But she was filthy rich and I reckon he found out her daddy had a pretty close hold on the purse strings."

"See — I told you. Shall I top up your tea?"

He nods, mouth full of bacon and bread. After a few moments he asks if there was any particular reason I was looking for a dress.

I smile, relieved the conversation has moved on. "Faculty drinks reception this week — and the DSD Christmas party. It'll have to do for both. I hate clothes shopping."

"Me too." He indicates his black sweatshirt which carries an advert for a local beer. "I pick up freebies whenever I can. It's my own brand of sartorial elegance."

"And it suits you."

"I don't get invited to smart parties; I don't need an extensive wardrobe. I've got one posh shirt which I wear with my best black jeans and that's about it."

"Would you like to give them an outing?"

He puts his head on one side, the gold hoop in his ear glinting under the strip light.

"Come to the DSD party with me. It'll be much more fun if I don't have to go on my own."

"When is it? We've got a lot of gigs coming up over Christmas."

"Nineteenth of December. It's a Tuesday. Free dinner and booze."

He pulls a slim diary from the pocket of his donkey jacket and grins. "That works for me."

I grin back. At least I won't look like Billy No Mates anymore.

CHAPTER 15

It's a shame I can't take Jem to the faculty reception as well, because by the time I arrive the gallery in the Art, Architecture and Design building is packed full of people I don't know. Normally a quiet place for ten minutes' contemplation, this evening it's a buzzing, glass-chinking mass of high heels and suit jackets. I take a deep breath and dive in.

Thankfully it's easy to spot Davina watching proceedings from one end of the makeshift bar, looking stunning in a fantastically embroidered full-length navy velvet skirt and matching waistcoat. I feel positively pedestrian in my plain red shift dress and I tell her so.

She snorts as she looks me up and down. "Sex on legs — that's what you look like. Very long legs, at that. If I wasn't a happily civil partnered woman, even I'd think about taking you home."

"Shut up and pass me a drink — lord knows I need one to get through this."

She shoves a glass of warmish white wine into my hand. "Here — it's marginally less disgusting than the red. Let's go and hide behind that sculpture and people watch."

The sculpture is a gleaming metal monstrosity but at least it has bulk and a good view of the door. Davina treats me to acid thumbnails of professors from other departments and even the dean himself. But our amusement is cut short when I spot Jonathan Daubney.

Jonathan has been cornered by the head of business studies, Professor Gerard, and he has a blonde clinging to his arm. The blonde is not the one I saw him with outside Ask. This one is less brassy, with fine hair trimmed an inch or two below her shoulders. She is wearing classically cut evening trousers but even so her cleavage is struggling to remain hidden under her sequined top.

Jonathan nods in my direction and Davina and I walk over. My own cleavage seems to be the object of some inspection as I am introduced to Professor Gerard and I am almost sure I see Jonathan smirk. He introduces me to Fiona, who remains glued to his arm, although she does offer a few snippets of semi-intelligent conversation.

Little is expected of me as Professor Gerard holds court. I spin my empty wine glass between my fingers, refusing a top up from a passing waitress. Jonathan does the same.

"So," Gerard asks him, "perhaps next year you'll actually sponsor a post? I understand you have the lovely Rachel doing some freelance work for you at the moment."

Jonathan shakes his head. "I doubt it. It's expensive and I would need to see a return. So far we haven't been busy enough to justify a luxury item like a sponsorship but our arrangement with Dr Ward suits me just fine."

I raise my eyebrows. "Just as long as you're getting value for money."

"Of course." Is it another smirk, or a smile?

"Well, if you'll excuse me I need to circulate." I turn to Fiona. "Nice to meet you."

Davina walks away with me. "That your Jonathan Daubney? He's quite a looker … if you like that sort of thing."

"He's an irritating, money-obsessed shit."

"Oh, so you don't."

"Don't what?"

"Like that sort of thing."

I sigh. "I don't like him very much at the moment. Trouble is, sometimes he can be quite nice — superficially at least. I guess now he's just showing off in front of his new girlfriend."

"That's men for you."

"I suppose so. But they have their uses." I wink.

The departmental corridor is eerily quiet when I go upstairs to find my flat shoes for the walk home, but there are lights on in the conservation lab. I'm tired, I want a proper drink, but I'm drawn to the room like a lonely moth. Just see if there are any students around first...

Ben is packing away his tools as I approach. He looks up and whistles. "Wow, Dr Ward, you look absolutely stunning. Going anywhere special?"

"I've been at the faculty cocktail party for Lincoln's great, good and especially the wealthy."

"What a waste of that dress." He, too, is making no bones about staring at my chest and running his eyes up and down my legs. It's making the hairs on the back of my neck stand on end and not in an entirely unpleasant way.

"Very sweet of you to say so. How are you getting on with your project?"

"I've been taking a break this evening, working on your coin. Only I'm not sure it is a coin."

"Oh?"

"I was going to see you about it tomorrow but as it isn't really university business why don't we discuss it over a drink instead? There's a new wine bar opened in Western Parade..."

"I was really on my way home."

But he can sense me wavering, even though I'm avoiding his coal black eyes. "Come on ... just the one."

Of course the one turns out to be a bottle. And a platter of bread and cheese to mop up the classy Argentinian red. The girl behind the bar is finding it hard to take her eyes off Ben and something deep in my belly is stirring. Stop it, Rachel — there'd be so many strings attached to this particular hook up it could never be worth it.

Once we've finished the cheese he pulls a fat square of tissue out of his pocket.

"This coin, Rachel … it doesn't seem right." He puts the package on the table and opens it, long fingers peeling away the paper one layer at a time. In the middle is a circle of domed brass, still badly corroded, and he picks it up and hands it to me. Instantly I know what he means.

"So what do you think?" I ask.

"It's curved, not flat. Not that you could tell with all that earth on it — you could only see the edge, after all. But there is a pattern — looks to me like some sort of military insignia."

"That would make sense given I found it at the old airfield at Hemswell. Hopefully when it's fully cleaned I can link it with one of the squadrons based there."

"So it's not very old?"

"Archaeology doesn't always have to be, although if I'm right it will be one of the more recent finds I've come across. I think it might be a uniform button of some sort. Can you tell if there's anything on the back?"

The insignia is balanced on the centre of my palm. Ben moves to pick it up, but instead runs his finger around it, the warmth of his skin brushing mine before he stops and looks up at me.

Hauling my shattering willpower back together I pick up the button and place it in his hovering hand. Before I can pull away he closes his fingers around mine.

"Rachel … you must know … must have guessed … I'm crazy about you."

"I'm your tutor, Ben."

"Please — tell me — don't you like me even just a little bit…"

I pull my fingers away and place my hands deliberately in my lap. "Of course I like you — as a person. Anything else would be inappropriate."

"And you can switch off your feelings, just like that? Because that's not what's been in your eyes tonight."

Shit. "OK, Ben — you're a very attractive young man and you know it. I'm not made of stone and perhaps in other circumstances…" I jerk my head up. "But we're not in other circumstances and I need to maintain a professional distance. Understood?"

"But I don't see why…"

I stand and pull on my coat. "Ben — it's been a great evening and I've really enjoyed your company. Don't spoil it, huh? Go finish the bottle with the barmaid — I reckon you've got a more than even chance of getting lucky there."

"I don't want some moony kid — I want a real woman. I want you."

"Ben, don't be silly. We can be friends, but that's all. And as long as you stop sulking."

He has the good grace to look up and grin. A very sexy grin. A familiar shiver runs down my spine — I haven't had sex for so long this could be dangerous. Ignoring the tremble in my thighs I take two steps towards the door.

"Goodnight, Ben."

He nods, and pours the remainder of the wine into his glass.

CHAPTER 16

I buy a single latte and a single chocolate brownie and settle myself at a table next to the window. Weak sunshine filters into the café as Christmas carols swirl around me. I was so looking forward to bringing Esther to Hemswell for some seasonal shopping but she phoned last night to say she has a cold and isn't feeling up to it.

Being on my own is rather the way of things at the moment, but as Gran would have said, it doesn't do to dwell. Term is finished and in just over a week I'll be making my way to the Cotswolds to spend Christmas with Jessie and her family at her parents' house. I've known them since I was a student but since Gran died they've wrapped themselves around me like a comforting blanket and I'll be forever grateful.

But first, presents. I never know what to buy for the children so Jessie sees to that, but with the adults I have no such excuse. The men are easy; Highland Park whisky for her father and a bottle of Grey Goose vodka for Paul. Jessie's mum is a keen cook and I'm looking forward to hunting for a beautiful brass jelly mould, but it's Jessie herself that's always the problem.

It's a problem in a good way. The present needs to be something special, something a bit unusual, something she would never buy herself. And right at this moment I don't have a clue what that might be.

There is plenty of kitchenalia in the labyrinth of rooms opposite the coffee shop. My hand hovers over a vintage coffee grinder, picturing it on the dresser at home in Southampton, but that's not why I'm here. A butter stamp with a plump cow under a stylised tree is worth considering, but it isn't very practical. Useful and beautiful is what I'm looking for.

Soon I find myself at the back of the building. The sun is stronger now, competing with the electric light to illuminate the little rooms. I stop in a doorway and frown. In front of me is a scrubbed table, bare save for three powder compacts and a small basket of jewellery. To the right a rail of vintage clothing, the vaguest hint of lily-of-the-valley in the air. Why couldn't I find this room last time? I step inside — it's the same, I'm sure it is. As I flick through the dresses I recognise some of them and the forget-me-not tablecloth is still there. I weigh up in my mind if it would be a good present for Jessie's mum, but decide against it.

At the end of the rail, closest to the wall, is a flying jacket. The brown leather is cracked, the colour faded from the arms and the sheepskin around the neck and cuffs closer to rust than their original cream. I run my fingers along a sleeve. It's a thing of rare beauty, rugged yet soft, its story etched into every crease. I look for a price label but there isn't one and I know that although I want it, it isn't for me. It's made for a man and would swamp my scrawny frame. God, I wish I had someone to buy it for.

It's that thought more than any other which shakes me from my reverie. *For goodness sake, Rachel. Sort yourself out.*

I turn my back on the rail and start to trawl through the contents of the jewellery basket. There are some pretty brooches; one a butterfly with red and orange enamelled wings, another a bird studded with diamante, but brooches aren't quite Jessie. There's a string of seed pearls but they look far too delicate, and a cheap cameo on a wide-looped chain. But underneath is a ring and I pull it out to examine it.

Rings are dodgy to buy as gifts because of the sizing, but I place it over my middle finger and it's a bit too big so it would probably fit Jessie. And it's a really characterful thing; silver, with a square cut paste diamond flanked by three paisley mounts on either side, a round diamante rather badly set into each. It's by no means perfect but I'm drawn to it and I know Jessie will be too. I could buy better finished jewellery on the high street but that isn't the point.

That's one gift sorted but I still need to find a jelly mould. Upstairs I wander through yet more rooms, but although I'm distracted by Moorcroft vases and a white china art deco fish that Gran would have loved, my search is fruitless. I pay for the ring and mention the jelly mould to the lady at reception who explains they have four buildings in all, and then I remember walking past another one just a hundred or so yards away, so I decide to try it next.

It is identical in every way to the first, with its run of large and small rooms front and back, linked by a long corridor with a staircase at either end. They could only have been barrack blocks and I find myself wondering about the layout as I wander around. Were the small rooms for officers and the larger ones for other ranks? Were some of them communal areas, or for services? Esther said she worked in the laundry. Where was that? She didn't seem to think I'd be interested but I am so I really must ask her again.

In one of the larger rooms to the right of the front staircase I strike gold. Not the jelly mould I'd envisaged but a wonderful enamelled vintage bread bin, still perfectly serviceable and decorative to boot. I'll need a whole roll of paper to wrap it, but I don't care. I can picture it now next to Jessie's mum's Aga. It'll look perfect.

The drive to Winteringham is relatively short and I find the village in its seasonal glad rags. The shop is strung with coloured lights and a Christmas tree fights for space with the silver birches on the grassy space next to the crossroads. There is another small tree balanced on top of the porch at The Firs, firmly anchored to the wall by thick wires. A holly wreath festooned with red ribbon on the front door completes the festive look.

Esther is in the dayroom, next to one of the tall Georgian windows. Outside the garden is bare of vegetation, a glossy blackbird feeding beneath the bird table. At first I think she is watching him but then I realise he's beyond her range of vision.

She seems to start when the carer tells her I'm here, but then she turns towards me, smiling. "Hello, Rachel. This is a lovely surprise."

"My shopping didn't take too long so I thought I'd come to see how you are."

"Not too bad, thank you. I'm hoping my cold won't come to much. I certainly feel better today than I did yesterday."

I sit down and shrug off my coat. "That's good news. And there's a lot of walking at Hemswell if you aren't feeling one hundred per cent, although I could have always left you in the coffee shop."

"There's a coffee shop? I don't suppose I'd recognise any of it now. Still, I was only there for about eighteen months and that was over seventy years ago."

"I'm not sure it's changed that much. I'd guess the antiques' centre buildings must have been barrack blocks because they're more or less identical and there are several of them around the square."

"Yes, that would be right. Oh look, here's the tea. Will you put your own milk, my dear? I struggle to see it in the white cups but I can do mine by feel. Now come on, what did you buy?"

I tell Esther about the bread bin, which she thinks is a fine idea, then pull the ring from my handbag. The lady on the till found a little box for it and I angle it to the light for Esther to see.

"It's very sparkly," she says. "Is your friend a sparkly kind of person?"

I laugh. "Bouncy's a better description than sparkly, but it's hard to find a bouncy present. I think she'll like it though."

"I suspect she'd like anything you bought her. Do you always spend Christmas together?"

"Only since Gran died. It's good to have somewhere to go."

"Do you ever see your parents, Rachel?"

"They come over sometimes and Dad makes the effort to meet up. He's a typical army type and we were never that close but I'm quite fond of him really. Mum and I are better off apart."

Esther puts her head on one side. "I don't mean to pry, but did anything specific happen?"

My pat answer is 'no, it's just one of those things,' but somehow it's hard to lie to Esther. Even harder to find the words to tell the truth, but I can't say nothing. "We never really got on but after I left school … things didn't go according to plan and … she wasn't very supportive." I grind to a halt, biting my lip.

"It's all right, Rachel, I understand. My daughter and I didn't get on that well either and when you say it, it sounds like a crime, but sometimes that's just the way it is. Of course, there are times I regret it now she's gone."

"Do you have any other family?"

"Oh yes. My son-in-law is very good. He's in the oil industry so he spends most of his time offshore but he visits when he can. In fact I'm expecting him before Christmas, which will be nice. It's just a shame Cassie, my granddaughter, can't come too, but she manages the fabrics section at Liberty and they're manic at this time of year."

"I expect they are. For me it's rather quietened down with the end of term."

A carer appears behind Esther's chair. "Rachel, do you think you could move your car? You're parked quite close to Ted's and he's afraid he'll scratch it — he's not always the best at reversing."

"Of course. I won't be a minute, Esther."

When I come back Esther is holding the ring just inches away from her eyes. I can see her reflection in the window, her face initially full of curiosity, but then she recoils and all but drops the box back onto the table. I stand for a moment before advancing with a loud, "Goodness, it's cold out there now."

Her skin is pale but her voice resolute. "Then you'd best be going, Rachel, before the roads freeze. I'd only worry otherwise."

"Yes … you're probably right. Take care, Esther." I bend to kiss her cheek then pick up the ring and put it in my handbag. She recognised it, I'm sure she did. And it gave her quite a shock. If only I had the courage to ask her why.

CHAPTER 17

The chain of Christmas lights running along the wharf sway gently in the icy east wind as I wait for Jem before entering the venue booked for the DSD Christmas party. I pull my winter coat more firmly over my dress, cursing Jem for his lateness. I sneeze three times. I hope I'm not getting Esther's cold.

I turn when I hear footsteps pounding towards me. Not Jem, but Ben, grinning but clearly out of breath.

"I'm sorry, Rachel, Jem's got the runs real bad — came on in the last hour and he's glued to the toilet. I'm afraid I'm his sub. We didn't want to let you down."

I arch my eyebrows. "Oh, really?"

"Am I so awful?"

"Of course not — but you're one of my students."

"I don't have to be — not tonight. No one will know — if anyone asks I'll say I'm a conservator — it'll be true in a few months anyway. Come on, Rachel, give me a chance."

I try not to smile through my chattering teeth. "All right. It's too damn cold to stand here arguing about it anyway."

The Electric Bar is packed with revellers. As the Maître D' takes our coats, Ben breathes, "Wow — you're wearing that dress again — I hoped you might be." He hasn't scrubbed up too badly himself, in dark grey tailored trousers and a matching shirt with a button-down collar open at the neck. His hair is sleeked back and in his left ear is a single diamond stud. As he gazes down at me the butterflies in my stomach erupt into a seething mass. This is going to be hard.

As soon as I spy Jonathan holding court at the bar I am glad about Ben. At his side is a tall blonde with hair reaching halfway down her black-sequinned mini-skirt. Not Denise, not Fiona — someone completely different. Talk about a new woman for every night of the week. Does she know how disposable she is? Does she care? Or is it enough to be on the arm of a wealthy, good-looking man for a night or two?

Ben nudges me. "Come on — aren't you going to introduce me?"

"Let's get a drink first."

As we weave closer to the bar Jonathan hails us. "Evening, Rachel — what would you and your guest like?"

"Gin and tonic for me. Ben?"

"Pint of lager, please."

We forge further forwards and introductions are made. When I explain Ben is a colleague at the university, Jonathan raises an eyebrow.

"I didn't see you at the cocktail party?"

"Oh — I'm just a conservator — not high enough up the food chain to be invited."

The blonde isn't even introduced and we are dismissed when Jonathan turns to greet two of the project managers and their wives.

At dinner we are seated next to Caroline and her husband. They're excellent company and the evening passes quickly with food and wine flowing. Especially the wine. Ben is most attentive topping up our glasses and as each bottle empties another one appears. Whatever sort of boss Jonathan is, he isn't mean at Christmas.

He and blondie are at the far end of the long table. Whenever I glance in their direction she is gazing at him like a lovelorn sheep. Her affection is returned by an occasional stroke of her hand, and later, once the meal is over and coffee is brought, Jonathan leans back in his chair with his arm around her shoulder.

Ben nudges me. "Got a thing about the boss?" he whispers.

"Of course not. Why do you say that?"

"You keep looking at him."

"Rubbish."

He raises his eyebrows and opens his mouth to speak but I beat a hasty retreat to the ladies. Hasty, and slightly stumbling. *Woah, Rachel — you've had way too much to drink.* I peer into the mirror, haloes of light splashing off every surface. I need to down about a gallon of water and get home as fast as I can.

Caroline is at the bar before me, clearly with the same objective. "Your Ben's a bit too good at topping up the glasses," she giggles.

"He's not my Ben — he's just a friend."

"A very good-looking friend. Almost as good-looking as Jonathan."

"Much better-looking than Jonathan. Younger, sexier. Same issues with women, though."

"Issues?" Caroline takes a slug of her water.

"You know — think they're god's gift — change their girlfriends more often than their underwear."

"Oh — come on, Jonathan's not really like that."

"Of course he is; first I see him with Denise, then the other week it was Fiona, and now it's whatever her name is with the hair longer than her dress. All blonde, all big tits. Like a production line for self-styled sex god Jonathan Daubney. If they weren't so stupid I'd feel sorry for them."

"Not, of course, that it's any of your business."

I spin around at Jonathan's words. His face is whiter than white, with high spots of colour on his cheeks.

Caroline nudges me. "Rachel, apologise — quick," she whispers.

"Why? I've nothing to apologise for; it's the truth."

Jonathan's voice sounds strained. "Except you were unbelievably rude. Even by your normal standards."

"By my normal standards? What do you mean by that?"

"Well, it's not the first time you've made a deeply offensive comment and quite frankly I'm getting rather fed up with it."

"And I'm getting rather…"

Ben is at my elbow. "Come on, Rachel — time we were going."

"No, I…"

"For god's sake, do as he says. Do as someone says, for once," Jonathan snaps and turns on his heel to walk away.

Ben takes me by the arm. "Let's find our coats."

I down my water in one gulp and slam the glass on the bar. "Can't wait to get out of here." I'm slurring. How drunk am I?

The next morning, the rain bouncing off the canal is the merest echo of the drumming in my head. Bloody Ben, refilling my glass like that. Bloody Ben — bloody men. I had a text from him this morning, asking if I was all right. No thanks to you, I told him. I don't even remember giving him my number.

One thing I am sure of — I owe Jonathan an apology. I'm working up to that one. I can't face my iPad just yet. Not until my head stops thudding and my stomach stops swirling. Not until I've had a coffee and a shower. I crawl back under the duvet.

I don't wake again until almost twelve but at least I feel halfway human. I make a mug of coffee and sit up in bed with my iPad on my lap, staring into space. Rain trickles down the window and the sound of a hoover comes from the apartment upstairs. How best to phrase what I need to say?

What I should do is pick up the phone but I'm lacking moral courage. A text is pretty much out of the question — far too casual. So an email it must be. Short and to the point, or long and rambling? What do I actually want to say? I was drunk, I was out of order, and I'm very sorry. But is that enough? Should I explain? But the memory of his casual cruelty to Denise is what makes me so angry and the reason for that is buried far too deep.

Drink talking is my only defence. That and an honest request for forgiveness. Not too mealy-mouthed, though — I don't want him thinking he can walk all over me like he does those other women. Except I'm probably exempt because I'm not blonde. Thank goodness.

I take a sip of coffee but it's cold. *Come on, Rachel, enough prevaricating. Get this done.*

When I log into my inbox there are three emails waiting and one of them is from Jonathan. The heading is rather ominously 'our agreement' but it isn't until I open it the full impact hits home: *Dr Ward, I have decided to terminate our agreement with immediate effect. Please email my PA your invoice for hours spent to date. Jonathan Daubney, Managing Director.*

Tears burn my eyes but before they spill over, abject humiliation is swept away by anger. He is just so up himself. When did he send it? Half past seven this morning — he didn't even give me a chance to apologise and I'm not going to do it now. Over-bearing shit. I hate him. I hate him. And I'm definitely not crying over this either. I fling back the duvet, my iPad hitting the carpet with a soft thud as I stalk to the shower.

CHAPTER 18

The few days left before Christmas drag. No students and no other work to do. Technical reading up to date. Jem too busy with gigs to come out to play, and although he invites me along I'm definitely avoiding Ben. I'm much too vulnerable to even go near him at the moment.

I run through crisp cold mornings and misty afternoons, white spirals floating from the canal as I pound past The Pyewipe then follow the towpath beyond the marina to Saxilby and back. I've screwed up big time — and because of it I've lost the opportunity to work on a real dig again. At the back of my brain is the slow insistence something has to change. Someone has to change. The thought it could be me scares me rigid.

On Friday morning the rain is coming down in stair rods so I drive to Waitrose and buy the biggest box of chocolates I can find for Esther. Back in the car I peel off my sodden gloves and fight with the end of the Sellotape and a roll of red and gold paper to wrap them. I may not be feeling particularly festive but it's time I went to play Father Christmas.

At The Firs, Pat answers the door. When I tell her I've come to see Esther she shakes her head. "I'm afraid she's out — her son-in-law's down from Scotland and they've gone for a meal and to do their Christmas visiting."

"She did mention he was coming but I don't think she knew when. Can you give her this?"

As she takes the parcel from me our hands touch. She grasps mine. "Goodness, Rachel, you're freezing. At least come in for a cuppa to warm up before you drive back."

Pat's office is a modest room with a view of the dustbin store. There are two armchairs in front of the mahogany desk and she motions to me to sit in one while she bustles around making mugs of tea and I ask about her plans for Christmas.

"I work on Christmas Day." She smiles. "I can't expect the staff to do what I'm not prepared to and it's important to make the place as homely as possible for the residents who don't have any family. It's the little things, really — like putting out bowls of sweets and nuts and making sure we finish lunch in good time for the Queen's speech. Jonathan helps too — even plays Santa if we can't find a resident who feels up to doing it."

"That I can't imagine," I murmur and Pat shoots me a frown.

"Why ever not?"

"Well … it just doesn't seem to go with his business persona…" I mumble.

"I wouldn't know about that." Pat laughs. "But he's always had a sense of fun. Of course, there was a dark time when we lost his father, and when Christopher disappeared I thought for a while it might break him, but he's always risen above things. He's like me in that respect."

"So do you work all Christmas?"

"No. On Boxing Day we go to Winteringham Fields with my daughter and her lot. Big family get together and it's great fun. They even arrange games for the kids. Anna's bringing a friend this year — it'll be a difficult time for her so we thought it would cheer her up. She was in a terrible car accident in the summer — killed her fiancé and left her with two smashed up legs. Come to think of it, you might have met her — Fiona — Jonathan took her to the university cocktail party. It was the first time she'd been out in ages."

"Oh, I thought she was his girlfriend."

"I wish! Actually, no, I don't wish because although she's lovely it's far too soon for her and I don't honestly think she's bright enough for him. Wouldn't hold his interest."

I take the mug of tea she's offering and she sits down in the chair opposite me.

"I had the distinct impression they were an item — the way she was hanging onto him…"

Pat rolls her eyes. "I don't expect the silly girl had her sticks with her. She struggles to walk but she hates them with a passion. Says they make her feel like an old lady."

"Oh, I see…" And I do. The tea trickles down my throat.

"So, what are you doing for Christmas? Esther said you're going away?"

"Yes — to a university friend in the Cotswolds."

"You don't have any family?"

"My parents are in Cyprus." I'm aware that isn't really a reason and I shrug. "I'm not into the officers' club social scene. Rather be yomping over the fields with my godson and his sister."

"So you like children?"

I laugh. "Only other people's."

"That's exactly what Jonathan says. Can't see I'm going to get any grandchildren from that quarter, but to be fair I'm blessed with Anna's little ones. I know I'm biased but they are totally adorable and such fun." She picks up a photo of two rosy-cheeked girls in royal blue school sweatshirts. "Go on — say they're lovely and then I'll stop boring you about them."

"Pat — you're not boring — you've barely mentioned them." I drain my mug. "But even so I really do have to go — it's almost dark and I want to get back to Lincoln before the roads start to freeze."

"Good call. It's a weight off my mind Jonathan has a flat in the city so he doesn't have to commute every day. Especially not with the hours he has to work. All hands to the pump at DSD at the moment I understand — I'm just glad they finish for Christmas today so he can have a rest."

CHAPTER 19

On the day after Boxing Day Jessie and I have a chance to escape. We leave Abbie and George with their grandparents, and Paul to nurse the hangover brought on by a surfeit of festive port. We drive to Chedworth Roman villa, a place I've been coming to for many years.

The low winter sun is creeping into the valley as we park under the trees. Frost sparkles on the grass and ahead of us a family is making their way towards the entrance, a boy of about eight or nine running ahead with a gleeful energy I envy with every bone in my body.

Jessie tucks her arm into mine. "You love this place, don't you?"

"I always have. It's not the best I've seen or even the best preserved, but it's the way it's tucked into the head of the valley, so far removed from the present day. Here more than anywhere you can close your eyes and imagine what it would have been like. There's so much more to discover too." I turn to her. "I need a project like this, Jessie, not some field on the edge of an RAF base where I'm unlikely to find anything more than a brass button. Although … even that won't happen now."

"Isn't the development going ahead?"

"It's not that. I've rather upset Mr Daubney I'm afraid."

"Why? What's happened?"

"Let's go for a coffee and I'll tell you."

One of the more recent additions to Chedworth is a low Cotswold Stone building housing the shop and tea room. Jessie looks mournfully at the chocolate fudge cake under its plastic dome.

"Go on — have a piece," I tempt her.

"You must be joking — my diet's gone to hell with Christmas. It's all right for you — you're still built like a bloody racing snake."

"All legs and tiny tits."

She sighs. "Better than saggy tits and an enormous arse."

"Jessie — you're cuddly — and it's contentment. I bet Paul still loves every acre of you."

"Cheeky cow!" But there is a glow about her as she adds. "You're right, you know. He does. And I'm very lucky."

"You have two small children and you probably get more sex than I do," I grumble. "That's not how it's meant to be."

"Don't tell me there aren't any attractive men in Lincoln."

"Oh there are — well, one at least — but I told you about Ben and he's strictly out of bounds."

"Until May."

I groan. "I've already been living like a nun since last summer — I can't go another five months."

"So from what you said outside, Jonathan isn't in the running?"

"No. I got rather drunk at the DSD Christmas party and didn't realise he was eavesdropping on my conversation. And eavesdroppers never hear any good about themselves." I stir the froth into my cappuccino.

Jessie rests her elbows on the table. "Go on. What did you say?" There is a resigned note in her voice.

"Something about the number of women he gets through. I mean, it's true —"

"But none of your business."

"That's what he said. But the thing is … a few days before I actually met him I saw him in Ask and he was being unbelievably cruel to his girlfriend. That's what makes it so easy for me to get angry with him."

"Why? What was he saying?"

"More or less telling her that if she was pregnant he'd expect her to have a termination."

Jessie's hand is over her mouth. "Rachel, that's awful."

I nod. "I know. But sometimes I've seen him be so kind I almost forget about it. Then he acts like a total prick and I bite. At least it won't happen again because he's terminated our agreement."

"Is that such a bad thing?"

"Only because getting back to the coalface is what I think I want to do. I love teaching but I'm scared I'll end up a dried old academic who knows nothing about anything other than Romans. But making the change is scary too. I'll never get a job as a site director without more practical experience under my belt so it means more or less starting again."

Jessie laughs. "You say it's scary but your eyes are glowing. Why not just find a dig over the summer — even if you volunteer — that should remind you how it feels to be filthy, wet and cold with dirt under your fingernails all the time."

"Oh come on, it's not all bad."

"I know. And if I didn't have the children I'd come with you like a shot. Remember when we first started at uni — getting our hands on a trowel was all we wanted to do."

I shake my head. "It seems so long ago."

"What's thirteen years between friends?"

I put my hand over hers. "And what would I have done without you all that time?"

CHAPTER 20

Almost as soon as I return to my flat in Lincoln and start to unpack my bag Ben texts me. *Lights on — are you home?*

I lean against the kitchen unit. *Unless I've got burglars.*

Can I come over — been working on the button over Christmas — want to show you?

Oh god, not now. My head is pounding after the drive and my nose is red and raw. All I want to do is take a huge slug of Night Nurse and go to sleep. *Tomorrow? I've got a stinking cold.*

On my way in half an hour with a hot toddy. Won't stay long — promise.

The boy's insufferable.

All the same, it's nice someone cares. By the time a double dose of Night Nurse has worked its magic and I manage to repair the damage to my nose with a bit of make-up, I feel halfway human when Ben buzzes the entry phone.

He follows me along the hall to the living area. "Wow — this is cool. And it's great to see it from the inside not just a glimpse through the window."

"You're not meant to be looking through my windows."

He shrugs. "Can't help it. The old bloke on the ground floor isn't much to write home about."

I shake my head. "You're impossible."

"Besotted, yes. Impossible, no." He puts a Tesco carrier bag on the counter. "Right — it's hard to miss that kettle but where are the mugs?"

"What are you doing?"

"Making you the hot toddy I promised — although I'll stick to neat scotch myself."

The wonderfully warming mixture of whisky, honey and lemon slides down my throat and tingles all the way to my toes. I curl up on the sofa and Ben sits in the armchair by the window and we talk about our Christmases. He stayed with his mother for the minimum of time — duty visit, no more, no less. So I say how a trip to my parents would feel the same.

"You grow away, I guess," I tell him and he nods.

"Isn't just that, though. I'm not close to Mum and I've never met my dad. Don't even know who he is."

"And does that bother you?"

He takes a sip of his whisky. "Nah. He didn't want me, so why should I want him? And Mum's so rubbish at choosing men he was probably a right tosser anyway. All my life it's been one after the other; alkies, druggies; abusers the whole lot of them."

"You mean they abuse her?"

"She wouldn't see it like that, she's so desperate. Laps it up, whatever they do. It's pathetic."

"And sad," I murmur.

"Oh, she's happy enough in her own way. But I had to get out. And just look at me now, sitting talking to a university lecturer — a doctor, no less. I've certainly moved up and if I have anything to do with it I'm going even further."

I nod. "Education opens so many doors."

He stands and walks across my line of vision to refill his whisky and make me another toddy. As he brings our drinks back to the living area he tells me to budge up on the sofa so he can show me the button. The intoxicating mixture of kindness and the warmth of his body threatens to overwhelm. I screw up my face and concentrate on what he's showing me.

"You were right, it is a button," he says as he hands me the metal object. "Not only can you tell the engraving's an eagle, but I've found where the bar on the back went. You can't really see without a microscope, but you can feel." He closes his fingers around one of mine and guides it along the flat surface of the disc. Sure enough there are two slight dips, a roughness. I turn it over to look at the pattern on the front and his hand drops away, landing on my thigh.

"Ben, no."

"It isn't a button?"

"That's not what I mean."

"You're doing it again, Rachel — your words telling me one thing and your eyes telling me another."

"You have to believe my words." But my voice is trembling and my stomach cartwheeling at the weight of his palm through my jeans.

"No, I don't. No one need know. It's only for a couple of months and then it'll be all right. It's not as if you don't want me…" And he begins to slide his hand upwards. This is the moment. This is the moment to leap up, tell him to go home. Instead I turn my face towards his and he kisses me, his fingers exploring the buttons of my jeans, easing them open, one at a time.

Daylight is forcing its way around the bedroom curtains and slanting across the floor to illuminate three denim legs emerging from a tangle of clothes. A white sports sock strays under the bedroom chair and my bra nestles in the corner next to the bin. Although I am alone, the other side of the bed is warm and I bury my nose in the pillow, listening to Ben's whistling drowning out the boiling of the kettle.

The genie is well and truly out of the bottle. Wrong, so wrong — but reasons and excuses flood my brain; it's not like he's a kid, after all. He's a grown man, knows his own mind.

And I'm not made of stone. The echo of his hand on my breast tells me that.

He's a man born to be naked, an impression reinforced as he strolls into the bedroom with a mug in each hand.

He sits on the bed and strokes my hair. "How are you feeling, sex goddess? Has Doctor Ben's magical cure chased away that cold?"

I smile up at him. "I don't know… I might need a bit more treatment just to be sure."

"I got no plans for the day." His hand traces my collar bone. "Have you?"

I'd been going to see Esther but the cold is a good excuse. "No. But Ben … before we go any further…"

He puts his finger over my lips. "Later. We'll talk about it later."

He manages to avoid later with great aplomb for a couple of hours but there comes a point when even the sexual appetites of a twenty-eight year old are sated. Temporarily at least. I rustle up cheese on toast and we eat it in bed, gritty crumbs chasing down our bodies and into the duvet.

I turn to him. "We do need to talk."

"Women always want to talk," he replies through a mouthful.

"Well, in this case there's very good reason."

"Look, Rachel, there's no need to worry — now that I've got you, why would I want to jeopardise everything by letting on? You want us to be a secret and I promise we will be. Teacher and student by day, lovers by night — what could be sexier than that? I'll be in the front row for all your lectures, just imagining what I'm going to do to you later to make you scream my name."

"You should be concentrating, not daydreaming." I laugh. "I can see I'm going to have to be very strict with you."

"Yes please, teacher," he grins.

"Ben — you're incorrigible."

"Incorrigible, impossible … inconvenient too, I guess. But that doesn't alter the fact you can't keep your hands off me, Dr Ward. And the feeling is perfectly mutual. In fact, it's not only my hands…" With that he slides down the bed, his empty plate thudding onto the carpet as his tongue chases a path through the crumbs.

CHAPTER 21

"My goodness — what's happened to you?"

I look myself up and down as I put my lecture notes on my desk. Shoes shiny, no visible spills on my trousers, blouse buttons in an unbroken line. "I'm not sure what you mean, Davina…"

"You're positively glowing — not what I expect to see in Lincoln at the start of the January term."

I shrug. "It's probably because I've spent the last hour sniggering to myself. Ben Carter turned up to one of my first-year lectures — I told him he needed some background — and those poor little eighteen-year-old girls didn't know where to put themselves. Except the one who sat so close to him she was almost in his lap."

"Hmph. No wonder he thinks he's god's gift to women. Coffee?"

"Oh — please. How was your Christmas?"

"Wonderful. No students for three whole weeks. Just chilling at home with Sylvie and the cats. It was bliss. What about you?"

"I had a really nice time with my friend's family but then I was laid up with a cold. Perhaps the enforced rest did me good — I'm ready to be up and at 'em for the new term."

Davina rolls her eyes. "Well, can you pass some of that energy on to me? I keep wondering if it's time to retire."

There is the faintest of knocks on the door and Ben's head appears around it. "Doctor Ward? Oh, hello, Ms Short — good break?"

"Yes thanks, Ben — and you?"

"Christmas was so-so but I've had a great time since I got back." He winks at Davina and she rolls her eyes.

"Then I can only guess what you've been up to."

"Working hard on my dissertation. Talking of which — Dr Ward, there were a few things in the lecture I didn't quite understand — can we book some time to go through them?"

I look at my watch. "I've got almost an hour before my tutor group. Would we be disturbing you, Davina?"

She shakes her head. "I need to be getting down to the labs anyway." She sweeps her notebook into her shoulder bag and, coffee in hand, stands to leave. Ben steps to one side and opens the door to let her pass, closing it behind her.

I swivel my chair around to face the low sofa which is meant for guests and Ben sits down.

"So — what can I help you with?"

"I wish you were wearing a skirt — I'd be able to see right up it from here."

"Another good reason to wear trousers. Come on, Ben, get to the point."

"Honestly, Rachel? I think I'm still going to struggle. You say I should be starting to write up by now but I just don't feel I have the knowledge — even if I came to all your lectures. And I really, really want a good grade. I'd love to be able to stay and do a Masters…"

I rock back in my chair. "You surprise me. I wouldn't necessarily see you as an academic…"

"Well, it's not a bad life, is it? Before I started here I had a job in the parts department of a motorbike dealer and real work was rubbish." He frowns for a moment, looking uncertain. "But that aside I want to show you there's a bit more about me… I guess I'm worried you'll get bored if I'm not educated enough."

I shake my head. "You must never, ever, base your career choices on what you think someone else would want you to do. Follow your own star and be yourself. You won't be happy otherwise."

"That's exactly what a lecturer would say. But what I want to know is what would my lover think?"

"You should ask her — when you next see her."

For a moment Ben looks confused, but then he nods. "Oh, I get it. I have to pretend we're not sleeping together even when there's no-one else around. Makes the sex more exciting for you, does it?"

"Ben, shut up."

He holds up his hands. "All right... I'm off to do some work. Catch you later, sex goddess."

He is barely out of the room before Andrew walks in. Did he hear anything? His expression gives nothing away, but as he shuffles the papers on his desk the risk I'm taking begins to hit home.

CHAPTER 22

The lights from The Firs' cast a cheerful beam through the glass in the front door, brightening the dank morning. I smile to myself as I ring the bell. Inside a vacuum cleaner stops then warm air floods out to meet me.

"Hello, Rachel — how are you?" To my shame I can't remember the carer's name, but we exchange pleasantries before she tells me Esther isn't feeling too well and she disappears to find out if she's up to visitors.

I sit down on one of the high-backed chairs but before I even have chance to start worrying about Esther the carer calls down the stairs. "It's fine, Rachel — she'd love to see you. Leave your coat on the hook and come up."

She leads me to a bedroom at the front of the house with a bay window containing a round table flanked by two armchairs. Esther is shrunk into one of them, swamped by a cream cable knit cardigan. Her hair is neatly combed but her face devoid of the subtle make-up she normally wears. However it isn't so much Esther who draws my eyes; it's the white hand-embroidered cloth covering the table, a chain of forget-me-nots dancing around its border.

"Come on, Rachel," Esther laughs, "surely I don't look that poorly?"

I shake myself and bend to kiss her. "Well, you don't look quite yourself. What's wrong, Esther?"

"The aches and pains of old age, I'm afraid. Sometimes they make it hard to get up in the morning but I always do. Getting downstairs, however, can be another matter."

"And why should you when you don't have to?" The carer intervenes. "Now, shall I get you and Rachel a nice pot of tea?"

"That would be lovely, Julie, thank you."

To my left is a bureau packed on top with photographs, which proves a distraction while I pluck up the courage to ask about the tablecloth. A black and white wedding picture in a gilt frame is taking pride of place. Esther stands ramrod straight in an elegant full length dress, carrying a spray of roses, next to a portly man with a beaming face.

"You look very happy in your wedding photo," I say, and she smiles.

"Why wouldn't I? Ralph was the love of my life."

"How wonderful — to meet someone you want to spend the rest of your days with."

She puts her head on one side. "I take it that hasn't happened for you?"

"Oh, I'm not looking. I don't have a very good track record for picking men as it happens. Best left to my own devices."

"Well, marriage doesn't suit everyone, my dear."

Next to the wedding photo is a picture of a couple with a small girl on what appears to be a Mediterranean harbour front. The woman has dark wavy hair and her husband towers above her, a protective arm around her shoulder. The little girl has been distracted by a passing cat, which is just in the corner of the frame, and she's pulling away from her mother's hand. It must be Esther's daughter's family, but I hesitate to ask.

"Aren't you going to sit down?"

"Sorry. I got side-tracked by your photographs."

"Dust gatherers, more like. Of course, if I could see them properly I wouldn't say that. Sometimes I potter over and take a closer look but they're all so stiff and still — the real memories are in my head."

"It must be hard…" I venture.

"Sometimes. But I'm old enough now that when I doze a bit sometimes I think they're still around. Well, of course, some of them are — and Cassie's coming to see me tomorrow — I can't wait."

"How lovely for you."

"Yes. She'll tell me all about her whirlwind life in London and I won't understand half of it. She's a wonderful granddaughter but I do worry whether she was damaged by what happened to her mother. I know she was picked on in school because Sally drank so much. It was only Jonathan who saved her from being really bullied."

"Jonathan?"

"Yes — he's three years older so he had a bit of clout with the other kids on the school bus — rather nipped any trouble in the bud I believe. He was a kind lad, even then."

I finger the tablecloth. "This is pretty, Esther. Was it a Christmas present?"

"Yes, but a very long time ago. Someone I knew embroidered it." Her smile seems to come from a long way away and she nods, but any further explanation she may have given is lost when Julie reappears with the tea tray.

All the way home I try to rationalise what Esther said about the tablecloth. I saw it at Hemswell Antique Centres — more than once. But Esther said she's had it for years. Maybe there was more than one — maybe somebody made a lot of them to sell. If you were that skilled at embroidery it wouldn't be hard to make them identical. But all the same… I'm missing something here and it's bothering me.

When I get home I decide to go for a run. The rain is heavier here and before I even reach the park my hair is clinging to my skull, my sweatshirt sticky cold against my chest. Once around isn't enough so I splash along the towpath to The Pyewipe, its lights a warming beacon in the damp afternoon. Further on I go, the traffic on the concrete bridge thudding above my head, until my body is exhausted but my mind refuses to be still.

I shelter under an oak and stretch my fingers to the sky. The clouds weigh heavy, sailing slowly into the dusk. What wild imaginings there? But now I have stopped I'm shivering so I turn back towards the city, distant streetlights flickering into life as it rises out of the mist.

I take my time in the shower, piling the lather onto my hair and scrubbing myself with scented oil and sea salt. Wrapped in my dressing gown I sip wine as I wait for the clock to scrape past five. Ben will have left the university by now — it's safe to call him. I get his voicemail but I dare not leave a message. This whole thing is beginning to make me feel very uneasy, but right now I need him. I need his touch.

It's past seven by the time he turns up and the bottle is almost empty. We're hungrier for each other than for the fish and chips he's brought, but as we lick and kiss and tumble and touch, gratitude wells within me and I cling to him like never before.

Inevitably he notices. As I heat the oven in an attempt to rescue our forgotten meal he asks what's wrong.

I furrow my forehead. "Nothing. What makes you say that?"

"I don't know for sure … lover's instinct?"

"Then it's a little off beam. I feel more like the cat who got the cream, to be honest."

He laughs. "I like it when you purr."

"I like it when you make me."

I pull my dressing gown more firmly around me. "While I was waiting for you I spent some time looking up the insignia on the button. It's definitely an eagle and it's definitely Polish — you can tell because it's wearing a crown. There were Polish squadrons based at Hemswell during the war, so it makes perfect sense."

"I wonder why they chose an eagle? After all, it's the same emblem as Germany and they were at war."

"The eagles go back much further than that, over a thousand years — and besides, the German one is a black eagle and the Polish is white."

"God, Rachel — how do you know where to look for all this stuff?"

I shrug. "It's my job. And if you have ambitions you're going to have to find out too."

"You could always show me … you know, in return for services rendered…"

I shake my head in exasperation. As I sprinkle vinegar on our chips I ask him how his transcription's going.

"Really well — it should be finished in the next day or two so we can start working through it. I was thinking, though … the next thing I need to get into is stratification — you said perhaps you could recommend some papers for me to read?"

"I've got a great book on it — much better."

"A whole book? Rachel, I'll never have the time. Isn't there a quicker way?"

"It's not a thick book — couple of hundred pages — and lots of diagrams. Honestly, Ben, if you put your mind to it you could read it over the weekend."

"I've got other plans for the weekend."

"Like what?" I fold my arms.

"Like spending it in bed with you."

"Ben … you've got to get some work done…"

He pinches a chip from my plate. "Oh no, Rachel, you can't nag me here — that's for the university, remember?"

"I can nag you where the hell I like."

"Oh, can you? Then maybe I can flirt with you anywhere too."

The batter is soggy, the vinegar bitter in my throat. I don't like where this is going one bit, but all the same I need to keep things light. "So don't tell me you've never had a nagging girlfriend before," I wink.

And he smiles, reaching over to steal another chip. "Sometimes, Rachel, you're just too bloody clever for me. Just as well I have other skills, huh?"

CHAPTER 23

Inevitably, at half past six in the morning, the car park in front of DSD is deserted. It took me twenty-four hours of hunting to remember I lent the book I promised Ben to one of the project managers and now I can only hope my security pass still works.

The LED on the lock glows green and I push the door. Inside DSD's reception I fumble for the light switch but in the moment I find it I notice Jonathan's workspace is illuminated by a desk lamp. And he is there; slumped in front of his computer, his glasses next to his sprawling right arm.

The strip light blinks around me — there is no escape. But he doesn't move and a new kind of panic grips me. I take three steps towards his desk.

"Jonathan?" My voice sounds high-pitched and strangled. There is no response. I creep closer and try again, clearing my throat before I speak. "Jonathan — are you all right?"

He turns his head to one side and lifts it slightly. His face is pale and blotchy, his blinking eyes staring at me with an empty gaze. Is he drunk? Had a stroke or something?

I crouch next to his desk. "What's wrong?"

"Christopher — he's dead."

My shoulders drop as the tension floods from me but I am careful to keep the relief from my voice. "What happened?"

"They found his body in his tent … in some woods…" He hauls himself up on his hands and sits back in his chair, closing his eyes.

"Do they know how…?"

He shakes his head. "Not yet. He'd been there quite a while. Oh, god, Rachel — to die alone like that when he had so much to live for…"

"Caroline told me he went travelling to get his head straight after his divorce."

"It shouldn't have come to that — I should have seen … helped him more…"

"From what Caroline told me you did quite a lot."

He rubs his hands over his face. "I can't believe he's gone. We went looking for him, his brother Dave and I, when he disappeared. Nothing. No trace. But I always thought … he's out there, somewhere. For Charlotte's sake as much as anything. I still don't understand how he could have ended it all."

"You don't know he did."

"That's what Dave said when he phoned me. I was at a Chamber of Commerce dinner — couldn't take it in. Got a taxi back here to read the last emails he sent. Hunting for clues. He seemed so much better — look."

He wiggles his mouse and the screen in front of us comes to life. Three erudite paragraphs describe the beauty of the foothills around Mount Cook and how without the haze of antidepressants they look so much more vibrant and real, that he was going to grab the chance to go off-grid for a while. No clues, except…

"When my friend Jessie was doing her finals she was struggling so they gave her some antidepressants. You have to be really careful how you come off them — they can play tricks with your mind."

But Jonathan isn't listening — he's staring at the screen, his eyes filling with tears.

I stand. "Come on — I'll drive you back to your flat. You don't want anyone to see you like this, do you? And you'll feel better after you've put your head down for a few hours." His nod is almost imperceptible but he reaches for his glasses and starts to log out of his computer.

I pick up the book from the library in the conference room then he follows me out of the office and into the car park. Even though it's still dark the sound of traffic reaches us from the main road and a lone bird chirps. Jonathan gives me concise directions then falls silent, his chin slumped on his chest. This isn't any of the Jonathans I've seen before — this is an empty husk of Jonathan. It feels as though I'm seeing him naked and my toes curl with embarrassment.

Even at the beginning of the rush hour the journey is a short one and we pull up outside a red brick former mill, its tower dominating the residential street around it. Its preservation looks perfect — a far cry from the sterile modernity of Willow Gardens.

"One of yours?" I ask.

He has already undone his seatbelt and is half out of the car. "One of Chris's." He picks up his briefcase from the footwell and I watch as he passes in front of me, slow and bent as the pensioner on the pavement opposite. He's clearly hurting so much, and whatever's passed between us I can't help but feel desperately sorry for him.

"Who's been buying you flowers?" Ben's question has a sneer to it, which puts me on my guard.

I shrug. "Did someone a good turn, that's all. They're a thank you."

"Pretty elaborate thank you." He runs his hand over the enormous tiger lilies, brown dust from the stamen scattering over the coffee table and onto the carpet.

"Careful — that stuff's awful to clean up."

He clasps his hands behind his back. "So — who gave them to you?"

"When I went into DSD to collect that book for you one of the girls was upset — a friend had died. I was a handy shoulder to cry on, that's all."

I watch as Ben picks up the card propped at the base of the vase. He reads it out loud. "With sincere thanks to my good Samaritan — and apologies I was too spaced out to say it at the time. J."

I put my hands on my hips. "Happy now?"

"The only girl I remember meeting at the Christmas party was Caroline…"

"Not everyone went," I snap. "Ben — what's this all about?"

"Sorry… I'm just stressed out over my project I guess."

"Well, how about instead of stressing you actually do some work? You could make a start on that book while I do some marking."

He flops down on the sofa. "Come on, Rachel, give me a break. I'm knackered and I've got no money for speed until after Saturday's gig."

Speed. So that's how it is. The warning bell that's been tinkling away in the back of my head since the beginning of term goes into red alert. How the hell can I trust him to keep his mouth shut when he's high? God, I've been beyond stupid. I turn away from him and power up my computer.

"Rachel?"

"I'm working even if you're not."

I am aware of him moving around the apartment. He picks up the kettle, puts it down. Opens a kitchen drawer. A floorboard creaks as he pads along the hall to the bedroom. My bedroom. I'm acutely aware he's invading my space, and yet I invited him in. What have I done?

I put my laptop on the coffee table and follow Ben into the bedroom. He's lying on top of the duvet, tapping on his phone.

"You'd better go."

He looks up. "Go?"

"Yes. Go."

"It's fine. I won't bother you while you're working. I'll just chill here until it's bedtime … sex time."

I walk over to the window, fold my arms. "No, Ben, I'd like you to go. This whole thing was a mistake on my part and I'm sorry, but it's over."

He's on his feet in a flash. "You can't mean that. We're so good together, Rachel. Don't tell me I'm not worth it."

"I'm sorry, Ben. It's over."

"But you can't…" His face is inches away from mine. "What if I choose to kiss and tell?"

I should have seen that coming. Should have known. "It's a risk I'll have to take. But you need to think carefully before you do, because who other than me can help you with your dissertation?"

He steps back. "You're threatening me…"

"Oh no, Ben. Just pointing out we hold fairly balanced hands."

"You're not so bloody clever, Dr Ward, and I'll make sure everyone knows it."

The front door slams. I even hear the door in the entrance lobby slam. Eventually I move, and with shaking hands pour myself the last of the scotch.

CHAPTER 24

"I don't care what you think, this office is not a counselling service for junior staff." Andrew has drawn himself up to his full five foot eight inches, his puffy face a quiver of indignation above his grey jumper.

"Now listen here..." Davina thrusts her legs in front of her and he takes a step back. "This is not just your office, it's our office — there are three of us..."

"And she," Andrew jerks his thumb in my direction, "always takes your side, so what chance do I have of doing any serious work? Students traipsing in and out like they own the place..."

I've had a terrible weekend worrying about Ben and quite frankly I can do without their bickering. I put my bag on my desk and unbutton my coat. "Well, students are rather the reason we're here."

"Rubbish," spits Andrew. "We're here for the advancement of knowledge — not that there's a great deal of that going on in this room most of the time."

"Oh, come on, we're not that bad..."

"You're heartless, Dr Pleat," Davina cuts across me. "How could I turn that poor child away when she was sobbing her heart out? And anyway, you weren't even here at the time."

Andrew thumps his fist on Davina's desk, making the assorted biros and paperclips dance. "I am not putting up with your insults or your behaviour anymore. I'm going to see Professor Stephens."

"You do that, you..." But her words are lost beneath the slamming of the door.

I check the water in the kettle and flick it on. "What's got his goat so early in the morning?"

"It's that weasel one-man tutor group of yours, creating havoc again."

"What, Ben?"

Davina rolls her eyes. "You know Monica, the new secretary?" My hand hovers over the coffee jar as I nod. "He only got her to transcribe all his final project notes. Hours and hours of them, apparently."

"The sneaky little sod — he told me he typed them himself. Did she get into trouble with the prof for doing it?"

"I don't think she knows anything about it; not yet anyway. No, it's Ben's lothario tendencies — honest to god, someone ought to tie a knot in it for him."

Keeping my back to Davina, I carry my mug over to my desk, put it down, and start hunting in my drawer. I grunt noncommittally.

"He led her completely up the garden path; took her out to that swanky new wine bar so she agreed to do the transcript as a favour. Poor little thing — like a lamb to the slaughter. Probably took very little to persuade her into bed and keep her there just long enough to get the job done. And this morning he texted her when she was on the bus to work telling her it's over because he wouldn't want his girlfriend to find out. Little shit."

His girlfriend? Did he mean me, or... "Little shit indeed."

"Wow — you said that with some venom, Rachel."

"It's men, isn't it? And he's a prime example of how low they stoop. No wonder Monica was upset. Are you going to do anything about it?"

"Actually, I was going to ask you. You're his tutor after all."

"I'm not responsible for his sexual misdemeanours though, thank god." I wipe my palms on my trousers but I can taste bile in my throat. It's all going to come out. I just know it is.

But Davina is still talking. "No, but will you speak to him? It's not acceptable behaviour — he has to understand that."

I glance at my watch. "I need to run to the library before my seminar. Can we pick up on this later?"

"Rachel?" Davina's head is on one side and I wonder for a moment if I've been rumbled. "You will say something to Ben, won't you?"

"Of course…" I promise as I all but run from the room.

With shaking hands I leave a note in Ben's workspace summoning him to a meeting at three o'clock. Andrew will be lecturing but Davina should be there to chaperone. And if anything comes out … well, I like to think I could trust her. Even if she'll know me for the fool I undoubtedly am.

It's almost ten past when there's a knock on the door just seconds before it pushes open and Ben strolls in. "Afternoon, Ra… Dr Ward, Ms Short."

"You're late," I tell him.

"Yeah — sorry — I only just got the note." He settles himself on the sofa and grins at me. "Anyway, what can I do for you?"

"I've had a complaint that you have misused college resources and before taking it any further I want to hear your side of the story."

A flash of concern travels across his eyes. "I'm not sure what you mean."

"Your transcription. You didn't do it yourself, did you? Despite what you told me."

"I didn't ever say I was doing it…"

"Don't get slippery with me, Ben — just tell the truth."

"The whole truth?" The threat is barely veiled and Davina looks around from the essay she is pretending to mark.

I'm going to have to call him out. "Of course."

He looks from one to the other of us, but says nothing. Davina opens her mouth but I shoot her a warning glance and she closes it again.

Ben leans back and stretches his arm along the sofa. "OK, so I asked Monica to do it for me. But as a favour, not work. It's not my problem if she did it in the office. It's her you should be talking to, not me."

"That's right — blame the poor kid for being hoodwinked by your so-called charm…" Davina can hold her anger no longer but I motion her to silence with an outstretched arm.

"So, Ben, you fully explained to Monica that the transcription was a personal favour and should not be done in university time?"

He shifts a little. "Not in so many words…"

"Then you need to take some responsibility for this. She's new — she doesn't know what she should and shouldn't do. There are plenty of paid transcription services you could have used."

"That's all right if you've got any money…"

Davina cuts across him. "I doubt it would have cost more than dinner for two at a wine bar."

"And I might have actually got my notes…"

"She didn't give them to you? Well, good for her." She folds her arms. "Finished with her a bit too quickly, did you?"

"That's none of your business. But she's in more trouble than I am, so what are you going to do about it?"

Davina is momentarily at a loss so I step in. "Ben — I would like you to apologise to Monica. If you're lucky she may not take her complaint any further and we can close the book on this whole sorry affair."

"Good call — I might even get the transcript." Ben turns to Davina, "See, I knew Dr Ward would be on my side."

"Don't bet on it." My tone of voice wipes the grin off his face. "I also wanted to talk to you about progress — or rather lack of it — on your dissertation. You are way behind so by the end of the week I want a detailed plan with regular milestones I expect you to keep to. Is that understood?"

Ben nods. "Perhaps we can book a tutorial to discuss it?"

"No, Ben. There's been quite enough discussion; I expect to see evidence of actual progress from now on. You'd better get to it." I turn back to my desk and punch my keyboard to bring my computer screen to life. My shoulders drop as Ben closes the door behind him.

CHAPTER 25

By half past five on Friday the department has fallen silent. I check my emails one last time. No work plan from Ben. Did I really expect it?

I stare into space as my computer powers down. I've been on edge all day, wondering what Ben's next move will be. Will his desire for revenge win out over needing my help to complete his degree? But can I continue to tutor him? Just thinking of what happened fills me with self-loathing. I've breached an essential trust, just to fulfil a sexual need, and the growing realisation of how low I've stooped is making me feel sick to the core.

Trying to force back the bitter tide I pull on my coat and pick up my briefcase then turn off the lights in the office and walk down the corridor, the click of my heels bouncing off the walls. I'm going to get home, get drunk and forget about it all.

My hand is on the door of the stairwell when I see Ben through the glass. He's sitting on the top step, playing with his phone, and I have just a moment to compose myself before he looks up and smiles.

"Rachel — I was hoping to see you."

"To give me your dissertation plan in person? I've been in my office for the last couple of hours."

"I haven't done it. Rachel... Did you mean it? Is it really over between us?"

I look down and there is anguish in his eyes. To give him credit he's a bloody good actor. "Yes, Ben. It should never have started so least said soonest mended. Let's both move on."

I put my hand on the bannister but he stretches his legs to block my way. "I can't. I need you too much."

"You need me to write your dissertation, that's all. And that isn't going to happen so you'd better get on with it yourself."

"Please, Rachel, can't we go back to your place and talk about it?"

"No. Shift your legs, Ben, I want to go home."

He doesn't move and I am aware of the silence around us. No-one works late on a Friday. I take a deep breath.

"OK," I tell him. "I'll take the lift."

The walk back down the corridor seems endless, but the only footsteps are my own. At least I've told him. And in no uncertain terms. The doors of the lift open and I step in, pressing the button for the ground floor. The face gazing back at me from the mirrored wall is pale, mascara impeccable but lipstick rather worn. It doesn't matter. The only thing going to see me tonight is that bottle of wine.

When I step out into the entrance hall, Ben is waiting. My stomach muscles clench but I freeze the smile onto my face. At the reception desk the security guard is fiddling with his CCTV screens and outside students hurry along the path towards the bar.

"Still here, Ben?" I ask.

His coal black eyes fix mine. "I'll always be here. You can't dump me just like that."

"I can, and I have. I don't sleep with guys who lie and cheat." I keep my voice low but Ben doesn't bother.

"Monica was nothing. Means to an end." He shrugs.

"Goodnight, Ben." I turn towards the door, but perhaps I won't walk home. Maybe a taxi from the rank outside the station would be a better idea.

I am walking to the university through the Monday morning drizzle when my mobile rings. I almost don't hear it, what with the buses and lorries thundering over the canal bridge, and when I see the number is DSD's I almost don't pick up.

"Rachel?" Caroline sounds anxious.

"Yes."

"Thank goodness I've caught you. Look, we need to meet — are you free at all today? At lunch perhaps?"

"Well, yes — any time between twelve and three — but what's going on? You sound really worried."

"I'd rather not say on the phone. Do you know the bookshop on Portland Street? There's a little café upstairs — shall we meet there at about twelve fifteen?"

Her anxiety is infectious and I can do nothing but agree.

As luck would have it my tutorial overruns and it takes longer than I thought to walk to the bookshop. Caroline is already waiting, a mug of coffee and a sandwich in front of her. I queue at the small counter, the aroma of homemade vegetable soup too much to resist on this dank day.

I smile as I sit down. "How are you? It's been a while."

She looks at her hands. "I know, and I'm sorry. I feel perhaps I should have done more to keep in touch."

"There's no need. I'm persona non grata as far as DSD's concerned since Jonathan…"

She shakes her head. "This is nothing to do with Jonathan." She reaches into her handbag and pulls out a handwritten envelope, pushing it across the table. "Luckily I open his post."

I put down my spoon and pull out a single sheet of paper. The message is typed but I know the block capitals on the envelope as Ben's: *Dr Ward is an immoral predator. She is a disgrace to her profession who uses students for her sexual ends and you would be wise to get rid of her before I go public with the evidence in my possession.*

Holy shit.

"Not very nice, is it?"

My throat is too dry to answer. It's all I can do to shake my head.

"I'm assuming," she carries on, "that it isn't true."

I take a sip of water. "No. It isn't. But all the same... Caroline — I've been monumentally stupid."

"Do you want to tell me?"

"I slept with a student. Remember Ben, from the Christmas party?"

"I thought he said he was a colleague..."

"He lied. We lied. There was nothing going on then — it hadn't started — I was determined it wouldn't but..."

She puts her hand on mine. "Rachel — he's a good-looking man and he seemed so nice..."

"However good-looking and nice I thought he was I shouldn't have slept with him. It was wrong on every level and now I've finished it ... and, well ... it looks as though he's out for revenge. Which is pretty rich given he was only after me because he thought I'd write his bloody dissertation for him."

"What are you going to do?"

I put my head in my hands. "Oh, god — I don't know. Resign, probably. I bet my head of department's got one of these letters too."

"But you can't — not over this — you can't let it ruin your career, everything you've worked for. It seems such a small thing by comparison."

"I don't know, Caroline, I really don't know. I was so careful, but what if he does have evidence? I can't drag the university through the mud because I've been so stupid. I just need time to think."

"Promise me you won't do anything rash. And if you want to talk it through, you know where I am."

"Thanks, Caroline. I really appreciate you doing this." I push the letter back across the table towards her.

"Don't you want to keep it?"

"I never want to see it again." Blinded by tears I push back my chair and head down the stairs as quickly as I can.

I deliver my afternoon lecture on automatic pilot then go straight home and change into my running gear. Thud, thud, thud along the towpath into the early dusk, the rain misting my face. I'm not just a lowlife but I'm a bloody stupid lowlife. How totally senseless to think Ben would put his dissertation before revenge. Hell has no fury like a man scorned, or a woman scorned... both can do seriously stupid things.

I stop in my tracks, on the quiet section of path beyond The Pyewipe. Canal merges with rain, which merges with mud and the dripping vegetation. A train passes on the opposite bank, the oblongs of light from its windows blurring into one. I try to force my mind back, back, to the long road home after Tommy... blistering heat... blisters on my feet... and blood... I think there was blood... I squeeze my eyes shut but I can only hear the clickety-clack of the carriages fading into the distance.

I make it home in what must be record time, despite my thudding heart and trembling limbs. After my shower the wine bottle calls, but it wouldn't be a good idea. I'm in trouble so deep clarity is my only friend. I sit on the sofa in my dressing gown trying to forge a plan. At least deal with the practicalities. I fully expect a summons from Professor Stephens so I have to be ready. To lie, or come clean and face the music? I don't know, I just don't know...

My neck and shoulders are stiff when I wake, still on the sofa with the lights on all around me. I check my phone — it's just before four and I've never felt so low — and so alone. But it isn't my heart that's breaking. It's something else inside me, something else beginning to crumble.

And suddenly I know. I know what I should do. Phone still in hand, I send a text. Then I stand, stretch, and head for my bedroom to get dressed.

CHAPTER 26

I park my car under the dripping trees and circle my shoulders to release the tension. Red brick Victorian terraces line the road and in my rear-view mirror I watch as mothers leave their offspring at the brightly painted school gate. Jessie will be one of them. I left so early, the journey to Manchester was quicker than I thought, and despite the service station coffee my eyelids close.

I come to with a sharp rap on the window. Jessie's mouth forms the words, "I'll put the kettle on," and I struggle out of the car and follow her into the house.

Light floods the kitchen from the patio doors and she turns and wraps her arms around me. "Honey — what gives? You look absolutely terrible." And then I am crying, for the second time in two days, and she rocks me to her, stroking my hair, just as if I was Abbie or George.

Slowly, the story comes out. At first I'm scared she'll be angry I kept the secret from her but she is strong and calm, and I realise how much motherhood has changed her. She has grown, and I am being left behind in a way I barely understand.

I finish by telling her about the note.

"The little shit…" she breathes.

"I know. Jessie — I'm going to have to resign."

She shakes her head. "Come on, Rachel — that might not be necessary. Think — what evidence could he have?"

"Believe me, I've thought of little else. I've gone through the texts — there's nothing there. There aren't very many and if anything they read as though he's the one chasing me. I never left him a note, a voicemail… He wanted to take a selfie of us but I wouldn't let him. Thank god. Because now I understand his motive."

"Could he have taken a photo without you knowing?"

"Jessie — his phone was in the bedroom — of course he could. And if that's the case then it isn't going to be pretty."

"I'll tear his bloody guts out…"

"No," I shake my head. "This is my fault too. I should never have put myself in this position. I tell you, Jessie — I'm through with men."

Jessie leans back in her chair and picks up her mug. "Perhaps it's not so much men, as you and men. Or rather — your attitude towards them."

"How do you mean?" But I know what's coming.

"I've known you for what … thirteen years? And in all that time I've never known you to have a proper relationship."

I trace a wavy line through the toast crumbs on the table. "Depends how you define a relationship."

"You and I — we have a relationship. We trust each other, care about each other, we're always there for each other."

"You can't expect that from a man."

"Yes, you can. You have every right to, in fact — but only if you're prepared to trust and love in return. And you're not."

"There isn't any point…"

"It depends on what you want. It's like anything, you put in what you get out. You use men, Rachel, so you end up being used."

"I know… I suppose I'm just as bad as Ben is." I gaze over her shoulder into the garden.

"I'm not saying that. I don't want to add to your guilt — I can see you're overburdened by it as it is. There's no way you deserve what he's threatening — no way at all. But he's part of a pattern of behaviour as far as you're concerned, and it isn't healthy."

I rub my hand over my eyes. "I'm sorry, Jessie — I can't deal with this now. It's all I can do to cope with the practicalities. I need to resign, I know that. I guess whether or not I work my notice will depend on what comes out. It could be very awkward."

"You don't have to resign, you know."

"Yes, but I think I actually need to. I want to get my head straight and anyway, in the middle of all this mess there's a glimmer of light, and that's freedom. It's like I said at Christmas — I'm turning into the sort of academic we always despised — too far from the coalface." I hold out my hands to show her my perfectly manicured fingernails. "I don't want these anymore. I want to do what I should have done in the first place. I want to dig."

She looks at me, eyes locked into mine. "Rach — you're smiling."

"I know. It's probably a sign of madness." I walk around the table and hug her as tight as I can. "Come on — help me draft those resignation letters then I'll buy you lunch to celebrate."

It was one thing sitting in the warmth of Jessie's kitchen writing the letters to the heads of department at Lincoln and Southampton and emailing them off, but quite another when the summons arrives from Professor Stephens to explain myself in person.

The walk along the corridor never felt so long. Monica sits in the outer office, her hair far from clean and black circles under her eyes. Seeing her like this strengthens my resolve.

Professor Stephens is asking for an explanation even before I have closed the door. I'm damned if I'm going to stand in front of her like a naughty schoolgirl so I make myself comfortable in the chair opposite her desk.

"Your letter says — and I quote — that you are resigning 'because you fear your actions may have brought the department into disrepute'. What the hell have you done?"

There's no beating about the bush. "I slept with Ben Carter. I've ended it now, but it was unprofessional to say the least."

She rocks back in her chair. "I agree. But if it was a cause for resignation then I can name at least three male lecturers and one head of faculty who wouldn't be working. Lecturers who are married and who aren't as gifted as you, Dr Ward."

"It's very kind of you to say so, but I have every reason to believe Ben will go public and I don't want to drag the university through the mud. It's better this way."

"I appreciate your concern about our reputation, but what makes you think your ... er ... affair will come out?"

"You didn't get an anonymous letter?"

She leans forwards. "Has he threatened one?"

"He's actually sent one — to DSD where I've been freelancing — but the MD's secretary intercepted it, thank god."

"And you're sure it was him?"

I smile. "Oh yes — the letter may have been typed but the envelope was handwritten."

"For a final year student, he's not very bright. Thankfully. Well, that's fairly straightforward; I'll phone DSD, get hold of the letter — and the envelope — and challenge him. That should nip things in the bud and mean you can stay." She folds her arms in triumph.

I take a deep breath. "It's very kind of you, but my resignation stands. What I did may not be unusual but it was wrong. I need to sort myself out — do something different for a while. Of course it's up to you if I work my notice…"

"I was rather hoping you'd work more than your notice — I was intending to offer you a permanent full time position at the end of your secondment."

I look down at my lap. "I'm so sorry…"

Her voice softens. "What will you do?"

"Get my hands dirty, I think. Find a dig to work on while I consider my options."

"If you could commit to coming back in October…"

"I'm sorry, Professor Stephens, I can't commit to anything right now."

She takes off her glasses and puts them on her desk. "This has shaken you, Rachel, hasn't it?"

"Yes, it has. I find myself in a position which is both indefensible and strangely outside my control. I'm not used to that."

"Would it help you to take a few days off?"

"In all honesty I'd be better placed sounding out a few contacts about taking over my lectures as soon as possible, because if push comes to shove I don't want to leave you in the lurch. The way I see it, I need to resign pretty immediately and openly to stop Ben going public — with all the furore around 'me too' this could make quite a story."

"If DSD still have the envelope I can put a stop to that."

"It might make matters worse. As soon as he knows I've resigned there'll be nothing to threaten me — or the university — with."

"Well, if you're sure…"

I nod. "I'm sure."

Professor Stephens nods, then stands. I do the same and we shake hands across her desk. "Just remember, Rachel," she tells me, "when you're ready to come back to the academic world, make sure I'm the first to know."

CHAPTER 27

Saturday morning brings an email from Jonathan and a note in my mailbox from Jem. One more welcome than the other, but both with the same fundamental message: we need to talk.

I ponder the email for some time, sipping coffee as the rain bounces off the canal in stair rods.

Dear Rachel,

Caroline has told me about your resignation from the university and the reasons for it. I would like to invite you to breakfast to discuss and suggest the Double Tree Hotel at 8am on Tuesday. Please let me know by return if not convenient.

Regards,

Jonathan

So I've been summoned by Mr Daubney, for no apparent reason I can see. He probably just wants to rub my nose in it over his full English. I'm not sure I'll even reply.

Jem's note is a far more intriguing proposition; 'our young friend' as he calls Ben, is apparently furious because he's been 'beaten all ends up' and Jem can't wait to tell me. Quite frankly I can't wait to hear so I use the mobile number scrawled on the bottom to text Jem to invite him and Toast to lunch at The Pyewipe.

Hope you've got waterproofs, I add. *We'll get soaked, but I'm desperate for some air.*

Toast is waterproof, Jem texts back. *We'll stroll by just after 12.*

In the event Jem's beaten up black umbrella keeps us both fairly dry for the walk along the towpath as Toast scampers ahead, oblivious to his darkening fur. When we arrive at The Pyewipe, Jem pulls an old towel from the satchel slung over his shoulder and rubs him down, damp dog smells filling the lobby.

He wrinkles his nose. "I hope nobody minds…"

"He can't help it — we'll just hide him under our table until he dries off."

But the barmaid even gives Toast a dog biscuit which he crunches noisily as we order our drinks.

The rain means the pub is unusually quiet and we choose a table next to the fireplace.

"So how are you, Rachel?" Jem asks.

"So-so. Really pleased to have this week behind me. It's been truly awful — Ben threatened to… Well, anyway, I've had to resign. But that's OK — I mean, I realised I wanted to anyway, go back to the real world. I've ridden the flak and my boss was really good about it. It's in the back of my mind Ben still might kick off, but I'm banking on the fact he's too lazy."

"You do realise what little sense all that made?"

"God, no. Was I gabbling?"

"Just a bit. I do know some from what Ben said last night — but perhaps you'd better start from the beginning and explain it properly."

So I do. Right from the moment Caroline called, while Jem sips his pint and nods in all the right places. Toast's damp weight is heavy on my foot and somehow my neck unknots itself and my shoulders relax.

When I finally stop, Jem looks grim. "Ben did have that evidence he bragged about and he did plan to use it. But thanks to your friend Jonathan Daubney you've got no worries on that score."

I turn my glass in my hand. "Now you're being obscure. Jonathan isn't exactly a friend…"

"Right at this moment I'd be hard pressed to think of a better one … present company excepted, of course," he winks.

"Of course," I grin back at him. "Go on then — tell me what happened."

"Well, Ben came back yesterday teatime in an absolute rage. To be honest, I was amazed because like you I thought he was too fundamentally lazy to get that worked up. But no — his face was red, his eyes were bulging and he could hardly speak for the stream of f-words coming out of his mouth. And all because your Jonathan Daubney had dropped his voice recorder into Brayford Pool."

"What? How the hell…"

"That's what I wanted to know. Not only how the hell, but why the hell too." We pause as the waiter brings two enormous plates of sausage and mash. Toast shifts under the table.

"Eventually Ben calmed down enough to admit he'd sent a note to Daubney saying he was going public on your affair unless he sacked you. Well, I nearly threw him out there and then but I wanted to know the full story. He said nothing happened for a few days but on Thursday the students were told you'd resigned. He said although he knew he'd won he still wanted revenge because you'd stuffed up his dissertation and his chance of a good degree.

"All the same I think he was pretty surprised to see Jonathan Daubney outside the faculty when he left on Friday. He went up to Ben and said he understood he had something of interest to him, and could they talk? It sounds as though there was some implication money could change hands so of course Ben was there like a rat up a drainpipe. They walked towards Brayford Wharf and he told Daubney what he had…"

I put my fork down, a lump of sausage stuck in my throat. "Do you know what it was?"

Jem shakes his head. "Given it was on his voice recorder my guess would be some rather intimate audio."

"Oh my god…"

Jem reaches over and puts his hand on mine. "He must have left it recording in your bedroom. But it's OK — no one will ever hear it now."

I want to pick up my glass but my hand is shaking too much. "So what happened?"

"Jonathan insisted on verifying the quality of the evidence. Ben tried to play it to him but he said he couldn't hear properly so he handed the device over. Next thing Ben knew it was in the bottom of the canal. Daubney claimed it slipped out of his hand but Ben said there was no way… I'm afraid I just started to laugh — it was so pathetic…"

I am trembling from head to foot. "You're sure — Ben didn't have it backed up anywhere…"

"Of course not — he was screaming he'd lost his dissertation notes as well — you're safe, Rachel, I promise you. You're really safe. You won't even have to worry about him leering at you from the barge because I told him to pack his bags and leave."

"Jem — you didn't have to do that."

"Yes I did. I couldn't live under the same roof as that scumbag for a moment longer. I put a card on the noticeboard in the Tap last night and I've already had a few calls so I won't be much out of pocket."

Tears are pricking the back of my eyes again — what the hell's got into me? "It's at times like this you find out who your friends really are," I sniff.

"Yes," Jem nods. "Me and that Jonathan bloke."

I manage a smile. "I know which one I'd rather spend the afternoon getting drunk with."

Jem leaps to his feet. "Right — I'll get the next round in."

CHAPTER 28

Jonathan rises to shake my hand as the waiter shows me to his table. The muted clatter of cutlery and early morning music fill the air, coffee and bacon drifting around my nostrils making me feel slightly sick. But given what Jem told me, I rather felt I had to come.

"So, Rachel," he asks as we sit down, "how are you?"

"Hugely in your debt, so I understand."

He raises an eyebrow. "In what way?"

"Ben Carter's voice recorder."

"You could say it was an unfortunate accident. I told him if he contacted Caroline she'd get him another one but we haven't heard anything yet." His voice is smooth, telling me nothing.

The waiter reappears. Jonathan orders another espresso and a bircher muesli while I go for a latte with pain au chocolat. I might just be able to force it down and it will give me at least some energy to face whatever the rest of the day brings.

I clear my throat. "You wanted to see me?"

Jonathan nods. "It's probably not for me to say but I was a little surprised you felt you had to resign from the university over Carter. However as you'll have some time on your hands I wanted to let you know you're welcome at DSD."

"But you ended out agreement weeks ago!"

He looks away. "Yes, well, I've just got the nod for pre-planning at Hemswell, and what with demolition starting at Burton Road it'll be all hands to the pump from now on."

"Well of course, I'll do what I can."

"Are you working your notice at the university?"

The waiter brings our breakfast.

"I'm handing over to the new lecturer next week. A former PhD student of mine."

Jonathan smiles. "That's good. I was rather hoping I could steal some more of your time."

"You really are that desperate?" I try to make it sound like a joke.

"There could be a great deal to do. It depends on what you find from your initial research. What's your gut feel?"

"About Hemswell?"

He frowns. "What else?"

About coming back? About the water that's gone under the bridge between us? "It isn't that far from Ermine Street so Roman is a possibility and of course there might be something from when the airfield was operational. Or any time in between, really. I'm sorry to be so vague but I need to look at the history."

"Would the modern airfield stuff be classed as archaeology?"

"It depends how modern and what it is. There's quite an interest in improving our understanding of the first and second world wars, so it's possible — probable even."

"Well that increases the risk significantly."

I pick up my pain au chocolat and tear off a piece. "Not so much it would stop your development, but there'd be a delay while we excavated."

He nods. "I suppose I should expect that. And if it happened … would you stay after your notice period to run the dig? I'd pay you of course, and you could keep the flat."

Deep breath. "I really wanted the time to find a dig to work on during the summer."

Jonathan leans back and folds him arms. "But you'd have a dig to work on here."

How can I explain the difference between a site of real significance and a muddy field in the middle of nowhere? "Look," I plough on, "let's just see if we can work together again. We've had our ups and downs, after all."

"Rachel — I can work with anyone. And you're not half as prickly as you like to pretend either."

I feel the colour rising from my chest to my neck, fiery under my cashmere jumper. His steely grey eyes are fixed on me so hard he must see it too. My gaze drops away. I don't have the energy to fight him. I see Ben's voice recorder dropping, dropping, through the murky water.

From somewhere deep in my chagrin I summon a smile. "I'll try my best."

"I know you will. You've shown a lot of professionalism and moral courage this last week. After what you've been through, working with me should be a doddle."

The most logical thing to do with the rest of my day would be to start my desk research, but instead I find myself drawn along Ermine Street to Hemswell. The sky is leaden as I walk from the central car park to the dig site, clipboard tucked under my arm. It's official now — I'm allowed to be here.

I stand at the corner of the field and sketch its shape, noting the position of hedges and trees as the wind swoops in from the distant wolds bringing the merest hint of snow. The chances are there's nothing in this desolate corner of Lincolnshire but I need to prove that to the planners before work can start on whatever Jonathan's intending to build. I should have asked, but my head's still spinning. I expected to be sacked, not welcomed back into the fold. I expected Jonathan to be disgusted, but he was pretty nice about it all.

Sketch finished, I crouch down and crumble a handful of soil beneath my fingers. The frost has bitten into the surface, making it damp and cold, but the structure seems good and it shouldn't be too hard to put in some test pits. Research and field walk first. Then I'll know.

Back in my car I peel off my gloves and go to clean my hands with wet wipes, realising at the last moment I bought lemon-scented ones by mistake. The synthetic bitterness makes me gag and I slam them into the glove box and throw open the door to let in the freezing air. Freezing, daylight, birdsong. Not the heat and cicadas of a Mediterranean night. But every bloody time it takes me back.

It's OK — you can breathe, Rachel, breathe. And calm down. I wipe my shaking hands on my woollen hat then toss it into the back seat and give my hair a cursory comb in the rear-view mirror. I need company — and a hot cup of tea.

Esther is waiting for me in the hall. "It's so lovely to see you. After you phoned I told Pat you'd be staying for lunch. I hope that's OK?"

A hint of rosemary and roasting vegetables wafts from the direction of the kitchens. "Oh yes, it smells wonderful."

She tucks her arm into mine. "Come on — I've got something to show you first."

We make our slow progress to the living room where the woollen suited ladies I remember from the talk are sipping sherry. They acknowledge us then return to their conversation.

On Esther's favourite table is a gleaming new iPad. "Is this yours?" I ask as we sit down.

She nods. "Cassie had one when she came to see me and I took rather a shine to it. It seemed so much easier than the computer and she said if I got one too we could Facetime or whatever the youngsters call it. So I asked Pat to order it for

147

me and Jonathan spent most of Sunday morning setting it up and showing me how to use it. I've hardly put it down since. I can read books with it too — in really large print. It's wonderful."

"So how is Cassie?"

"I'm a bit worried about her to be honest. She wouldn't visit her mother's grave this time; says she blames her too much for not being able to cope, for making her feel as though she wasn't important. I tried to explain it wasn't like that. She said she knew really, and that she'll deal with it all better now she's acknowledged her anger so she can work through it. The things kids come up with."

"I guess there always has to be blame, doesn't there?"

"No, I don't think so. Sometimes things just happen; people are what they are. Believe me, Rachel, I've racked my brains for what Ralph and I could have done to make Sally the way she was, but it's a pretty pointless exercise — except at three in the morning when I can't sleep."

I look out of the window. Do I blame my mother? About as much as I blame myself — but telling Esther that won't help. Instead I laugh. "Oh, those pesky three in the morning thoughts. There's a scientific reason for them, you know, but I can't quite remember what it is at the moment. Anyway, I have some news of my own — Jonathan's ready for me to start investigating the field he's buying at Hemswell. Isn't that exciting?"

Esther still looks pale. "Oh, so you weren't shopping this morning?"

"No, I was making a sketch and generally getting the lie of the land."

I'm delving into my handbag for my car keys to fetch my clipboard when Pat appears. "Hello, Rachel. I can't tell you how sorry I am to hear about your resignation."

Esther looks up. "Resignation?"

Pat flushes red. "Oh lord, I haven't put my size sevens in it, have I?"

I fiddle with my key fob. "I hadn't got around to telling Esther yet — I've only been here about ten minutes."

"Oh, I am sorry. Look — why don't you go through to the dining room then you can bring her up to date over lunch."

Esther's eyes seem to have lost their milkiness as they bore into mine.

"I've resigned from the university," I tell her, then grind to a halt.

"But, Rachel, why? Are you unhappy in Lincoln?"

I shake my head. "Properly resigned. From my post at home too." She gazes at me, saying nothing. "It's … it came to a head quite quickly but it's been in the back of my mind for a while. I've been in the academic world too long — too far from the coalface. I need to get back to what I love doing."

"Well, that sounds like a wonderful idea to me."

"It does? You don't think I'm crazy to quit a cushy job…"

She puts her head on one side. "I am assuming, of course, you've worked out how you're going to eat and pay the rent?"

"Not really. But Jonathan has more than one project on the go at the moment so I'll be OK for the next few months — maybe longer."

Esther beams at me. "You brave and clever girl. There aren't many women who'd have your courage."

The drive back to Lincoln feels interminable. The temperature gauge hovers around zero and for part of the way I follow the gritting lorry, its flashing lights making my eyes ache. I couldn't tell Esther, could I? Couldn't tell her the truth.

Why? Well that's obvious. I'd never want her to know I was stupid enough to jeopardise my career for sex. The seeds of truth in what Jessie said are beginning to itch in a most uncomfortable manner. I'm not clever, I'm not brave — I'm just a liability. And I'm going to have to do something about it.

CHAPTER 29

I figure the best way to cope with my first day back at DSD is to go into the office and get my head down, but Caroline has other ideas, perching on the corner of my desk and filling me in on all the gossip about people I hardly know. Luckily, Jonathan is out, so I can nod and smile without feeling too guilty, and eventually the phone rings and she drifts off.

My inbox is mainly full of out-of-date all-staff emails. Over the last few days there have been a few from Jonathan, pointing me in the direction of the Hemswell development file, asking for a timetable for my initial report and giving me the contact details for archaeological liaison at the council. All as if I've never been away.

It's always best to start with what's gone before and it isn't long before I unearth a report on an extensive dig in the fields immediately north of Jonathan's plot. I print out the plan of the trenches to get my bearings and start to read.

Even given the proximity to Ermine Street, my expectations were pretty low, but to my delight there were Roman finds in one area; evidence of quarrying and limestone walling, a cobbled floor surface and some reasonably high status pottery — amphorae from southern Spain, a tiny shard of Samian from Gaul, as well as colour-coated wares from the Nene Valley. A small assemblage, but certainly indicative. Hints of Iron Age occupation too.

I check the position of the trenches on the plan and find they are no more than 150 metres from the northern tip of the site, so that's where I'll start. Excitement fizzes through me and it takes me a moment to remember if I do find something,

Jonathan will not be pleased. Well, I can't help that — what's there is there — and I didn't choose where to build.

Hunger reminds me the morning has gone so I pick up my handbag and wander down the road to Greggs for a sandwich. It's a fresh, crisp day but the cold seeps into my bones so I buy a paper cup of tomato soup as well and sit in my car to eat.

I nibble and sip, watching the slow progress of the traffic on the main road beyond the copper beech hedge. Jonathan's Jag pulls up, but he doesn't see me as he jumps out and strides into the office. I look at my watch. I can steal another twenty minutes if I want. Perhaps he'll go out again.

Bored now, I turn to my phone. No new emails in my personal inbox but a text from Jem reminding me his band has a gig tomorrow night. I did say I wanted to see them — out of curiosity as much as anything. Having exhausted all other possibilities, I turn to Facebook. A notification asks permission to add a post I've been tagged in to my timeline. I click on it and almost spill the last of my soup. It's a picture of me posted by Ben, with the words: *Meet the ex — Rachel Ward — don't get vindictive with me, love — remember I know your dirty little secrets.*

Jessie picks up her phone almost straight away.

"Are you in Facebook?" I blurt out.

"No — but I can be. Hang on a tic." There is a furious tapping on her keyboard. "OK — now what?"

"My timeline — can you see a post from Ben?"

Tap, tap, tap. "No — nothing. Last thing is the picture I put up at Christmas."

I sit back in my seat and exhale. "Thank god for that."

"Why — what's he done?"

"Gone public on us … not that half the university doesn't know already. At least none of my friends can see it."

Tap, tap, tap. "Except it's a public post pinned to the top of his timeline. And it's been shared four times already. Bastard."

"What can I do?"

"You could try reporting it to Facebook — they'd probably take it down if you said it was libellous. But I doubt that would be the end of it."

"Probably not. I'll just have to ride it out, Jessie. I finish at the university next week anyway, once I've handed over. It's not nice — but it's not the end of the world."

"That's my girl — rise above the crap and get on with your life. Are you at the uni now?"

"No — it's my first day back at DSD — nice meaty project to get my teeth stuck into. Which Jonathan Daubney won't like because it's going to cost him money, but that's not my fault."

Jessie chuckles. "I love it when you're all guns blazing."

"Thanks. Anyway, I'd best blaze back into the office and give him the good news. Speak soon."

The silence in the car is deafening. I read the Facebook post then press the button to ignore it. If I get it removed, he'll only do it again — perhaps something worse. Let it stay there and rot. Sticks and stones can break my bones but words…

A phrase springs from nowhere, accompanied by laughter and the pump of music over the beach: *Tommy, control your woman.* Humiliation. Cicadas. The hot well of pain dragging between my thighs.

CHAPTER 30

The development area at Hemswell is so bleak and windswept I wonder how I'm ever going to work here. Flecks of snow whirl in the wind and I wrap my scarf more firmly around my neck as the council liaison officer walks me around, an aerial photograph showing the position of the old runways in the field to the west flapping in his hand. Our site is right at the end of one of them and the area is pockmarked with half a dozen hotspots where metal detectorists have had strong signals but weren't allowed to dig.

Jonathan will not be pleased. I look across to where he is standing next to the hedge, phone pressed to his ear. The old aircraft hangars rise in the middle distance behind him and in his long black overcoat he looks every inch a spy from a cold war thriller.

Call over, he strides towards us. "What do you think?" he asks while he is still several feet away.

"There's nothing on the ground but the hotspots are in the area closest to the Roman finds from the dig just north of here. It gives me a clear target for some initial test pits, but I'm going to field walk the whole site first and we've just been discussing some geophysics."

He turns to the council officer. "I know what that means with you guys — you're more or less telling us to do it. How much is that going to cost, Rachel?"

"I'll need to get some quotes and…"

"Then do it. These bills are going to add up." He folds his arms and the set of his mouth should have warned me but I plough on regardless.

"Not to mention delays if we find something from the initial surveys. There are scheduled sites around the village and if we have to get the historic monuments people involved that will certainly hold things up."

The liaison officer shifts from foot to foot. "Do you think that's likely, Doctor Ward?"

I smile at him. "Impossible to say. We'll just have to take it one stage at a time."

Jonathan is silent as we walk back to where the cars are parked on the verge, speaking only to shake the officer's hand and bid him goodbye. As he unlocks the Jag, he turns to me. "Those costings — I'll need best and worst case scenarios. This one's tight."

"Aren't they all?"

"When can I have them?"

"I'll do them by Tuesday."

He grunts and starts the engine. This is going to be a long trip back to Lincoln. I glance at his profile, spikey and hard. He turns on the radio. Wagner. How appropriate.

As soon as Jonathan drops me at Willow Gardens I race upstairs and change into my tracksuit, lacing my trainers with a fury beyond my comprehension. I gulp down a glass of water then it's out into the sleet and along the towpath towards The Pyewipe, my bobbing headtorch lighting the way.

I run past the pub and under the road bridge with the clunk and thud of traffic above me. A commuter train passes along the opposite bank, its carriages illuminating the countryside in square flashes. Then there is silence as I follow the canal through fields until I can pound the path no more.

My journey back is at a slower pace, needles of icy rain soaking my clothing and pitting my cheeks. I am spent, but although my thighs are burning, my shoulders feel more relaxed, and my thoughts turn towards a huge bowl of pasta with tons of grated cheese and a glass of red.

Despite the weather, I am not alone. Ahead of me the light from a torch arcs in the rhythm of a slow jog, sweeping the path and verges as it approaches. Someone's even more knackered than I am, by the look of it. As they come into the range of my light I glance up, but they are head down against the rain, oblivious to my presence.

It's over in a moment. Arms then bodies collide and I lose my footing, sliding from mud to damp grass, on and on in a desperate scramble through the leaves and decaying brambles until I hit the water with a scream. I reach up, up, expecting the torch — a hand — but there is no-one there.

The icy water has knocked the breath from my body, but my mind is racing. Some instinct keeps me silent and still, clinging to the reeds at the edge of the canal until I hear the footsteps fade in the direction of The Pyewipe. They must have known. They must have known what they'd done.

I follow the reeds until I come to a grassy patch on the bank and I lever myself out of the water. My torch is nowhere to be seen, but ahead of me are the streetlights of Willow Gardens and I run like never before; along the towpath, across the car park and up the stairs, locking my front door behind me and sliding the safety chain into place.

I sink to the floor in the hall and try to regain my breath.

My wet clothes soak their chill into my bones and the base of my spine is numb from where it's pressing into the skirting board, but movement is beyond me. There's a pain in my ribs that could be exertion or could be the beginnings of a bruise. Could the jogger have been Ben?

When the shivering starts it could be fear, it could be shock, or it could be cold. It is beyond me to separate the sensations; beyond me to see anything but the blackness of the canal as I slide into it. The shock of cold was bad enough, but I was soaked through and frozen anyway. Was that what saved me? What if it hadn't? What if I'd injured myself so I couldn't climb out?

My arms circle my drawn-up legs, my head drops and with a kind of wonder I realise that my eye sockets fit my knee caps perfectly.

It couldn't have been an accident or the other runner would have helped me. Most people know their attackers. Bile rises in my throat, carrying with it the stench of synthetic lemons.

I've never been hated like this. The chill reaches deep into my bones but my skin smarts with the heat of the Mediterranean evening; throat parched, stumbling steps. Has one somehow led to the other? Was Jessie right? *What have I done?*

I'm cold now, really cold. There are pins and needles in my feet. I raise my head. The strip of light from under the door casts a glow on my right leg as I extend it in front of me, pressing my sole against the opposite wall as cramp bites. Is he watching, waiting? Dare I move from the hallway, let him know I'm in here? He might try something else.

All the same, I have to get warm before a chill sets in. As I run my bath I watch the door. Once the taps are quiet I will hear if he comes. I pull off my running gear and throw it in the washbasin before sinking under the foamy crust.

I ease myself down the bath until only my nose is sticking out. I'm breathing lavender, not the dank waters of the canal. Slowly, I push the what ifs away. I will not snivel. I will not be scared.

I grab the foothold of control and haul myself up on it. First, I'm going to draw the curtains and put on all the lights. Next, I'll pour a glass of wine and stick a frozen pizza in the oven. Then I'll start researching the minutiae of the Roman history of northern Lincolnshire.

It's almost one in the morning by the time I remember I need to sleep. As I check my bedroom curtains I see a lone light in the barge, towards the back where Jem's cabin is. Unwinding after a gig, probably, with Toast curled at his feet. Have I put him in danger too? The thought stops me in my tracks. Somehow, this has to stop.

CHAPTER 31

The next morning I drop in to see Caroline at DSD's offices. Jonathan has gone to London and the project managers are scattered to the four winds as usual so she is on her own. She clucks over me and makes me coffee.

"You look bloody awful — what's happened?"

I raise my eyebrows. "Thanks. It's only sleep deprivation and actually I feel all right."

She turns from the coffee machine. "My question still stands — what happened?"

"While I was running last night someone pushed me into the canal."

"What?" The mug wobbles in her hand as she passes it over.

"It's OK — I got myself out quite easily. But I'll need to replace the carpet in the hall. I'm afraid it got rather wet and smelly."

"Sounds more like a job for our insurers. Did you call the police?"

I shake my head and sink onto the sofa opposite her desk. "Not yet."

"And why the hell not?"

"I would have done if I'd been convinced it was some random nutter."

She sits down next to me. "You think it could be Ben, don't you? Rachel — you're not safe. You must go to the police. Now."

"I'll feel safer once the key code to the block has been changed. I was stupid enough to give it to him. How do I go about making that happen?"

"We've handed it over to a management company but I'll call them. And if they're in one of their less helpful moods I'll get Jonathan on the case."

"Thank you. If Ben can't get into the building then..."

"But you can't stay a prisoner there."

"I know. But it may not have been him. I just don't know. He may have been vindictive, but I'm still struggling to believe he'd do something like this."

"You don't know that, Rachel. Really — you hardly knew him."

I hang my head. That makes it even worse. "I should never have taken the risk," I mumble.

Caroline takes my hand. "No, but you ended it pretty quickly. And you can stop beating yourself up about it as well. As Jonathan said, you've behaved impeccably professionally over this — better than most men would have done. He really respects you for it and so do I."

"He does?"

"Of course he does. He's not as black as you paint him, you know."

"I know that really, but he was in a filthy mood again yesterday."

"Yes, well. Let's just say there's a lot going on for him too at the moment. The New Zealand authorities have released Christopher's body. That's where he's gone today — he and Chris's brother have an appointment at the High Commission in London to try to sort out bringing him home."

"So did they find out how he died?"

She shakes her head and puts her empty mug on her desk. "No. Open verdict. He was there a long time before they found him..."

I squeeze her hand. "I'm sorry. It must be so hard."

She nods and grips my fingers back. "But come on, let's change what we can. Shall I phone the police for you?"

"No. I need that envelope with Ben's handwriting on. It's the only physical proof I have. And then I promise you, it's straight from here to the police station."

I'm not expecting a knock on the door. The police left about an hour ago. As far as they're concerned, Ben has an alibi — he was with the girls he's moved in with. All I've done since is stare out of the window at the lights shimmering onto the canal from Jem's houseboat.

"Who is it?" I call, my hand hovering over the handle.

"It's me, Jonathan."

Another surprise. "Come to inspect the damage?"

As the door swings open he looks down towards my feet at the damp stain on the cream carpet. "Can't really miss it, can you?"

"No. I'm sorry…"

He crouches down and prods at it. "It's nothing that can't be fixed." He looks up at me. "What did the police say?"

"Come in and I'll tell you. Coffee?"

He steadies himself on the wall as he pushes himself up. "Please."

"I can't do espresso but I can make it black and strong."

"Anything as long as it isn't decaf."

"Long day?"

"You could say that."

He switches on the light then takes command of the armchair while I fill the kettle and set it to boil.

"Can I offer you something stronger?"

He shakes his head. "I've got the car. Tell me, were you sitting here in the dark?"

I shrug. "You don't need the light on to think."

"So what are the police going to do?"

"They've questioned Ben, but he has an alibi. He was at home with two of his housemates."

Jonathan raises his eyebrows. "And how likely is that?" I shake my head mutely and he carries on, "Caroline said you were going to show them the blackmail note — finally."

"I know — I should have done it straight away. But I never thought … and I wouldn't listen to her. I'm not that great at listening when it comes to advice — even good advice."

"Will you listen to me now?"

I hand him his coffee, which he downs in one gulp. "Another?"

"Please."

I retreat to the kitchen area. "Aren't you permanently wired, the amount you drink?"

He smiles. "It's like any drug — the more you use, the more you need." I put a second spoonful of granules into the cup while he looks at me. "You haven't said whether you're going to listen."

"Do you really mean listen, or do you mean do as you say?"

"Preferably the latter, but hearing me out would be a start."

At least he's being honest. He takes off his glasses and closes his eyes while he waits for my answer, revealing dark smudges under surprisingly long lashes.

I put both our cups on the coffee table and sink onto the sofa. "I'm all ears."

"OK. Ben's alibi might be real or it might be not, but it isn't a risk I'd like to take. I'm off to New Zealand tomorrow for a week or so and I'd like you to use my house in Winteringham while I'm away. Let the whole thing simmer down. It'll be safer — and closer for you to get on with your work at Hemswell."

"That's very kind…"

He shrugs. "Kills two birds with one stone."

"Can I sleep on it? Let you know tomorrow?"

"I'm leaving for the airport pretty early."

"Oh. Caroline said they've released Christopher's body."

"Don't change the subject." He picks up his glasses and spins them around his fingers. "I'd rather you just said yes."

"At the moment everything needs careful consideration. My brain…"

"As far as I can see this is a no-brainer."

I stand up. "Don't push me, Jonathan." My voice is shaking and I struggle to control it. "I'm really grateful for your offer — it's tremendously kind of you — but I want to think it through, OK?"

He stands too and picks up his coat. "Then I'll leave you to phone Mum and let her know. She'll give you the keys, show you what's what."

"I will. I'll call her first thing. And … have a good trip, won't you?" I put my hand on his arm.

He half smiles, shaking his head.

CHAPTER 32

I swing my car into the drive and look up. Pat told me it was the house with the conservatory on the roof and now I see exactly what she meant. Jutting out from the honeyed bricks and red tiles is a room made completely of glass with a terrace in front, no doubt giving fabulous views over the Humber.

I'm still gawping when Pat opens the door. I jump out of my car and to my surprise she gives me a hug.

"I'm so glad you decided to come," she says. "You must have been through hell."

Her warmth makes it hard for me to speak but eventually I manage. "It's good to get away."

She leads me through a square hall with some impressive pieces of abstract art on the walls and down a corridor to the right. The guest room is plain and functional with a bathroom opposite. The bed is made up with crisp white linen and the towels folded on one corner match the blue in the curtains. There are hothouse tulips in a vase on the dressing table.

I turn to Pat. "I've put you to so much trouble..."

"It's no trouble at all. When Jonathan told me what happened, I could barely believe it. But you'll be safe here while things simmer down."

"And I can get on with project Hemswell. And see more of Esther."

Pat laughs. "She'd like that, but perhaps the circumstances of you staying here would worry her."

"Then shall we just say it's so I can be closer to the site?"

"Good idea."

Pat explains she has her own rooms at the other end of the house, beyond the kitchen and lounge. "I don't use them that often but sometimes it's nice to get away from The Firs when I'm off duty. It means Jonathan and I don't get under each other's feet too much. His part of the house is upstairs."

"You mean the conservatory?"

"Yes. It's his living room, but you're most welcome to use it. The views are stunning."

She leads me up a light oak staircase to a galleried landing. The glass room opens directly from one end of it, flooding light into the whole area. I'd expected modern furnishings, but instead there is a low chesterfield sofa in cracked brown leather and a battered trunk serving as a coffee table. In the far corner, facing the Humber, is an Edwardian bureau with an old-fashioned swivel office chair in front of it.

"His father's things," Pat smiles. "I was so glad he wanted to keep them. And the bureau would be a good place for you to work if you need to. He and Christopher used to brainstorm stuff up here — Jonathan would talk and he'd sketch. He said it inspired him."

"They were good friends, weren't they?"

Pat shakes her head. "More than that, much more. Chris was the most important person in Jonathan's life. After me of course." She forces a laugh.

I follow Pat downstairs, pondering her words. *Is Jonathan gay? No — he can't be — Denise thought she was pregnant. Bisexual then? Forget it, Rachel. It's no concern of yours.*

"How long will Jonathan be gone for?" I ask.

"As long as it takes."

"Caroline said they've released Christopher's body. I thought … you know … the authorities might just fly it back."

"It's not that simple apparently — Dave and Jonathan had quite a tussle at the High Commission. The easiest option would have been to bury him there but the boys felt it was important for Charlotte and for Chris's parents to bring him home but that wasn't feasible. So they've struck a compromise that the magistrate who led the inquest will sign a cremation certificate so they can at least bring his ashes back. But I have a feeling Jonathan's estimate of a week might be wildly optimistic."

"Oh lord — he'll be tearing his hair out."

Pat nods. "He wasn't in the best of moods anyway. Said there was a lot going on here he could do without as well." I look away, out over the garden, but she carries on. "I think he feels it, you know, running that business on his own, but I can't ever see him getting another partner. Caroline's a great support, bless her, but he needs someone who will challenge his thinking a bit, talk around all the different angles." She puts her hand on my shoulder.

"From what I've seen he doesn't much like his thinking challenged. He almost told me as much — admitted that when he said he wanted me to listen what he actually meant was he wanted me to do as I was told."

Pat frowns. "In his personal life he's usually quite laidback."

I shake my head. "This was business. Our relationship is … business." For some reason the colour is rising up my neck.

"I'm sorry — I didn't mean to embarrass you. It's just that of all the people in Jonathan's life I think you're the one he could talk to as an equal."

I shake my head. "I don't think he sees me like that. But it's OK, really. We get on much better than we did and anyway, I'll be gone in a few months."

"What are you going to do, Rachel?"

"Get my hands properly dirty — and I can't wait."

Once Pat's gone I wander into the kitchen to make myself a cup of tea. While the kettle boils, I open one cupboard after another to get my bearings. Spices, couscous, three sorts of rice. Boxes of pods for the Nespresso machine. Almonds, brazil nuts, raisins, dried apricots and sugar-free muesli. An extensive range of plain white Villeroy & Boch crockery — there must be a plate or bowl for every eventuality. All very … metrosexual.

I identify the tea caddy by the fact it has a tiny spoon built into its wooden lid, but thankfully there are bags inside so I don't have to reach for the teapot and risk breaking it. I carry my mug upstairs and stand looking down over the village at the Humber beyond. As I sip I watch the clouds fill the sky from the east, racing towards me until the rain starts to patter on the glass.

On the one solid wall is a family tree in a light oak frame. At the bottom are Jonathan and Anna. He'll be forty next year and she's two years younger. Pat's only sixty-one — she must have been a young bride in 1978 — but her husband, Charles, was fourteen years older. There's no date for his death so I imagine tracing the Daubney family was his project. And he's done it well — right back to 1605 and all in Lincolnshire, with a footnote that the name originated in Norman France and was known in the county at the time of Edward I.

So this is Jonathan's pedigree. Perhaps you would be a bit arrogant with that lot behind you. As I sit down on the sofa, I realise I know nothing of my family further than my gran. But to be honest, that's all I need to know. Gran helped me, healed me even, when my parents wouldn't.

The rain on the glass is strangely comforting and I set the remains of my tea on the trunk before kicking off my shoes and swinging my legs onto the chesterfield.

Within moments I am asleep.

CHAPTER 33

There is little change between the grey of dawn and full morning light as the rain continues to sweep up the Humber. The vegetables are ready in their pans, potatoes and pork prepared for the oven. I have two hours to fill before Jem arrives, so I abuse the Nespresso machine by making a second latte and take it up to the conservatory to examine the geophysics quotes for Hemswell.

Even through the curtain of rain it's hard not to be distracted by the view. The soft red bricks and tiles of the village slope down before me, giving way to the dark band of ploughed earth in the fields closest to the river. On the other side the industrial ugliness of Brough is a damp blur, hills rising behind it. I sit in the swivel chair and open the bureau, trying to drag my eyes downwards.

There's a calmness about this place that's healing me, making me whole. I had nightmares about the canal on Friday, and that's what really made up my mind to come here. Last night I slept like a log. It's early days, I know, but already I'm scared to go back to Lincoln. Not so much that Ben will try something else, more I'm afraid of my fear. Afraid there'll be triggers, flashbacks ... like last time. And I really can't take any more.

I hold my head in my hands, but tears don't come.

Jem whistles as he scans the living room. "Wow — am I allowed to put Toast down? I've already lowered the tone of the area by parking the band's van outside."

"I don't see why not. He might skid around the wooden floor a bit but he can't hurt it, and I can always hoover the sofa later if he jumps up."

Toast trots off to sniff around the patio doors while Jem studies a photograph on the bleached oak bookcase. "This your Jonathan? He's a real good-looking guy."

"He's not *my* Jonathan."

He steps back and looks at me with his head on one side. "Have I touched a nerve?"

I give him a little hug. "Sorry. Come on, let's get a drink before lunch."

"I have to say — something smells good."

"I think it's having a proper kitchen — it's inspired me. It's absolutely enormous — come and see."

Jem follows me with Toast close to his heels. He puts the bottle of wine he's brought on the table as I light the gas under the gravy to warm it through. "Will you have any if you're driving?"

"Just the one."

I open the oven and shake the potatoes in the pan before bringing the pork out to rest, Toast giving me his undivided attention. I look down at him. "It's OK, fella, there'll be some for you."

"You spoil that dog."

"So do you. Has your new lodger moved in yet?"

"On Friday — and so far, so good. Did I tell you she's a music teacher? Goes around schools and youth groups teaching the sax. It's fair to say our tastes clash but it's good to have another muso around. You never know, she might even convert me to jazz if she stays long enough."

"Rather you than me. Now, how hungry are you?" Toast pricks up his ears. "You'll have to be a bit patient, fella — it needs to cool first."

As I am dishing up the roasties my mobile buzzes. Jem looks at it, questioning. I shake my head. "Just an email — won't be important." I angle the screen so that I can see it. "It's from Jonathan."

"You don't want to read it?"

"It can wait. He's probably worried I'm trashing his house."

"As if!"

"Maybe he's bored. They've only just arrived and I reckon there'll be some major hanging around for a slot at the crematorium."

"Christ! I hope it's better than it is here — when the barmaid at the Tap's mother died they were waiting for weeks."

"He'll do his nut if that happens — glad I won't be the one in the firing line."

"Got a bit of a temper, has he?"

"God, yes — he can have. But at other times … and I have to say I'm very grateful to him for letting me borrow his house."

Jem carries the gravy to the table. "From that point of view, the longer he's away the better."

I gaze at our plates. "I need to find somewhere else to live, Jem. I don't want to go back to the flat. It doesn't matter whether it was Ben or not, I still won't feel safe when I go out, and I have to run for my sanity."

"Shall I ask around? See if anyone's got a room?"

"Not yet. It might be better if I was nearer Hemswell — most of my work's going to be there, after all." I put my hand over his. "I'll let you know if I need any help. And I'll keep in

171

touch. I might just miss Toast if I didn't. Not to mention his owner."

Jem turns his palm upwards, intertwines his fingers with mine, and squeezes them. For a moment my heart thuds in my chest but then he laughs. "Oh, if only I was twenty years younger. You're not even a bad cook." He winks.

I laugh, and it's an easy laugh. There's no sexual tension between us and I like that. Perhaps Jem's beginning to show me that a man can be a friend.

Later, as I wash the pans and stack the dishwasher, I wonder if I could be friends with Jonathan too. I am actually beginning to like him and he's been extraordinarily kind, but his cruel words to Denise continue to haunt me.

Some gravy's burnt on the hob and I crouch to open the cupboard under the sink. Synthetic lemon spills out all around me and I topple back onto the tiles. The pains ripple through my abdomen, blood spilling onto the floor. The white tiled floor of my mother's bathroom. Then the memory fades and I'm left with the stink of the lemon cleaner.

CHAPTER 34

There is no first light this morning; just the grey of dawn melting imperceptibly into a thick curtain of mist. I stand at the kitchen sink and sip a long glass of ice cold water. All night long the memory came and went, blurred with the sensation of sliding into the canal, but I don't suppose the second bottle of wine helped. I know what happened in the beach bar in Cyprus and I know what the end result was — so why can I never recall it properly?

My head is pounding too much to even think about running, but tossing and turning in bed any longer isn't an option either. I put down my glass and pad along the hall to the bathroom where I shrug off my dressing gown and turn on the shower, praying the jets will wash the night away.

In my car, I inch through the village and along the lane south, headlamps struggling to pierce the fog. A van looms from the opposite direction, bearing down on me in slow motion before rumbling past towards Winteringham. It's a cotton wool world, inside my head and out.

At Hemswell it's the same. Pale haloes from the bollard lamps guide me as I edge along the road, but once I reach the track to Jonathan's field there is nothing except the damp glow of the lights from the grain yard to my left. There's a chalky layby on the long straight edge of the field and I abandon my car with its parking lights on.

I wonder how much I can do when I can't even see from one end of the site to the other, but for fieldwalking the focus is so narrow it doesn't really matter. And maybe this strange, enclosed world will help me to concentrate, because my head's still all over the place, memories flicking with every thud from the dark waters of the canal to the crescendo of cicadas in a smothering Mediterranean heat.

I take a deep breath, my lungs filling with damp, vegetal air, and then I start. I work along the straight edge of the field, keeping the stubby hawthorn hedge to my right, the grinding gears of the lorries at the grain silos fading into the fog. I am the only living thing moving in this strange, blank world; not a bird is singing, no small mammal scurrying through the grass at my approach.

And I find — nothing. Just a Coke can thrown over the hedge and silver paper from a cigarette packet. My second transept back towards the invisible grain silos is the same and I can't even make out their mass until I am feet away from the low bank separating them from the field.

I turn and refocus, my eyes fixed on the scrappy grass beneath my feet. Away from the hedge it's harder to stay in a straight line, but my footsteps have left a shadow of a trail and I keep it in my field of vision to guide me. The fog is seeping through the downy lining of my anorak and coating my hair so it sticks to my head. My feet are like lead, I'm so damned tired.

I have no idea how far up the field I am when I find the flint so I take a flag from my rucksack and stick it in the earth so I can mark it properly later. Crouching low, I turn the object in my hand and run my finger along the worked edge. It's blunted by the years but it's still beautiful. It is not an entirely unexpected find, given there are crop marks indicating a Neolithic long barrow between here and Ermine Street.

It's as I stand I realise I am not alone. Coming out of the fog is a man; about six foot tall with a well-built physique masked by a short, thick jacket. I know the shape well; it's Jonathan, and I find myself smiling, about to call his name, before I realise it can't possibly be him. I look again, but there is no-one there. I step forwards and call 'hello', but my voice echoes back at me.

And then I hear it, a rumbling different to the lorries — an engine to my left, gathering pace, faster and faster as it races towards me; huge, invisible, lost in the wall of fog. I pick up my rucksack and stumble across the field before some instinct deep inside my befuddled brain tells me it's an aeroplane and I throw myself onto the ground.

There's a flash of light — a roar — a sound so loud it bursts my eardrums and I cover my head with my hands as the earth shakes beneath my feet. Then nothing. Nothing but silence and fog, and the image of Jonathan imprinted on my brain.

Slowly I sit up, feeling a bruise on my hand where I hit the earth. I'm expecting to hear running feet, sirens, the commotion that follows a dreadful accident, but there is nothing. The flash must have been an explosion, but I can't smell smoke and surely a fire would be visible even through this fog?

My legs are shaking as I stand; ears, eyes and nose straining for some tangible evidence of what I've just witnessed. More than that, I'm completely disoriented. I find a hedge, but it isn't the one I thought it was and I grope my way along it, increasingly mystified. I start to shiver. I need a hot bath and something to eat — I'm light-headed and sleep deprived; my mind playing tricks on me.

Eventually the grain silos loom in front of me and I'm able to cut the corner of the field towards the gate and the sanctuary of my car.

CHAPTER 35

It's almost as though Winteringham is wrapping me in its arms. In complete contrast to yesterday, the morning sun glistens off the Humber and after my run I decide to treat myself to a brownie and coffee in the village store. The owner greets me by name and asks how I'm enjoying house-sitting for Jonathan.

As I stir my coffee and gaze at the footpath map in the tiny room behind the shop, I am still struggling to understand what happened at Hemswell yesterday. I've even thought of asking Jonathan to send me a selfie from Christchurch to prove to myself he's there, but that would be idiocy. I know he is — there's no way he'd put up such an elaborate charade, because if there's one thing I've discovered about Jonathan Daubney, what you see is what you get.

So what *did* I see? And hear, just afterwards? Taking it apart and putting it back together again, every scrap of evidence tells me it was a plane coming down. Except there wasn't one. But Hemswell was a wartime airfield. I even googled 'Hemswell ghosts' and was slightly surprised when it came up with three or four of them; one of which is described as a pilot in flames on the runway after his plane crash landed. It shakes me for a moment, but what I heard sounded more like a plane taking off than coming down.

Of course, I could have imagined it all. But the bruise on my hand tells me that at the time it was real enough.

Esther is waiting in the dayroom at The Firs, struggling with a magnifying glass and *The Times*. She looks up when she sees me. "It's so frustrating — it's a really interesting article on birds of prey in Snowdonia but I can hardly see it, even with this thing."

I kiss her cheek and sit down opposite her. "Shall I read it to you?"

She folds the paper and looks at me, cheeks glowing. "No. Tell me what you wanted to pick my brains about. Is it something exciting?"

I shake my head. "Not really. It's just I'm enjoying being in the village so much I'd like to find a place to live locally. I don't like staying in a flat with no garden, not with spring coming on. The trouble is, I'm only looking for somewhere for a few months so none of the letting agents can help."

"Oh, Rachel, I do wish I hadn't sold my house…"

Pat bounces up behind us. "I've just heard from Jonathan. The cremation's on Friday so they've booked flights home for Sunday."

I look up at her and smile. "So not too much more than a week then?"

"No. I think he's relieved. Now it's my turn to worry."

"Worry? Why's that, my dear?" Esther asks.

"I hate it when he's anywhere near a plane — don't ask me why. I'm fine when it's Anna, but not Jonathan and I suppose in a way that makes it worse."

Pat's words wash down my spine like a trickle of icy water. *Oh my god. Could what I saw have been a premonition?*

Pat moves away to talk to another resident but I am sitting too close to Esther for her not to notice my sudden pallor.

"Goodness me, Rachel — whatever's wrong with you? Was it something Pat said?"

"Yes. You'll think I'm mad, Esther, but yesterday something happened which makes me scared about Jonathan flying too."

"What was it?"

"I was at Hemswell, at the proposed development site. It was really foggy but I was fieldwalking, and when I looked up I saw a man standing there and I could swear it was Jonathan, but when I looked again he'd gone. And straight after … straight after I heard what sounded like a plane taking off, then a huge explosion. But there was nothing. It didn't happen…" My voice is shaking and I grind to a halt.

Esther is silent. Eventually she says, "You care what happens to Jonathan, don't you?"

"Yes, because he matters to Pat, to you, to Caroline, and people depend on him for their jobs."

"I think what you saw was from the past, not the future."

"I did wonder about that. During the war there must have been accidents. I even googled Hemswell ghosts." My palms are sweating and I wipe them on my trousers.

Esther is looking at her hands. "There were accidents, yes. One in particular — a plane. It crashed on take-off, with a full load of bombs. I don't know what went wrong but one moment it was there and the next … well … the crew wouldn't have stood a chance." She shudders.

"Did you see it happen?"

She nods her head. "It became a bit of a tradition at the base. When there was a big raid, the civilian workers would stand by the runway to wave them off. I don't know, but Freddie may even have started it." She smiles. "Freddie ran the laundry where I worked and she was so kind to me. I was in awe of her at first, even in her overalls she looked glamourous — she was that kind of woman — but although she came over as hard she had a heart of pure gold.

"The airmen at the base were Polish and she fell in love with one of them. His name was Teodor but everyone called him Teo, and he was truly tall, blonde and handsome. He was a rear gunner — one of the most dangerous jobs — so she started to sneak out to wave him off. When other people around the base started to go as well, she used to take me with her. It was exciting in a way, standing on the airfield, seeing bomber after bomber take to the skies. We believed they were winning the war for us.

"Then one day, it would have been June 1942, high summer but it was damp and miserable, we were there as usual and we saw Teo's plane taxi past, and they all waved back at us then trundled to the end of the runway. Three planes took off before them, but Freddie and I always kept a special look out for Teo's. GR-F, it was — F for Freddie — they had the numbers painted near the tail. We watched as it gathered speed and it was off the ground, just over the end of the runway when it happened — like you said, a huge flash of white and an ear-splitting roar. Freddie started to run towards it but one of the men stopped her. She was crying and kicking and screaming… I don't know what happened next. They took me into one of the hangars and made me a cup of tea then one of the mechanics walked me home."

"Oh, Esther, how awful." My hand creeps across the table to cover hers. "No wonder you don't like talking about Hemswell."

She half smiles. "I'll probably have nightmares tonight, but it'll be worth it to stop you fretting over Jonathan."

"You really do believe I heard the ghost of the accident?"

"I wouldn't say ghost, perhaps more an echo of the past. Some things are so tragic, so strong, they leave a mark on the landscape. We can't understand everything in this world, can we?"

Esther's right — of course we can't — but all the same it doesn't sit comfortably with me. And it isn't until I am walking back through the dusk to Jonathan's house that I remember the man who looked like him. How does he fit into the story?

CHAPTER 36

The early spring sunshine follows me all the way to Hemswell on Tuesday morning. It burst through the fog just before the weekend so at least I had a little time to enjoy the view from Jonathan's rooftop conservatory before reluctantly moving back to Lincoln. I put a postcard in the window of Martha's shop before I left — and one on the noticeboard at the antiques' centre — but for the moment it seems the flat is my only option.

Today's plan is to finish the fieldwalking. My metal detector's in the boot of my car so I decide to sweep the area I've already covered first. The conditions couldn't be more different to last week and even the breeze has a breath of warmth and the birds are singing as I make my way up the hedge line.

Two thirds of the way along, the detector starts to bleep. The read out tells me there's some sort of ferrous metal about eight inches under the soil. I take my trowel from my rucksack and start to dig.

I am making good progress when a shadow falls across me.

"So have you found something?" No introduction, no preamble, just Jonathan on his haunches a few feet away. Really Jonathan this time.

I look up and smile. "Good morning. How are you?"

He laughs, but his face is pale and deeply lined. "Fine. How are you, Rachel?"

I point my trowel at the detector lying beside me. "I got a spike indicating ferrous metal so I'm trying to find it."

"What could it be?"

"Much too soon to say. I turned up a flint while I was fieldwalking last week but they're not particularly rare and the area is known for ancient occupation. So it could be anything. Or nothing."

"Let's hope it's the latter."

He stands, stretches, then walks across the field. I concentrate on my hole, carefully removing the soil until I find the curve of what looks like a piece of metal cable. I scrape more gently.

"Jonathan — I've found something."

He straightens, turns and marches towards me. "What is it?"

"Looks like some sort of metal cable."

"Modern then — not important."

"Not necessarily. Could be wartime."

"Are you sure that counts as archaeology?"

"I'm afraid so."

He watches as I scrape then crouches down. "Anything I can do?"

"Not at the moment. I need to see how far it extends."

The sun makes a feeble attempt to warm my shoulders as I work, and Jonathan settles himself on the grass next to the metal detector. After a while, I ask him how his trip went.

"Coming home was good — my extremely thoughtful ex-lodger left some homemade Bolognese in the fridge. It was very kind of her and the best thing I've eaten in over a week."

"Was the food out there so very awful?"

"No, not at all," he shrugs. "There's a lot of fusion stuff; interesting, but not very homely."

"Did you stay in Christchurch the whole time?"

He runs his finger around the detector's coil. "No. There was a lot of waiting around. Dave wanted to see where they found him so we went to Mount Cook. Beautiful country, breath-taking. One of the wardens took us."

"I've seen pictures — it does look marvellous."

"In different circumstances."

"Yes."

He closes his eyes and takes a shuddering breath.

"God, Jonathan — it must have been hard. You and Christopher were so close…"

"It was practically bloody impossible. But it's all growing back, the clearing where they found his tent. He's gone and he'll leave no mark."

"Of course he will. All those wonderful buildings — like your flat — and his daughter… Charlotte, is it? They're the mark he's left on the world." I ease my trowel under the metal and it gives slightly in the earth. I rock it from side to side, working further in. It's only a fragment — it's moving. "Hold your hands out, will you? As close and as flat as you can."

When the trowel is completely beneath the object, I cup my hand over the top to hold it steady. A gentle quarter turn and it's free to be lifted. It's a twist of metal cable, almost half an inch thick and about three inches long. I rest it on his upturned palms.

"What now?" Jonathan asks.

"Best leave the soil to dry a bit — it'll be easier to brush off." I stand. "I've got a flask and some sandwiches in the car. Want to share?"

He glances up. "I'm not hungry — my stomach thinks it's the middle of the night."

"Some tea then — warm your fingers."

"OK."

I pick up the detector and, with the find still lying on his hand, Jonathan follows me towards a gap in the hedge. The sky above us is an endless blue and sparrows scatter as I unlock my car. Opening the boot, I take the find from him and lay it in a plastic tray, then peel off my damp gloves and unscrew the thermos, pour the tea and hand the mug to him.

"What about you?"

"I'll drink it straight from the flask. I'm classy like that." I wink.

Finally he smiles.

We sit on the open tailgate, his fingers closed so tightly around the mug his knuckles are white and there's something about his expression that seems to be weighing me up. I pick up my sandwich and take a bite.

"Tell me about you and Chris."

He sounds wary when he asks, "What do you mean?"

"You know, your story. How you met, how you became friends. It might help you to talk about him."

He shakes his head. "Right at this minute, I don't think anything's going to help. Time's the only thing."

He sounds so sad, so desperately empty, that I balance the flask next to the finds tray and put my arm around his shoulder. He leans into me, human warmth mingling through our coats and I can smell the freshness of his shampoo, comfortable and comforting. The tug of emotion takes me by surprise.

Eventually he speaks, his voice scratchy and raw. "Actually, that does help — for the moment, anyway."

"I'm in no immediate hurry to get on. Not unless my boss is cracking the whip."

He shakes his head so we sit on with our arms around each other's shoulders as we finish our tea in silence, watching the sparrows peck at the gravel in the lane.

Eventually, Jonathan puts down his cup. "Amazing as that hug was, I've got a lot of catching up to do. And I suspect you're itching to get on as well." He gives my shoulder a squeeze then stands, stretching, fingers pointing to the sky.

"Jonathan? I do have time, you know, to listen."

He shakes his head. "Talking about Chris won't help, Rachel — it won't bring him back."

I stand too. "No, but talking about your feelings for him might."

"Feelings? We were mates, business partners."

"It seems to me you were closer than that. You clearly cared about him." The sun is too bright for me to see his eyes behind his Oakleys but I take a chance and plough on. "And Jonathan — nothing you could say would shock me. I know he was married and you have girlfriends but…"

His intake of breath is audible. "Are you implying what I think you're implying?"

"I'm not implying anything. All I'm saying is…"

He is three strides down the lane when he turns. "You don't know what the hell you're talking about. Stop interfering and leave me alone!"

I watch until he disappears around the curve of the road. Have I opened a door or closed one? I have a horrible feeling it's the latter and I feel slightly sick. My bloody enormous mouth again; just when I might have done a bit of good, all I've managed is to add to his anguish.

Still, that doesn't mean I should waste a day. I screw the lid back onto the flask, slam the boot of my car closed and return to the field. As I pick up the metal detector, I turn towards the grain silos. I have the strangest feeling someone's watching me, but when I look there is no-one there.

CHAPTER 37

Esther is in her usual seat at the dayroom window but she is not alone. In the chair opposite her is a woman with a round face and a blonde bob. She looks about my age but as I get closer the soft lines under her eyes give her away as about ten years older.

She stands as I cross the room and Esther introduces us. "Rachel, this is Lucy Caister. Lucy, this is my friend Rachel Ward, the archaeologist I've been telling you about."

We shake hands and I draw up a chair to sit between them.

"Lucy's mother Margaret is staying here at the moment, recovering from a stroke."

"I am sorry to hear that," I reply automatically. "Is she doing all right?"

Lucy looks down. "No, not really. Good days and bad but I'm not sure she'll ever be able to go home."

"And in the meantime," says Esther, "Margaret's house in the village is empty."

"And deteriorating, to be honest." Lucy looks at me. "It needs someone living in it and Esther mentioned you're looking. I don't suppose you'd consider house-sitting a potentially damp and leaky Georgian cottage?"

"Do you really mean that? Esther hasn't been twisting your arm, has she? She can be very persuasive."

Lucy laughs. "I know. She and Mum have been friends for years. It was her idea, but I think it's a great one."

My head is reeling. "I'd love to, Lucy — when can I move in?"

"You'd better see it first."

Esther looks from one of us to the other. "No time like the present, girls."

Bramble Cottage is one of the Georgian terraced houses I noticed near the crossroads on my first visit to Winteringham. Not the one that had pink roses clambering up its façade, but it has a dark green front door and an elegant brass knocker. Lucy fishes in her handbag for the keys while I gaze up at the dripping guttering with something close to pure joy.

The door swings open and Lucy stands back so I can step into the narrow hall. There is a staircase straight ahead of me and a hint of damp in the air, but it is mixed with beeswax polish and I turn to smile at her.

"Lucy — I'm going to love this."

"Let me show you first."

The living room is beautifully proportioned with a marble-mantel fireplace, its log burner shielded by an embroidered antique screen and the shelves either side home to a collection of Victorian china. A sash window at the front gives straight onto the pavement and at the opposite end French doors lead to a conservatory with elegant wicker furniture and a collection of orchids. At the back of the house a long, narrow kitchen extends into the garden with a small dining table nearest the door.

Upstairs, Lucy shows me the bedroom over the kitchen. There is a dark oak dressing table and wardrobe which crowd the space but their age gives them such rich beauty I don't care. Nearer the window is a double bed with an antique lace counterpane. Lucy's mum and I have very similar taste.

Lucy talks a lot about her mother while she is showing me around. It's clear she's struggling to come to terms with the changes in her. She can't live without her mother — I could never live with mine.

Our relationship ended in so much shame and anger we didn't even say goodbye. The things she said were unforgivable. Gran never forgave her either. At Gran's funeral Dad said I'd grown very like my grandmother. But she had a soft underbelly — a heart of gold, something I seem to lack. She was more than a mother to me and I miss her every day.

"I'd clear the cupboards for you," Lucy says, interrupting my thoughts. "Put it all in Mum's room." The door at the front end of the landing remains tactfully shut, but between the bedrooms is a bathroom and Lucy shows me how the shower works and where the heating controller is before we head back to the hall.

"Oh, Lucy, it's lovely," I tell her. "How much a week do you want for it?"

She shakes her head. "No. I won't rent it to you — but I'd love you to stay if you want to. Old houses deteriorate so quickly and I worry about the place being empty."

"At least let me pay the bills. I won't do it otherwise, but it would be such a shame because it would suit us both."

She's smiling at me — right to the depths of her tired eyes. "Then we have a deal. When would you like to move in?"

I close my eyes. Take the plunge. "Tomorrow? I don't have much stuff — the flat I'm in is fully furnished."

"Fab. I'm working in the morning but I can meet you here at two."

As I walk back to The Firs to tell Esther the good news I feel a weight lifting from my shoulders. Perhaps once I've left the flat for good the flashbacks will stop.

Esther looks up from her iPad. "Well? What do you think of Bramble Cottage?"

"It's gorgeous and I'm moving in tomorrow. I can't thank you enough."

"That's wonderful. Shall we have a sherry to celebrate?"

"Just a small one. Then I need to get back to Lincoln and start packing."

CHAPTER 38

I don't know if I'm avoiding Jonathan or Jonathan's avoiding me. Leastways, I've told Caroline I'm working from home while I'm waiting to hear about the geophysics. She seems to think it's a good idea.

For company, I visit Esther. Not that it's remotely a chore. When I arrive she's watching another resident making a fuss of her granddaughter's mongrel. I tell her it reminds me of my friend's dog, Toast.

She claps her hands together in delight. "That's such a marvellous name. What sort is he?"

"I'd say about eighty per cent terrier, but the rest it's hard to tell."

"One of the airmen at the base had a terrier. It went everywhere with him, right until the moment he got into his plane, and then one of the mechanics would take him and hand him over to the debriefing officer so he was there when he came back."

"And did he, you know, always come back?"

"Yes, he was one of the lucky ones. We had terrible losses in the early summer of 1942 and it wasn't sustainable. The crews who came after were moved to mine laying which was safer." She smiles. "Gardening, they called it."

"Esther, up until now I've had the distinct impression you didn't want to talk about what happened in the war."

"Then you were right. After I told you about Teo's crash I was expecting nightmares — I had them for so many years afterwards. But nothing happened. In fact, I felt a whole lot better for talking about it. So I wondered if perhaps you'd like to hear the whole story?"

"I would, very much."

"Then I'll tell you. But first, why don't you find Julie and ask her to bring us a pot of tea?"

We sit by the window as the pale sunlight illuminates the crocuses dotting the lawn and the blue tits swing on the feeder hanging from the lowest branches of the gnarled apple tree. Esther could see none of it, even if her eyes were open, but she sits back in her chair, bone china mug in hand, as her story unfolds.

When Esther's education was curtailed brutally at the age of fourteen, she went to help the war effort at the airbase at Hemswell. To her it seemed huge and forbidding, full of men speaking in a foreign language, and WAAFs with their noses in the air.

She was assigned to work in the laundry in one of the barrack blocks — two tiny rooms; one hot and steamy, the other hot and dry. At first, she was scared of Freddie too, with her perfectly coiffed black hair and her lipstick and rouge, faultless even when she was scrubbing sheets. She was glamour personified. She'd been bombed from her home in Coventry, her family lost, and believed she was helping the airmen strike back — if only by giving them clean sheets to sleep in and pristine uniforms to wear.

While the WAAFs were snooty, Freddie took Esther under her wing, helping her with the hardest work of putting bedding through the enormous mangle and showing her how to iron a perfect grain into shirts. They'd stop and listen to the bombers taking off through the dusk. 'Poor souls,' Freddie would say, tears glistening in her eyes. 'I'm never getting caught up with one of them.'

But of course she did. It was the first time Esther had witnessed love at close range and it made her teenage heart race just being on the edge of it. Teo was over six foot tall, with hair as fair as Freddie's was black, and pearl grey eyes. But it was his smile Esther remembered most; quick and ready, with a sense of fun that made it easy to laugh with him, even through the inevitable language barrier.

Freddie was smitten. There was a glow about her, and in the mornings she'd sing as they went about their work, sometimes making up new words to old songs, with Esther joining in the chorus. But on the days Teo was flying, there was a more sober mood and Freddie started to wait at the edge of the runway to see the planes off. Even when Esther went home, Freddie continued waiting, sewing in the airing room, making extra money from mending and remaking dresses and blouses from curtains, sheets and any worn bit of fabric people could find.

Then, in early June, she announced she and Teo were engaged. For Esther, it was the height of romance, and she'd listen to their wedding plans while Freddie embroidered a tablecloth for her bottom drawer. Next on her list was a bedspread, but that was barely started when Teo's Wellington exploded on take-off.

Esther opens her eyes and looks at me. "I have the tablecloth, you know. You'll have seen it — it's in my room. She said she hoped I'd have more use for it than she did."

"Was it the only one she made?"

"I believe so. That's why it's so special to me. She was a dressmaker by trade. She used to say she was no good at embroidery — kept pricking her fingers — but I thought it was wonderful work."

The air in the room seems suddenly so thick I can hardly breathe. How can I tell Esther what — and maybe even who — I saw in that tiny room in the old barrack block? My heart is pitter-pattering against my rib cage, but Esther carries on.

"There's something else I should tell you — something very strange. That ring you bought your friend for Christmas — it was Freddie's engagement ring, I'm sure it was. It was wartime so the settings were pretty rough and ready and the metal cheap — Teo promised her he'd have the diamond reset when it was all over."

I breathe out and try to stop my hands from shaking. "It wasn't a real diamond. It was paste — at least it was sold as paste — the ring wasn't that dear…"

"I suppose the stone could have been changed at some point, but nevertheless I'd ask your friend to have it checked. Just in case."

"Esther, were the laundry rooms by any chance at the back of the barracks? In the middle block to the east of the parade ground?"

She leans forwards. "Yes."

"That's where I found the ring. In a basket of other jewellery." But I can't tell her any more. I can't even process how a tablecloth could be in two places at once. Or in two times…

It's Julie who saves me when she asks if I'm staying for lunch. I make a show of looking out of the window at the pale sunshine, then decline. "I really must finish my fieldwalking," I tell her.

"And I think I'll have mine in my room," Esther adds. "I'm feeling quite exhausted."

We stand and I hug her goodbye. "I hope you're OK after that," I whisper.

"I'm fine, Rachel, fine. It's good exhausted, not bad, and this afternoon I expect I'll have a little sleep. I feel so much better, and I've only told you half the story. All the same, I'll need to be at my best to tell you the rest."

I hold her even tighter, her birdlike frame tiny beneath my arms. "All in your own time," I tell her before watching her grasp the bannister and climb the stairs one by one.

CHAPTER 39

Pat corners me as I'm leaving The Firs. "Rachel? A word, please." She marches off in the direction of her office, leaving me trailing behind her.

The moment I close the door she turns on me, her voice shaking. "Jonathan told me you didn't have the courtesy to tell him you'd moved out of the flat. He's got quite enough to worry about at the moment without you adding insult to injury."

"I wanted to tell him but, well, you see, when he got back from New Zealand I tried my best to help when he was upset and he told me to leave him alone."

Pat sits down. "Is that right?"

"Yes. He was pretty angry but I knew he was grieving so I brushed it off." I bite my lip. "The trouble was I'd made an assumption, hinted at something, and it made him angry. I thought you said his relationship with Christopher was much more than friendship and I thought you meant, you know, in a physical way..."

After an endless moment when all I can hear is the clock ticking, Pat reaches out and touches my hand. "Jonathan isn't gay, I can assure you, although he does forge close friendships with other men. His father was the same; a man's man, if you like."

For no apparent reason a tear escapes from my eye and I fish in my pocket for a tissue. "I'm sorry, Pat. It's been a tough few weeks but all the same I shouldn't let my emotions get the better of me."

"It mightn't be such a bad idea, you know. Emotions have their place." She moves away. "Shall I make us some tea?"

"No. I need to pull myself together then I need to talk to Jonathan. Where is he?"

"He's at home. Writing Chris's eulogy. Or trying to." As I stand, Pat hugs me. "Be gentle with him — he may not show it, but like you he's very fragile at the moment."

I play Pat's words over in my mind as I walk up the hill. Jonathan's Jag is in the driveway and my palms feel uncomfortably clammy as I edge past it. Whatever his reaction, unless he slams the door in my face, there is only one thing I need to say.

Jonathan answers the bell wearing jeans and a grey sweatshirt with a hole in the elbow. It drains the colour from his unshaven face and his fair hair is sticking up in spikes. He says nothing, just stands and stares at me as my willpower ebbs away.

"I'm so sorry," I stutter. "Pat told me ... but anyway, I want to apologise for what I thought ... for what I said... I didn't mean to..."

He raises an eyebrow. His 'really?' drips with disbelief.

"Yes, really. I was just so wound up... Anyway, it's not an excuse. I just want to apologise. Really apologise. From the very bottom of my heart."

"OK. Thank you."

"OK." There's nothing I can read in his face so I turn and edge back past his car. I am almost at the end of the drive when he calls.

"Rachel — are you doing anything tomorrow afternoon?"

"Nothing that can't wait."

"Do you fancy a walk along the dyke to South Ferriby for a quick one at the Hope and Anchor?"

I look over my shoulder. "As long as you're sure you want to."

"Not entirely." He shakes his head. "But I'll see you by the war memorial at two."

CHAPTER 40

I decide to waste some time at the antiques' centre before I meet Jonathan. Once I have my habitual latte in front of me, I spread the geophysics plots over the table. The scatter of blue blobs in the northern half of the field matches the ferrous spikes from the metal detecting almost exactly. There's a concentration in the north-east corner which will be my first target to dig, but otherwise they are completely random. I think about the exploding bomber. I need a ballistics expert to look at these — or to learn about ballistics pretty sharpish myself. And ask Esther exactly where the accident happened, although all things considered, I think I probably know.

The only other feature is a ditch which cuts the field in a crescent moon about half way down. Ditch cuts can be any age — you don't know until you dig them — so a section across that is target two. And then? Probably nothing. The southern half of my plan is completely blank.

If the archaeology liaison officer agrees with me, this could prove to be a pretty small dig — one I could perfectly well handle myself. My spine tingles at the thought, my fingers itching to grab my trowel and start scraping away at the earth. Over the ditch cut at least — if the ferrous spikes do turn out to be the bomber, I'm rather less sure I want to excavate that.

I'm shaking as I walk down the corridor and past the books at the bottom of the stairwell. I'd rather stay here and browse, but I have to know. Was it the second room or the third? I frown — I should be able to remember. I glance through the first door; the books have spread in here now, shelves lining the walls from floor to ceiling. Second door; Victoriana neatly displayed — two marble topped washstands, china bowls, vases, a mahogany hallstand with a selection of walking canes.

At the third door, I stop, holding onto the frame as I peep inside. There is condensation on the window, tiny droplets reflecting the harsh electric light. But there's nothing else to see — the room is completely empty.

The views are impressive walking east towards the mouth of the river, the Humber Bridge glistening in the distance. At first our conversation is polite, stilted, Jonathan's face tense and pale. It helps that in places the path topping the dyke is so narrow we need to go in single file. Only then is the silence between us remotely comfortable and I begin to wonder if this was such a good idea.

We brave the breeze to sit outside the Hope and Anchor with our drinks. The pub is on a platform next to the lock where the Ancholme meets the Humber and the tide is low, exposing the mud flats. Jonathan explains the pub was flooded a few years ago, left empty and forlorn until it was rescued by the owner of Winteringham Fields.

"Cash cow for him, probably," he says, "and a great pub to have as your local for the folks in the village." He takes a sip of his pint. "Keep their beer properly too."

I raise my glass and smile. "Definitely worth the walk. If only for the view of the cement works."

He twists to look over his shoulder. "Oh, lord — I'd forgotten about that — we'd better swap seats so you get to look at the river. Or you could come and sit on the bench next to me — I don't bite — not at weekends, anyway."

"You're sure about that?"

"Yes. Look, Rachel, you had the decency to apologise and so should I."

"It's OK, I know you have a lot on your mind."

"Yes." He traces the grain of the wood along the table with his index finger as we listen to the geese call in the distance.

I debate the possible outcomes of asking the question long and hard, but in the end my need to break the silence wins. "How's the eulogy coming along?"

Jonathan picks up his pint. "Not well. I can't see the point."

"Then why are you doing it?"

"Sometimes, Rachel, you have to do what's expected of you. However much you think it's a waste of time."

"But surely it will give some comfort? To his parents at least… I mean, that's why you went to bring him home, wasn't it?"

His finger traces the grain back again.

I put down my glass. "And maybe, once the funeral's over, you'll be able to start to move on too."

"Like anything's that convenient."

"No, think about it. Ceremonies for the dead are so deeply engrained in human nature they're almost part of our DNA. I've excavated sites going back millennia and although often we don't understand the specific practice there is no doubt there's been some sort of rite and a great deal of respect. As a species we must need to do it for some reason."

He looks up at me. "That sounds a bit too logical."

"And nothing like you feel?"

"I don't know how I feel."

"Then maybe you should try to work it out."

"You think I haven't been? It's like losing Dad all over again, only worse. Why should it be worse? I loved my father and whatever you may think about Chris and me, I didn't love him."

"Chris's circumstances were tragic and he was far too young. But also — don't fly off the handle — there's a difference between loving someone and being in love with them. The person I love most in the world is my best friend and if I lost her I'd be in pieces." I drain my glass. "Come on then — I'll shut up and you can do some more thinking on our walk back."

This time our silence is more comfortable and broken by Jonathan's occasional commentary on the bird life in the marshes edging the river. The wind picks up and clouds scud along behind us as the afternoon fades towards dusk.

Jonathan walks me back to Bramble Cottage and I invite him in for a drink. He settles himself into the leather armchair next to the log burner, stretching his long legs in front of him.

"It's a beautiful room, isn't it?" I say.

He looks around. "Comfortable, but not really my taste. But if you like this I can see why you weren't that keen on Willow Gardens."

"Well at least there's a silver lining come from being pushed into the canal." I try to sound cavalier, but I only wish I could believe it.

Jonathan takes a sip of his coffee. "So what happened between you and Ben, if you don't mind me asking?"

"It was just the stupidest mistake on my part. You never, ever sleep with a student but we became friends and one thing led to another. I should have seen he was using me, but I guess I was too busy using him."

Jonathan raises his eyebrows. "You? Using him?"

I force a laugh. "What I said to you at the Christmas party… I suppose you could say it was rather the pot calling the kettle black."

It is a while before Jonathan speaks. "What you said at the Christmas party — it was harsh — and some of your evidence was flawed — but it wasn't entirely unfair either. I suspect, looking back, it was the kernel of truth that made me so angry. The girl who was with me — I met at some dinner a week earlier. I saw her once afterwards. Before that... Denise... We were together for a while but we wanted different things. It ended when she told me she was pregnant. As it happened she wasn't but..."

I swing my feet off the sofa and lean forwards. "But if she had been you'd still have..."

"If she had been the baby couldn't have been mine. After Chris's divorce ... seeing him ripped apart by being away from Charlotte ... I had a vasectomy." He shrugs. "I never really wanted kids anyway."

"And Denise didn't know?"

"There never seemed to be a right time to tell her. It's hardly first date conversation and after that we just kind of slid into seeing each other. We never talked about any sort of commitment."

It's as if the scales are falling from my eyes; I can't remember his exact words to Denise but I must have taken them the wrong way — he couldn't have been talking about a child — he was talking about infidelity. As I look across at Jonathan I can no longer see the man with the scary Oakleys. I smile.

Jonathan reaches down and puts his empty coffee mug on the hearth. "I should be going. Comfortable as it is here, I have an eulogy to finish."

CHAPTER 41

I can tell from the scraps of paint that the piece of metal was once dark green. A ninety degree angle protrudes from the earth, almost an inch thick. I tuck a stray strand of hair back into my beanie hat and continue to scrape.

I've waited most of the week for the council liaison officer to get back to me, but he's playing it cautiously and has suggested two test pits over ferrous spikes before we decide what to do. The idea is to give a ballistics expert some finds to go on, and I may have struck proverbial pay dirt straight away. The metal looks as though it might have come from a plane, but the reality is it could also have fallen off a piece of farm machinery. I'd feel far more confident if it was a thousand or two years older.

There's drizzle in the air, making the limestone soil claggy, but it's not enough to force me to stop work.

Gradually more metal is revealed. It's almost upright in the soil and I stop to photograph its position. I am just putting my camera back in my finds tray when I see a man on the other side of the hedge, looking out over the airfield. Just like Jonathan was the day after he came back from New Zealand. Jonathan's height, Jonathan's build — but this time I don't call out. Instead, I lift my camera to my eye and squint against the drizzle. But through the viewfinder there's no-one there.

I jump to my feet but the man really has gone. Vanished into thin air, unless he's crawling along the other side of the hedge, and I rush over to check, feeling like a fool when the track is empty. There's nothing around me but the flatness of the fields and I am completely alone.

My hands are shaking as I go back to my scraping. I've read about Hemswell's ghosts and somehow that makes me feel better. I'm not the only one who's felt their presence. It's not that abnormal.

The rain eases to be replaced by the weakest spring sunshine and my soaking beanie hat joins my camera in the tray. I've found the bottom corner of the object now, the metal twisted and torn. If I'm not careful I'm going to cut myself. That's the only way the past can hurt me.

Except, of course, my own past. Since being pushed into the canal it's been creeping up behind me, invading my dreams, muddled with the murky waters. Esther said she felt so much better after she talked about Teo's plane crash. But how can I tell anyone what happened to me when the memory's buried so deep?

I pace the kitchen while the kettle boils then take my tea to the conservatory, the steady drumbeat of rain on the roof drilling into my skull. It started again when I was out for my run and I was already soaked through by the time I realised my house keys had dropped from my pocket. Luckily, there's a key safe half hidden behind the base of next door's climbing rose so I was at least able to get in and have a shower.

Everything about today's been disturbing and I need to talk to Jessie. But where the hell to start? Perhaps with the ring. It's not that I disbelieve Esther, but if the diamond is real it at least proves something.

Jessie's face flashes onto my iPad. "What are you up to?" she asks.

"Killing time. Looking at old fashioned recipes. I might ask Jonathan to supper."

"Ooo — might you?" Her head tilts to one side and she purses her lips.

"Not like that. He's going through a bad time and it's his best friend's funeral next week. That's all."

"Doesn't bear thinking about, does it? I don't plan on one of us having a funeral for at least sixty years."

"Don't even go there, Jessie. I couldn't…" From nowhere, tears threaten.

"Hey — what's wrong?"

"Weird stuff, Jessie, really weird. I thought I'd worked it out but it must be getting to me."

"What, Ben? Don't tell me he's tried something else?" Her voice rises in panic.

"No, no. All quiet on that front, thankfully. I reckon if it was him who pushed me, a brush with the police scared him off."

"Well that's something. So what's been going on? You mentioned the ring in your message."

"Possibly. I don't know. It's all so farfetched."

"Rachel — are you OK? You sound like you're having a real wobble."

"Jessie? How are you fixed this coming week? Is there a day we could meet up? There's so much more I should tell you."

"Tomorrow?"

"But it's the weekend…"

Her voice is sharp as she cuts across me. "Don't put this off. And a Saturday is actually easier as Paul can look after the kids. I want to see where you're living anyway so give me your address and I'll be there before lunchtime."

"OK. Oh, and Jessie — bring the ring too."

"Bring it? I wear it all the time."

Jessie's words warm me and after a little weep once she's hung up I turn my attention to reading all I can about the technical specification of Wellington bombers. It's tough but absorbing and when I finally look at the clock on the kitchen wall it's just after eight and I'm starving. I put a couple of slices of bread under the grill and open a bottle of wine. The boiler pops and sings, the stairs creak as the old house cloaks me with its peace and calm. I pour baked beans into a saucepan and add a generous slug of grated cheese.

It's only an hour or so later I decide to go to bed. I cork the remains of the wine and look for the keys which I always leave in the kitchen door — but of course they aren't there and I can't even unlock it if I want to get into the garden. I hadn't thought of that. I stand still and listen — it sounds as though the rain has stopped. If I just retrace the last part of my run around the village streets I might be lucky and find them.

I grab my almost dry leggings and a thick sweatshirt before pulling on my wellies and anorak. The breeze is whistling past the crossroads as I stride along the pavement, headtorch in my hand, sweeping the path in front of me. At this time of night Winteringham is quiet, with the exception of one house where someone is obviously having a party, but all the same I have the feeling of people around me and it's strangely comforting.

At the south west corner of the village I turn right and the road is bordered on one side by open fields. The wind cuts across and an owl hoots in the distance. Although I'm walking along a chain of streetlights the empty space is too much all of a sudden and I take to my heels and run, only stopping when I have houses on either side again. A couple walking a dog bid me good evening and the trembling inside me stops.

At the end of the street the pub door opens and the light spills a tall man onto the pavement. I realise almost at once it's Jonathan, but as we're on opposite sides of the road perhaps he won't notice me. At that moment he starts to cross.

"Rachel! What are you doing out at this time of night?"

"I went for a run and my keys must have dropped out of my pocket."

"You're not locked out, are you?"

I shake my head. "Thankfully there's a key safe. I just thought I'd take a look for them before turning in."

"You should have called. I'd have helped you — better than walking around on your own after dark."

"It's all right. I kept to the village — I'm not crazy enough to wander along the dyke in the pitch black."

He rubs his hands together against the cold. "Well at least some common sense prevailed. Come on, let me walk you home."

His voice is a little slurred and I smile up at him. "No, it's fine — honestly — I can practically see the cottage from here."

"Nevertheless…" He puts his hand on my elbow and leads me along the pavement, but says nothing more until I've removed the spare key from the safe and am putting it in the door.

"You can't be too careful, Rachel, remember that. You're one special lady." I raise an eyebrow and he laughs. "Not forgetting, of course, that I need you to run the dig at Hemswell."

"Of course," I wink. "Just as long as I'm useful."

"Absolutely." But before he turns away, he touches my cheek. By the time I've locked the door behind me I wonder if I imagined it.

CHAPTER 42

I'm cleaning my teeth, towel balanced on the top of my head after my shower, when a sharp knock echoes through the hall. Surely not Jessie already? I wrap another towel around me and run down the stairs to open the door and peer through the gap left by the chain.

Jonathan is standing in front of me, a set of keys dangling from his index finger.

"Where did you find them?"

"I took an early stroll along the dyke and hit the jackpot. They must have fallen out of your pocket when you climbed over the stile by the sailing club."

"That's so kind of you. Would you like a coffee or something?"

I fumble to release the chain but he shakes his head. "No — I need to get on. I'm taking Charlotte swimming this morning. It's the first time Ruby's let me have her so I can't be late. And anyway, I can see you're, well, not exactly ready to receive visitors."

I glance down to see there's a lot — and I mean an awful lot — of my left breast showing. I grab the keys and pull the towel closer around me. "I ... I can't thank you enough," I stutter.

He lowers his gaze to chest level. "The pleasure's all mine." Then he blushes ever so slightly. "Sorry ... that was more than a little crass. For goodness sake, go and put some clothes on." He winks at me then strolls across the road to where his Jag is waiting. I watch him drive away then go upstairs to dress.

Jonathan. The man who looks like Jonathan. The woman. The tablecloth. The ring. Then back to Jonathan again. Why am I so scared? Is it them frightening me, or is it myself? Their past or my own. Or my now. The flashbacks... I can't let that happen to me again. I can't live in a place where I can't remember, where there are only fragments. If I do, it will surely drive me mad.

I grip the edge of the kitchen table as hard as I can. The end could be far more frightening than the beginning and I need to go back there to understand. Talk about it, spew it all out. Even after seventy-five years, it helped Esther.

The kitchen clock seems stuck at quarter past ten. I need Jessie to be here. I need to tell her everything. But there are parts I can't truly remember myself.

I pull on my coat and race to the village store. In the far corner of the shop I delve amongst the bleach and washing up liquid until I find it. Toilet cleaner. Lemon zest. Something I have never bought in my life and with very good reason.

Under the sink at Bramble Cottage is a small china vase shaped like a scalloped bowl. I take it into the conservatory and shut the French doors to the living room behind me. If it's unbearable I can easily let the smell out into the garden. I set the vase on the table and hold my nose as I pour the toilet cleaner into it.

There comes a point when I have to breathe. The awful chemical lemoness sweeps up my nostrils and I force out the air, snotty and spluttering. I bend over the vase and fill my lungs until I am coughing and gagging. Writhing, on the floor of my mother's bathroom.

I am a red, blotchy mess when I open the door to Jessie.

"Oh my god, Rach." She pushes past me into the hall and wraps her arms around me. "I didn't know it was this bad."

"It has to be bad — to ever be good. I know that now."

"What on earth…"

I put my hand on her arm. "Let's make tea, eat biscuits and I'll explain. There's so much I haven't told you, Jessie. So much I couldn't tell anyone. Some of it I can't even remember properly and that's what I've been trying to do… But never mind that for the moment."

She follows me down the hall and hangs her coat over the back of one of the kitchen chairs. I put four teabags into the pot, set two mugs and the milk carton on the table and fish a box of chocolate chip cookies out of the cupboard.

I tell her everything. About being pregnant and fluffing my exams, losing my place at Oxford. About being swept along by my mother, ending up wanting my baby, the row with Tommy.

My hand shakes as I refill our mugs. "The row is the last thing I truly remember. I totally lost it with him. His friends were in the bar too and they were laughing, joking that he couldn't control his woman. Those words… they went round and round in my head. And then, somehow, I was down the steps in a heap on the sand. Maybe I remember a bruise in a ring around my arm but maybe I don't. I get these awful flashbacks — just fragments. Blood… on my feet from my flipflops cutting me — I tried to walk home — it was miles. Then blood running down the inside of my thigh from my shorts… And this terrible thirst.

"But I woke up in my own bed and my mother wouldn't speak to me. Not after telling me she would never forgive me for losing Tommy then coming home drunk with my clothing all messed up like the slut that I was. I had a miscarriage, Jessie, there in her bathroom… I was crying and calling for help, but all I heard was the front door slamming behind her."

There are tears running down my cheeks and Jessie takes my hand. "That is beyond unforgiveable, but what about your father?"

I sniff. "This was way out of his comfort zone. He's a very traditional army type. So he shipped me off to my gran's and it was the best thing he could have done."

Jessie smiles. "You always were very close to her, weren't you?"

"Yes. She put me back on track, but she was old school, you know, least said soonest mended. And for a long time that felt right." The very thought of her has brought my heart rate back to a more normal level.

"So what's changed?"

I take a deep breath. "Two things really. First, because I was starting to get flashbacks about the canal and I had to find a way to stop them growing into something like this. But also because I can see a path, a pattern. It was something you said, actually, when I came to see you after Ben — about not being able to form proper relationships. And it made me think about the reasons. I have to deal with it and I have to change, but I can't do it on my own."

She stands up and hugs me. "I'm so pleased, Rachel. So pleased it's me you're talking to about this."

"Who else would it be?"

She squeezes me again. "I just wondered, you know, if there was someone you wanted to change for."

I shake my head. "I'm doing this for me."

"I'm glad. That's always the best reason."

She sits back down and cradles her mug. The ring is glinting on her finger under the kitchen light. I take her hand and study the diamond. "I showed your ring to Esther when I bought it, and although she didn't tell me at the time she thinks she recognised it. And the last time she saw it, the diamond was real."

"What?"

"I found it in a basket of costume jewellery at the antiques' centre at Hemswell. Of course, the stone could have been changed but I suggest we go into Scunthorpe to the jeweller to find out."

"Good call. I'll be too terrified to wear it if it is real — it's huge."

"Promise me — whatever it is — you'll keep it right where it is on that finger."

Her eyes mist over behind her glasses. "Of course, Rachel. Of course I will."

CHAPTER 43

First thing on Monday I drive to Hemswell with my windscreen wipers on full blast and it's no better when I park up next to the field. I show my latest finds to the liaison officer and he seems quite happy with my plans, but neither of us has the least inclination to hang around outside so we shake hands and go our separate ways.

Back in my car there is a text from Jessie: *I've been looking up your Jonathan on LinkedIn. He's absolutely gorgeous.*

I start my engine then press the speed dial to call her. "You're meant to be insuring your ring, not looking up Jonathan."

She laughs. "I've done that too. I had to send the broker a photo but now it's on the policy."

"Thanks, Jessie — that's something of a relief."

"I know. I stuck a plaster over it all day yesterday in case it fell off while I was doing the housework."

"Idiot."

"That's me. How are you feeling now?"

"Much better. I slept like a log last night."

"You can come here any time, you know."

"I know — and I promise I will if I need to."

Next I want to call The Firs so I pull into the a layby to find the number on my phone. A breeze ripples across the hedgerow and a lorry thunders past, kicking up spray. It's just gone eleven o'clock. I can't leave it any later.

Pat answers after the third ring, so I ask if she thinks Esther would like to come out to lunch. She bustles off to find her then returns to tell me I've made Esther's day.

"Actually," she adds, "you made my day the other Friday when you went to talk to Jonathan. Feeling he'd lost you as well was just one negative too many for him at the moment."

"I didn't realise I was that important."

She laughs. "No, I don't think he did either."

I am surprised when Esther asks if we can go to the café at Hemswell for lunch. "I looked it up on my iPad," she tells me proudly, "it says they do home cooked food."

"Well if the cakes are anything to go by, it'll be delicious."

"Yes, and there's somewhere I want to show you."

I park in one of the disabled spaces right outside the antiques' centre and Esther fishes in her handbag for her blue badge, then hands it to me to prop on the dashboard.

"This is the right building?" I ask her.

She looks around the old parade ground as if to check her bearings. "Oh yes. It's seventy-five years since I've been here, but this is it."

I put my hand over hers. "Are you ready?"

"As I'll ever be."

The woman at reception nods as we pass. Esther's progress is slow but purposeful, not even glancing at the cabinets which line the corridor. But although she turns left at the bottom of the back staircase it is at the first room she stops, the dark and windowless hole packed with small furniture. She stands at the doorway for a long time, her eyes gazing only into the past, while I struggle to come to terms with my unexpected disappointment.

Finally, she turns to me. "Come on, I'll show you where the laundry was. It isn't far." And I know, before she moves on, which room she will lead me to.

The scrubbed pine table is empty but the flying jacket hangs forlornly at the end of the rail. Esther lifts her nose. "Can you smell lily-of-the-valley or am I imagining it? It was Freddie's favourite." She's right — there's just the faintest touch of it in the air.

Esther stands in the middle of floor and looks around. "This was the drying room — it was lined with slatted shelves where we'd air the linen and the ironing table was in the middle. That was such hard work. And Freddie had a little low chair in front of the window where the light was best so she could sew."

"So what was the other room you stopped at?" I ask.

"It was where Freddie died."

"What? You didn't tell me she died here too."

"Yes. About six months after Teo." Leaning heavily on her stick she walks over to the rail and fingers the jacket. She looks over her shoulder. "You should take this for Jonathan."

I follow her across the room. "I've seen it here before — it really is lovely. But then I couldn't think who to buy it for." I run my fingers over the soft leather, pick up the hem and the sleeves, but there is no label. "Anyway, it doesn't look as though it's for sale."

"It isn't. But you should still take it for him."

"I can't — not just like that."

Esther looks over to the window and whispers, "But she can, Freddie, can't she? That's why it's here."

A trail of ice runs up my spine, the hairs on the back of my neck standing on end. "Esther, can you see her?"

"No, but she's here all the same. Come on, put that jacket over my shoulders and we'll go to have some lunch."

"But you can't…"

"Rachel — I can't not."

Esther chooses a table near the window and I hang the flying jacket over the back of the chair next to her before heading off to the counter. I order two Lincolnshire sausage with onion gravy and mash and a large pot of tea. I pick up a couple of packets of sugar — they might just stop me from shaking.

While we're waiting for our meals to arrive, Esther talks. In the months that followed Teo's death, Freddie changed, not just becoming tearful and withdrawn, but physically too. "Of course, I was much too naïve to know what was happening, but I don't think anyone else realised she was pregnant either because there was a lot of bitchy talk about her letting herself go. I was just so sad about it — I didn't know what to do, but my mother told me to keep working hard and to be kind to Freddie, and she'd come around. Everyone did eventually.

"I think Freddie appreciated it. She stopped sewing herself but I made a clumsy attempt to embroider a handkerchief for her birthday and she hugged me and said she'd never had anything so beautiful to cry into. I'd seen love at its brightest and shiniest when she and Teo were together, and now I was witnessing her paying the price and I vowed I would never fall myself."

"But you did — you and Ralph…"

"Of course I did. I grew up — remember I was only fifteen at the time — and anyway when I met him I just couldn't help myself. The same as when Freddie met Teo. The same as lots of people when they meet the right one."

The waitress brings our food and Esther thanks her, picking up her knife and fork before carrying on. "I want to tell you what happened at the end. It's something I've regretted for years, but today … well, I'll come to that bit." She cuts a slice of sausage and puts it into her mouth, chews then smiles. "It was the 7th of January. I'll never forget it. It was the sort of day it never really gets properly light. There was always a quiet time in the barracks when the aircrews went for their briefing and Freddie said she was going to the toilet, but she was gone a very long time and I started to worry because she'd been complaining of a stomach ache.

"So I popped across the corridor and opened the door. There were two cubicles and a wash basin for us and the WAAFs to use and I heard Freddie groaning, so I asked if she was all right. At first she didn't answer, so I asked again, and if I should get anyone. Then she yelled at me — properly yelled — that if I did she'd never forgive me and told me to 'f' off. She used the full word too and I'd never heard her say anything like that before. I was so scared I ran straight out and went back to my ironing.

"But of course I couldn't concentrate. I carried on for almost an hour, but then I burnt a pillowcase. I can remember the mark of the iron on it now, and that horrible singed linen smell. I knew I couldn't leave her any longer, so I went back to the toilets and there was what seemed like a river of blood pooling across the floor and a baby crying. I'm afraid I just stood there and screamed.

"Some of the men who weren't flying that night heard me and came running. They started to break down the cubicle door but one of them, an older man called Henryk, took me to the office where the WAAFs were. For once they were very kind, but I haven't stepped back into this building from that day to this. I was allowed a few days off and my mother told me Freddie had died and I was absolutely heartbroken. I thought if I hadn't listened to her and gone for help she would have lived, but today I somehow knew that wasn't the case, and it was what she wanted — to be with Teo."

I put down my fork, a lump forming in my throat, but Esther looks so happy I have to smile. "Really? You really, really felt that?"

"Of course I did. She and Teo are together and at peace."

I clear my throat. "So what happened to the baby?"

"I didn't find out until a few months later; it wasn't really the sort of thing you asked about. I couldn't bear the thought of coming to this airfield every day so I asked to transfer to Blyton. It was only a short bike ride away and was being set up as a training centre. One of the WAAFs from the office came across too and she told me the baby had been taken in by a local family. It happened quite often in those days — another child would appear and no questions were asked. They lived in the next village so I was able to watch him grow up, but he never knew who his real parents were."

"That's so sad."

"No, it was of the time. He thought the people who brought him up were his family — he never knew any different. And he had a wonderful life — probably better than Freddie could have given him, and maybe she knew it. He went to grammar school, worked hard and set up his own business, married a lovely young girl when he was in his thirties and had a family of his own. She couldn't have wished for more for him."

"Do you still know where he is?"

She shakes her head. "Sadly he died a few years ago. Come on, Rachel, it's probably time we were going."

She stands and I follow suit.

"Don't forget the jacket," she says.

I'm about to argue, but one look silences me. I put it over her shoulders and we walk past the reception desk. No-one says a word, although I expect someone to run after us into the car park.

I help Esther into the passenger seat then put the jacket in the back, running my fingers over the soft, tawny sheepskin lining.

Esther looks over her shoulder. "It's for Jonathan, remember. But don't give it to him just yet."

CHAPTER 44

Driving to Lincoln without further flashbacks just a few days after spilling my heart out to Jessie feels like a major victory, but once I'm in the office my mood is short lived. From the goldfish bowl of the boardroom I watch Jonathan out of the corner of my eye. The Hemswell project manager, Stefan, and I are waiting, exchanging the normal pleasantries. Jonathan is at his desk, phone glued to his ear. He's scowling. He has been since I came in and my heart sinks. He didn't reply to the text I sent him about supper after the funeral either.

Jonathan's explanation is curt — there's an issue at Burton Road — vandalism overnight. Caroline brings him an espresso and I begin my presentation on the geophysics report and test pits at Hemswell, but it is Stefan who asks most of the questions. Jonathan is frowning, making monosyllabic notes on his pad.

He doesn't speak until I have explained my conclusions. "What do you recommend?"

"I've agreed with the liaison officer we need only two trenches; one over the large metal anomaly and the other over the ditch. But he also wants us to use a ballistics expert to assess the scatter of the ferrous spikes because a Wellington bomber crashed near there in World War Two. So that's something I've had to budget for."

Jonathan raises his eyebrows. "You've budgeted?"

"Well, I knew you'd want to see the figures."

Stefan laughs. "You're learning, Rachel — he always does."

Jonathan's smile is slow. "Yes — to pay your bloody wages. OK — what's the damage?"

We discuss the numbers for a while and Stefan plugs them into the project spreadsheet. It's less than my initial estimate and they seem pleased with the final result. The rows of numbers mean little to me — except they seem very large — a huge initial outlay and for the first time I wonder where the money comes from. There's a line for interest on the spreadsheet so I guess at least some of it must be borrowed. It'd scare the living daylights out of me to be that much in debt and I begin to understand Jonathan's obsession with the financial side of things.

I am picking up my iPad to leave when he asks me to hold on. Once Stefan closes the door behind him Jonathan turns to me.

"Thanks so much for the invite to supper on Friday. I'd love to say yes but I mightn't be very good company after the funeral."

I shrug. "There's quite a few DVDs in the cottage — we could always have a TV dinner with a box set."

"Now that could be just the thing."

"No pressure though, if you really don't feel like coming just text me."

He smiles. "It'll give me something to look forward to. And at least this time I've apologised in advance for being grumpy."

"I'll have my hard hat ready."

"You'll probably need it."

Despite the fine weather in Lincoln showers are chasing in from the coast, making it impossible to start work when I reach Hemswell. In a change from my normal habit I eat a sandwich in a different café, in the converted guardroom, cursing the patter of rain on the glass, but by the time I'm pouring the dregs of tea from my pot the sun is struggling from behind the clouds so I collect my car from the parade ground and drive through the industrial estate to the field.

I want to at least mark out my trenches so I pull on my wellies then take my measuring tape and the geophys plan out of the boot and trudge over the damp earth. Ominous grey clouds scud across the sky — I'm going to have to be quick.

All the same I am careful, measuring two or three times before I spray the trench outline on the grass with waterproof paint. I'm ready to move on to the ditch but the moment I pin one end of my tape to the ground the rain returns in venomous spikes. I grab the reel and run for my car, watching the downpour through the misty windscreen. Looking towards the wolds I can see the sky is blue so I grit my teeth and wait, gazing back across the field to where the airstrip would have been, my mind drifting towards Freddie and Teo's tragic love story.

Beyond the hedge, the man is there again. At least I think it's him — the shape is so familiar. I lean towards the passenger window to clear a circle in the glass and in doing so my elbow hits the horn, shattering the silence and making sparrows rise from the hedge in an untidy cloud. By the time I do manage to peer out there is no one to be seen.

That, at least, is normal, but something makes me reluctant to return to work. It's almost four o'clock and the rain is showing no sign of moving on. Even the patch of blue over the wolds has disappeared and the comforts of home beckon.

Bramble Cottage settles around me and the pipes wheeze as I lie in the bath, glass of red in hand. The apple tree sways beyond the frosted window as I push my toe against the tap to top up the hot water. I'm going to be good to myself tonight, make a big fluffy omelette and watch trash TV. Give my scrambled brain a rest.

Perhaps I need to get away. I wind the plug chain between my toes to pull it out, stand and wrap my towel around me, warm off the rail. I perch on the side of the bath and wine glass in hand, pick up my phone from the windowsill to check my emails before powering it off for the night.

The first one's a diary item from Jonathan — planning committee for Hemswell at 2pm next Monday with the note *thought you might be interested*. My first thought is 'as long as it's raining and I can't get on with my trench', but on the other hand... I click the option for maybe. I should have left the emails alone. But the next one really grabs my interest — an alert from an excavation in Orkney calling for diggers in July and August. Now that would be absolutely perfect. If it rains again tomorrow I'll reorganise my CV and send it off.

CHAPTER 45

Jonathan follows me down the hall and into the kitchen. I put the wine he's brought on the table and set about opening it while he takes off his fleece and hangs it on the back of a chair.

I peel the foil top off the bottle then reach for the corkscrew. "TV dinner, or do you feel half human?"

He smiles. "Half human just about covers it. Something smells good."

"Cottage pie. Classic comfort food. How did it go?" I pour us both a generous glassful and push his towards him.

"Started bad, got worse, ended better."

"Oh?"

He takes a long draft of wine. "Christ, that's good. Perhaps I should have brought two bottles."

"It's OK — I've got some in reserve. I just thought we should start with yours — it looks better quality."

He sits down as I flip the courgettes in the pan and put some frozen peas in the microwave. His voice is stiff when he asks, "So, how was your day?"

"Frustrating — this bloody rain…" And I tell him I've marked out both trenches and even removed the turf over the ditch target, but every time I managed to get my trowel within inches of the soil it started to tip down. And I explain I've downloaded a fancy new weather app, but it doesn't seem any more accurate than the BBC website. In fact, I prattle on until the aroma of rapidly caramelising courgettes stops me.

I scrape them off the bottom of the pan. "I knew something would go wrong."

Jonathan tops up our glasses. "It's fine — I like them crispy."

As we eat a little colour returns to his cheeks. "I didn't know I was so hungry," he tells me. "I got rather distracted at lunchtime."

"Oh?"

"Chris's mum. God, Rachel, she's aged. I couldn't believe it when I turned up at the churchyard for the internment. She used to be … well, glamourous granny didn't begin to cover it and in a really fun way. I was trying to work it out — she can't be much more than sixty-five but she looks like a little old lady. Horrible baggy black dress and coat — like she'd just bought the first thing she'd seen, and she used to spend hours shopping for the latest designer gear. And it was grim, I tell you, standing there while this tiny box was lowered into this tiny hole, and I was thinking — god — that's all that's left of that beanpole of a man…

"He was much taller than me — and I'm five eleven — always bending to look at something or leaning over his drawing board or my shoulder — and that was it — a tiny oak box with a brass plate on. Bizarre." He shakes his head and shovels a few forkfuls of pie into his mouth.

"This is lovely, Rachel. I didn't have much lunch. Chris's mum — she wanted to talk about him. It was only me and the family there and I got the impression she felt she'd already bored them all stupid. But it was good stuff — happy memories — from when he was a kid, mainly — all the games … the holidays … the birthdays … and how it broke her heart he'd never get to do those things with Charlotte and on, and on, and on.

"Of course I had to listen — she needed me to. But I don't mind admitting it tore me in half when she said about

Charlotte. I've got to see more of her, Rachel, make sure she doesn't miss out."

We take the third bottle of wine to the living room. "Do you mind if we talk?" He laughs. "I seem to have verbal diarrhoea this evening — can't stop. Perhaps if you said something…"

I wave an arm in his general direction. "I'm happy listening. Spit it out, Daubney. Another glass and I'll have forgotten what you've said by the morning. Lie down on the couch and tell Doctor Ward all about it."

He kicks off his shoes and does just that. His feet look enormous hanging over the end of the sofa and he stuffs a cushion under his head and stares at the ceiling. There is a long silence.

"Tell me about the memorial service," I prompt him. "How did the eulogy go?"

"I spent the first hymn sweating like a pig and wanting to throw up. I had to sit near the front with the family but Caroline sneaked in next to me and, bless her, she held my hand. All through the prayers, right until the moment I had to stand up to walk to the lectern. She'll never know how much that meant to me — she's amazing.

"I started off with what I'd prepared — all the formal stuff and the platitudes — it felt as though I was reading his CV. Then I looked down at his mum and she had a slightly puzzled expression on her face and I knew I'd got it all wrong. But instead of being a bad moment it was a really good one. Does that make sense? I put my speech to one side and I just said — look, folks, over lunch Maggie told me about her son — now I'm going to talk to you about my friend, and why we should be genuinely celebrating his too short life.

"I couldn't tell you what I said, but I do remember everyone laughing — more than once — and I went on far too long. But by the time I'd finished I knew — I just knew — that it wasn't so important how he died — or that we'll never be sure one way or the other — but it was how he lived that mattered — and how we remember him. I'm going to do something, Rachel, something proper … like a scholarship in his name … I feel so much better now I've decided."

"That's good, really good."

Jonathan rolls onto his side and picks up his wine. "You said that like you cared."

"I do. We may have started out on the wrong foot, but…"

"We did? I thought you were like that with everyone."

The amount of wine we've consumed makes me bold. "There was no reason for you to have realised. You know you told me about Denise and how it ended? I was at Ask that lunchtime and I overheard everything. To be fair, half the restaurant probably did but for me…" I bite my lip. *Oh god, I've gone too far…*

His grey eyes are focussed on mine as he says, "I'm listening, Rachel. It's your turn to talk."

I pour the last of the wine into my glass and swirl it around, mesmerised by the ruby glow reflecting from the log burner. "When I was eighteen I got pregnant. I agonised over what to do about the baby, pushed and pulled this way and that by what other people thought. You sounded so cavalier about it to me… Of course, when you explained it made perfect sense, but for a long time it seriously coloured my view of you."

The clock ticks in the hall. "And what did you decide to do about your baby?"

"I didn't have to. I… I miscarried. But the whole experience… It's the reason I started using men — that way you don't get hurt. It's been one disastrous fling after another, really. I was only sent to Lincoln because I'd been sleeping with my head of department and his wife found out." I stand up and stretch. "Shall we open another bottle or would you prefer a coffee?"

He gives me a long look I can't quite fathom, then nods. "Coffee sounds good — another drink and I'll be incapable of movement…"

He's not the only one. I clutch at the back of the armchair to steady myself then feel my way along the wall to the kitchen. The remains of supper cover every surface but I ignore them, and while the kettle boils drink glass after glass of icy water from the tap. As an afterthought I add some soluble paracetamol to the last one.

Jonathan's eyes are closed and when I put the coffee on the floor next to him he doesn't stir. He's taken off his glasses and his long lashes dip towards his cheekbones. There may be dark shadows under his eyes but his nose is straight and beautifully proportioned. I allow myself a long moment to gaze at him before the intensity of my feelings shocks me into action, stumbling upstairs to hunt for my sleeping bag.

I can hardly look at Jonathan as I lay the cover over him. I scold myself — it's the drink — it must be the drink. But as I replace his coffee with a glass of water I know that isn't the case.

CHAPTER 46

At first light I pull on my running gear and trainers. I creep down the stairs and peep into the living room but Jonathan is fast asleep, his feet escaping from the bottom of the makeshift duvet. I close the front door as quietly as I can before turning towards the crossroads then jogging down the slope towards the Humber.

As I pass The Firs I quicken my pace into a proper run. Ahead of me the hills rise on the other side of the river, the heavy industry at Brough shrouded in early morning mist. I cut past the sailing club and onto the dyke, the grass slippery beneath my feet, but the clouds scudding past are white and benign. Hopefully the rain will stay away.

Last night's water has saved me from a hangover but my world is cocooned in a fug I'm struggling to outrun. I descend the dyke and cross the field, the footpath lined with a bright green fuzz of new corn. The farm dogs bark as I hit the metalled track, turning towards the village and home.

By the time I slow to cross the wooden bridge below the church I'm gasping for breath. I lean on the rail and gaze into the water flowing sluggishly at the bottom of the dyke. Under the hedgerow are some early primroses and I bend to pick them then wander up the path to the lychgate. If I stay away long enough Jonathan might wake and go home. And anyway, I need somewhere to put the flowers.

Esther's daughter's ashes are buried with her father. It takes me a while to find them, tramping the wet grass between the rows of graves, reading the names and dates. Carved into black marble is a simple memorial to Ralph Moore but it shocks me to see Esther has been alone for almost thirty years, the bottom half of the stone virgin and waiting for her name. The pot of daffodils has blown over and I bend to right it, digging it into the soft soil.

The inscription on the square of quartz placed over Ralph's heart is simple: *Sally Nickelson wife, mother, daughter. Forever missed.* The primroses are wilting from the warmth of my hand but all the same I scatter them around the stone. As I stand I notice Jonathan's father's grave on the opposite side of the path. He's only been gone three years. Same as Gran. I pat the top of the stone. "You should be very proud of your son, Charles Frederick Daubney," I whisper.

I creep into the house as quietly as I can but the hall is dark, the door to the kitchen closed. From behind it come faint sounds of washing up.

Jonathan turns and smiles as I open it. "Oh hello — I thought you were still asleep."

"I've been up for ages — I've been for a run. How are you feeling?"

"Not my brightest and best, I'm afraid, but given the bottle count that isn't surprising. I've helped myself to some of your paracetamol though and they're beginning to kick in. By the time you've had a shower I should have sorted out this mess and with any luck my head will have stopped pounding."

"You don't have to do that, you know, you could just slump on the sofa with a coffee."

He shakes his head. "And probably fall straight back to sleep and wake up at lunchtime feeling like shit. No thank you."

By the time I've dressed, every surface in the kitchen is sparkling and Jonathan is filling the kettle.

"You're positively glowing, Rachel — how do you do it? I feel about a hundred and fifty."

"You should have come for a run…"

He groans. "Not after a couple of bottles of wine. I'd have thrown up within twenty yards."

"The sad fact is I'm a bit too practised at getting my head together the morning after. But at least I know it involves food. Fancy a bacon butty?"

He shakes his head.

"You wait until you smell it cooking," I tell him as I switch on the grill.

"I'll just stay for a coffee — then I need to get down to The Firs and prick Mum's balloon about the circumstances under which I spent the night here."

I open the fridge and spend an inordinately long time hunting for the butter. "She does seem to rather like the idea we could be … er…"

"Oh god, she hasn't been having a go at you as well, has she?"

"Not a go. She just said that with Chris gone you needed someone to challenge your thinking sometimes and I was the only person around you'd view as an intellectual equal."

"Crikey — she's way off beam."

I slam the fridge door and he winces.

"Oh, so I'm not up to your high standards?"

He's laughing now. "No — you're in a different league entirely — you've been to university — got a doctorate even… Two A-levels, a bit of commercial nous and a stomach for risk, that's all I have. No brains, as such. But then in my line of work I don't need them."

"How come Mister big shot Jonathan Daubney has developed a good line in self-deprecation all of a sudden? You were doing it last night too."

"Perhaps because Doctor PhD in taking offence easily Ward is only just beginning to get to know me? And anyway, great chunks of last night are hazy to say the least."

The silence is filled by the bacon beginning to crackle under the grill. Finally Jonathan ventures, "That does smell good."

"It's OK — I put in enough for you."

"Then you are getting to know me."

I turn to him and fold my arms. "It took me a while but I'm beginning to think you just might be worth the effort."

"Well, at least now I understand why you were so prickly at first." Oh, lord. Trust him to remember that bit.

The bread pops from the toaster and I slather it with butter before taking the bacon from under the grill and making the sandwiches. Jonathan brushes past me on his way to the window where he stands, looking out over the garden.

"It must have been hard, telling me," he says.

"Yes." I take the plates and set them down on the work surface in front of him.

"I feel very privileged you did. It makes me feel closer to you."

A robin hops around the apple tree, its quest for worms suddenly the most interesting thing in the world. Finally I say, "And is that a good thing?"

He continues to gaze down the garden. "You also said something … about using men. I don't want to be used, Rachel."

I trace an imaginary crumb across the work surface. "And I don't want to use you," I mumble.

Slowly he turns and his hands cradle my face. "My hedgehog breath notwithstanding, what I most want to do right now is kiss you. Really kiss you — seriously kiss you — for a very long time. But this is too important. I can't take any more hurt at the moment, Rachel, so if you don't think we have a chance then I…"

I raise my finger, put it on his lips. They are warm and firm and my first instinct is to melt into his body, make him want me and want me now. Instead, I hold his gaze. "Then we are on the same page. This feels as though it could be different. But right now I'm not sure I'm ready. There's stuff I need to finish working through first."

"Do you want to tell me what sort of stuff?"

I shake my head and his gaze drops away so I touch his cheek. "This is about me, not you."

"The biggest lie in relationships," he murmurs.

"Except in this case it's true." I slide my arms around his waist and he pulls me to him. "Please, Jonathan, I just need some more time. I really don't want to mess this up."

"Oh, Rachel," he murmurs into my hair and goosebumps run down my spine and over my buttocks. I bite my lip. "What do we do now?" he asks.

I look up at him and laugh. "Eat our bacon butties before they go cold?"

CHAPTER 47

Jonathan's question is running round and round in my head. What do we do now? Once he's gone home, giving me a gentle kiss on the cheek, I stand where we stood together at the kitchen window, pondering it.

I've never been in this position before, knowing someone so well before we've even started. And having them know me too — even my deepest secrets — well, some of my deepest secrets — and still wanting me. The sun slants between the branches of the apple tree. Maybe a little gardening would help me to think.

I go upstairs to change, pulling my digging trousers out of the laundry basket then hunting for a thick jumper. The flying jacket is hanging in the wardrobe and I take it out to inspect it in the daylight, the sheepskin soft under my hand. The cracked patina of the leather is wonderful — it's a thing of rare age and beauty — right down to the little linked metal chain inside the collar and the worn silk of the maker's label.

It's about the right size for Jonathan too, and I think it's probably his style. I can certainly picture him in it. And then I realise — the man I've seen at Hemswell wears one. I drop onto the bed, clutching it to me. The ring … now the jacket … they're real, not echoes. What the hell's going on?

Eventually I loosen my grip. *Leave it, Rachel, and get on with the garden.* In the abandoned shed I find a trug and a hand fork so set about weeding the borders. It's too soon for very much to be growing, but if it isn't done now there'll be chaos in a few months' time and I tease the weeds from between the bluebells pushing through the soil before giving the straggling roses a much overdue prune.

For the rest of the morning and all afternoon the flowerbeds bear the brunt of my tangled emotions. My arms and back are aching and I promise myself a long bath but as I undress in my bedroom the flying jacket distracts me again. Why did Esther say it was for Jonathan? And why should I not give it to him yet?

When I arrive at The Firs, Esther has just finished her supper, sharing a table with Graeme, who solemnly shakes my hand then tells me he's going to have an early night to finish his book.

"Has he settled in any better?" I ask Esther.

"Oh yes. But he still goes on and on about the RAF." She rolls her eyes. "Somehow I seem more able to handle it now."

"That's good, because it's Hemswell I want to talk to you about."

"Have you started to dig?"

"No, not really. It's not about the site, it's about last Monday."

She looks down. "It must have seemed very strange to you. It was strange enough for me."

"To be honest I'd decided not to think about it too hard. Other things have happened there too; the first time I visited I may have actually seen Freddie, but at the time I thought it was someone dressed up for the 40's fete."

Esther leans forwards. "Really? What was she like?"

"Beautiful dark wavy hair — and she was putting on lipstick. I smelt lily-of-the-valley then as well."

Esther sounds wistful. "Yes, that would have been her."

"And there's been a man too — more than once at the dig site — wearing a flying jacket. At first I thought it was

Jonathan — you remember, when he was in New Zealand and I was so scared about him flying home…" I stop as a piece of the puzzle falls into place. "Esther, there's a connection with Jonathan, isn't there? That's why he's to have the jacket."

She looks around the dining room but it's empty now. "I thought you might work it out. And that's probably for the best because I've been going this way and that, wondering whether to tell you. I've never told anyone and I suspect everyone else who knows is dead. But you're so caught up in this, Rachel, and Freddie and Teo seem to want you to be. Jonathan's their grandson. And what's more, he's grown to look so much like Teo, although Charles didn't at all."

"His father?"

She nods. "Rachel, I'm so tired. Quite worn through by all this. Would you mind if we talked another time?"

"Of course not." We stand and I give her a hug, then accompany her slow progress across the dining room and into the entrance hall.

"Good evening, ladies." Jonathan has his hand on the front door but turns and walks towards us with a smile.

"Oh, hello. I was just telling Esther about my day gardening."

"It was good to see some sunshine for a change," she adds.

"I probably went at it a bit too hard though so I'm off home for an early night."

"Then I'll walk you."

"No, it's fine…"

He smiles. "I was leaving anyway."

Esther looks from one of us to the other, her head on one side, but she simply bids us goodnight then grasps the bannister and starts to climb the stairs.

The breeze blowing up the Humber is surprisingly mild, but nevertheless Jonathan tucks me under his shoulder as we walk. I lean into his warmth, which seeps through me as he kisses the top of my head. It should feel good, but all I can think about is that he doesn't know about his father and I do. Not that I've had the chance to properly grasp it yet and my brain is spinning as I grapple with the implications.

He only speaks when we are outside my front door. "Any chance of a night cap?"

My reply is garbled through chattering teeth. "No... I'm really sorry but I'm so tired..." I fumble for my keys. "Goodnight, Jonathan." I lunge for the door and slam it behind me, dropping onto the bottom stair and sitting there in total darkness. It is a while before I hear his footsteps echo up the street.

CHAPTER 48

I wrap my hands around my coffee as the grey light edges into the garden and one by one the birds begin to sing. The solitary chirps merge into delighted chatter as colour washes the skeletal shape of the apple tree and the daffodils below become more and more yellow as the minutes pass by. I've been here for hours — overthinking it, probably. I put down my cup and stretch my aching shoulders towards the glass roof of the conservatory.

I'm overthinking because I'm thinking about Jonathan, trying to see things from his point of view. This is new territory for me. Jessie I understand implicitly, but a man? It shocks and scares me I care enough to even try, but all the same there's a glimmer of something inside I'm almost proud of.

The trouble is that knowing the truth about his father when he doesn't is a secret between us before we've even started. I don't want secrets and lies. Which also means somehow I need to find the courage to properly explain to him about how everything that happened around losing my baby has scarred and shaped my life. But what's the point if it isn't in my power to share what I know about him?

Around and around I go. I try to tell myself perhaps it wouldn't matter to Jonathan who his grandparents really were, but then I remember the Daubney crest at The Firs and the family tree on his living room wall. It's the backbone of who he is; his enviable confidence, which I'm afraid I misread for arrogance, the sense of entitlement, almost, that makes success come so easily. It's a part of him. Would knowing the truth change anything of that? And is he strong enough to take it right now?

I continue to ponder as I brush my teeth and throw on my digging clothes. The garden awaits my attentions, but as I make a cup of tea and pour cereal into my bowl I wonder if it's worth it. Will I be here to enjoy the fruits of my labour? Should I bail out while my heart's still intact? I fetch my laptop and start to prepare a CV appropriate for Orkney, but I'm strong on theory, weak on practice. Do I really have a chance to get a place on such a prestigious dig? Should I even be...

I don't even finish my cereal before my mind's back on Jonathan. How did I make him feel by rejecting him so soundly last night? Should I text him or not? Will he text me? God, I'm behaving like a lovesick teenager. Or rather, like I imagine one would be behave. Because quite frankly, I haven't been remotely close to this before.

I shove my phone across the table and slam the kitchen door behind me. The breeze is carrying the salt air of the Humber across the village, ruffling the daffodils under the tree. I scrunch my hands deep into my pockets as I watch the robin renew its quest for worms and for the hundredth time replay my conversation with Jonathan as we stood at the window. Am I about to throw away my chance for happiness because I'm too bloody scared? Am I putting non-existent obstacles in the way?

The laurel hedge bears the brunt of my emotions and by the time I've finished it looks distinctly worse for wear. I bite my lip. Maybe I've gone too far. I should have asked Lucy first. Without warning tears threaten. I pile the debris in the far corner away from the shed. Maybe I'll have a bonfire if the wind dies down.

To make amends for the damage I drive to the garden centre at Brigg. It's a trip out I know Esther would have loved but today I need to be alone. I still feel guilty, though, wandering through the plants and clothes and shoes and outdoor furniture. The place is more like a superstore and the scent of Sunday roast drifts from the restaurant. Instead of indulging I punish myself with a sandwich from the chill cabinet then go home to plant the primulas I've bought in the border and scatter some wildflower seeds under the remains of the hedge.

Only then do I look at my phone. Jonathan texted this morning to ask what I was up to today. So he isn't angry with me after all. But hurt. Maybe he was hurt. And I remember the look in his eyes when he told me he couldn't take any more hurt. I perch on the kitchen table to reply.

Sorry. Been in the garden all day. But it sounds like another brush off. Truly it does. So before I press send I add, *Shall I call you later?*

I haul myself up the stairs and start to run my bath. Except when I turn on the hot tap nothing happens. It splutters for a few seconds, then dribbles pathetically before grinding to a halt. I try the washbasin and it's exactly the same. The cold's working all right but I can't face an icy shower. In the airing cupboard the boiler stands silent and there's nothing I can do to coax it into life.

I stand on the landing for a long while hugging myself before I finally make my decision. I need to be clean. I need to be warm. I need to phone Jonathan. Try killing all three birds with one stone.

I remember the guest bathroom in Jonathan's house as stark and functional, but by the time I have rammed my toiletries and some clean clothes into my rucksack and walked up the village it has been transformed.

Jonathan opens the door with a flourish. "Your bath awaits."

He means it absolutely literally. The tub is filled almost to the brim with bubbles and the room is lit by two candles wafting jasmine towards me. On the heated rail are two dark blue fluffy towels.

I can't look at him in case he sees my tears. "Oh wow. You know how to make a tired woman happy."

"I have to admit I raided Mum's raffle box for the Jo Malone — you lucked out there. Now the only question remains, red or white? Or would you prefer a brandy?"

"Do you know? A brandy sounds lovely."

"I'd also offer to scrub your back, but all things considered I'd be better occupied trying to scrape us together a meal."

I lie under the bubbles and sip my drink, warming inside and out. Do I want him to scrub my back? Yes, and more. It's been a while since Ben … no, don't think of Ben. Not in the same breath. Don't think of any of them — this feels different. My hand moves down over my stomach — the physical need is still the same. I close my eyes and imagine Jonathan's naked body sliding into the water behind mine, his hands soaping my breasts, moving lower and lower.

Thankfully, under the bright lights of the kitchen normality is restored, although Jonathan looks no less attractive, freshly shaved and wearing a navy rugby shirt.

"I hope you don't mind but I've ordered a Chinese."

"No — that's fine." I put my brandy glass next to the sink.

"Have you settled on red or white?"

"It depends what you've ordered."

He doesn't seem to notice my emphasis on the 'you' and carries on, "Oh, the usual selection — bit of beef, bit of chicken, bit of prawn. And spring rolls, of course. You can't have a Chinese without spring rolls."

"And egg fried rice."

He frowns. "I ordered jasmine rice."

"Oh well, you can't always second guess what somebody else would want."

"No, that's true. Especially when you're only just getting to know them. Now, can I guess red?"

I put my head on one side. "White, please."

He laughs, and something in my chest does a funny little somersault.

After supper we move into the lounge but I wander around looking at the photos and pictures on the walls until Jonathan has settled on one of the sofas. Only then do I join him, carefully leaving about two feet of space between us.

He stretches his arm along the back of the seat behind my head. I pull one knee up onto the seat and swivel to face him.

"Thanks for the bath — and supper. It's been an absolute life saver."

"My pleasure. But I was worried about you, Rachel, you sounded almost tearful when you phoned. Are you OK?"

"I think I just got a bit overwrought, that's all."

"And last night?"

I can't look at him. "The same."

"Want to talk about it?" He makes the question sound harmlessly casual.

I fight the urge to shake my head and instead pick up my wine glass and nurse it in my hands. A half-truth is better than a lie. "When I was gardening I started to think about what I'm going to do once the dig at Hemswell is finished. I can only live on my freelance earnings because I'm not paying rent, and I don't see me being able to stay at Bramble Cottage long term.

Margaret's really not doing very well so I'd guess it's only a matter of time before Lucy needs to sell it to fund the care fees."

"And what would you like to do? Go back to lecturing?"

"No. Professor Stephens has left the door open for me, bless her, but it isn't what I want. I need to get my hands dirty again. I'd forgotten I loved it so much. I was in danger of becoming a dry old academic."

"Hardly that," he murmurs. "You know, Rachel, I could buy you time. All the time you need. You can stay at DSD and…"

"I don't know. You know, if you and I… I mean… I wouldn't want to be sleeping with my boss again." I manage a wink and a raise of my eyebrow but it feels a bit false.

He slides closer. "So have you thought any more about us?"

"I've thought of little else."

His arm drops and pulls me in. In the silence I can hear the steady beat of his heart under his rugby shirt. I want to reach inside the fabric, feel his warmth beneath my fingers, discover the pattern of hairs on his chest. But that would only lead to one thing and although the molten mess in my stomach is urging me on, this time my head has to win.

I sit up. "I'm going to have to be up early to call the plumber. And probably wait around all day for them but if I can get to the planning meeting tomorrow afternoon I will."

"You didn't really answer my question."

"No." I drain my wine and stand up.

He tips back his head and closes his eyes. "Rachel Ward, you are the…"

I put my finger on his lips to silence him. "Goodnight, Jonathan. See you tomorrow. Maybe."

CHAPTER 49

The plumber can't make it until at least twelve o'clock, so rather than twiddle my thumbs I decide to go to see Esther. The solitude I craved yesterday is threatening to overwhelm me today. Last night I even dreamt about Jonathan and it was the kind of dream that would make an honest woman blush.

Esther is in her room when I arrive. "Trying to escape the vicar's monthly visit," she explains. "Not that there's anything wrong with the woman, I'm just not feeling very religious at the moment."

I shrug my shoulders. "Fair enough. Can't say I'm much of a church-goer either."

"I don't even bother with funerals now — too many of them. And I certainly don't need reminding of my own mortality."

"No, it is rather a grim thought."

"I expect it seems well into the distance for you," she laughs, "you still have a future full of excitement."

"Well, I suppose…" I grind to a halt, uncertain how much to confide.

"Rachel, is something bothering you?"

Her eyes are bright behind her glasses, her head on one side in that familiar expression of enquiry. She is so dear to me. Will this hurt her too? "I'm thinking of applying to take part in a dig on Orkney this summer. Neolithic — incredible opportunity and of course I might not get it. Hemswell should be finished in time — we'll know about the planning this week… Today, in fact…"

The front door closes below us and two carers dash through the rain and leap into a car parked on the road outside.

"You haven't told me what's stopping you," murmurs Esther. "What, or who?"

"I don't know…"

She holds up a finger to silence me. "I may not be able to see very much, my dear, but because of that I can hear pretty well. Not only what people are saying but how they're saying it. And the way you and Jonathan talk to each other has changed."

"Oh, the other night, you mean. He was just being thoughtful walking me home. He didn't even come in…"

"Rachel — I'm not prying into where either of you spent the night," she laughs. "It's none of my business. I was trying to say that if it is Jonathan making you think twice about Orkney I know how you feel about him — and how he feels about you."

"Esther, how can you know how I feel when I'm not even sure?"

"Don't worry about 'sure', Rachel, 'sure' can come later. What you need to be thinking about is whether it could be love."

"I don't know what love feels like," I grumble. "And anyway, I thought you said when you met Ralph you couldn't help yourself — and it was the same with Freddie and Teo."

"Everyone's different, my dear. Sometimes love grows so slowly you hardly notice it. Especially if you don't want to. Then one day you realise that person has become the very centre of your world."

"I can't imagine Jonathan — or any man — being the centre of mine," I bluster.

"Perhaps not, but can you imagine your world without him?"

My heart seems to stop in my chest. "What if… I can't imagine it but he doesn't feel the same?"

"He does. I've known him since he was a child. The way he talks to you … talks about you … that's changed over the last few months. And I'm not aware he's even had a serious girlfriend before."

I swallow hard. "He's not my boyfriend. There's nothing going on." Her eyes don't believe me but she says nothing. "We have talked about it though," I concede. "It's just I've been so rubbish at relationships in the past we've decided to take it slowly."

"So slowly you're prepared to go to Orkney for the summer?"

"I need to get away."

"Or run away?"

I fiddle with the collar of my shirt. "I don't know."

"I think you do. Will you run forever, Rachel, or will you risk letting yourself be hurt?" I stare at the table, shake my head. "Let me tell you something. I've been without Ralph now almost as long as I was with him. When he died I thought the pain would never stop. But eventually it faded a little and what was I left with? Wonderful memories and the strength to carry on. It really is better to have loved and lost…"

"Than never loved at all," I whisper. There is a lump in my throat but I force it back down. "Thank you, Esther. I'll think about it, really I will." I lean over and squeeze her hand. "And I won't send off my application for Orkney just yet. But…"

"What?"

I finger the embroidered tablecloth, tracing the forget-me-nots along its edge. "I know something about Jonathan he doesn't even know himself."

Esther picks up the cloth on her side of the table, holding it to her cheek for a moment. "Then tell him. There has to be honesty in a relationship, Rachel, there has to be trust. Once you're sure you want to move forwards, tell him about his father and give him the flying jacket."

"Is the jacket Teo's?"

She shakes her head. "I just don't know. He should have been wearing his, you see, when … but maybe he wasn't, because the night it happened I am almost sure Freddie had one on. I've never forgotten that moment, seeing her run towards the fireball and one of the ground crew hauling her back. Maybe it was Teo's jacket or maybe not. Some things we can never be sure of."

In the end, the plumber doesn't turn up until just after four o'clock. Rather than ponder my conversation with Esther, I spend the time reading a new report from an archaeological investigation into a World War Two bomber crash in France. It gives me a few ideas about what to look for and is sufficiently distracting to draw me in. I'm itching to get back to Hemswell tomorrow, but the plumber needs a part to fix the boiler so it looks as though I'll have to wait in again.

I text Jonathan to tell him the bad news, and that I'll need to make use of his hot water again. To my surprise, the planning meeting has finished, and he calls to say he's on his way back to Winteringham with a couple of salmon steaks and a bottle of fizz to celebrate if I'd like to join him.

It would be churlish to refuse, but telling him about his father hangs heavily on my shoulders. Esther said not to until I was prepared to give us a go. But am I? Can I do it? I should really talk to Jessie, but I know exactly what she'd say. *Face it,*

Rachel, he's the only man you've ever really cared about — why are you still throwing up obstacles?

Dutch courage is the only way and I down a glass of red wine before making my way through the village to Jonathan's house. His Jag is already in the drive, but he's still in his suit when he answers the door.

"I take it we've got the green light?" I ask him.

He grins. "Through on the nod. Not a single objection."

I sit at the kitchen table with a glass of champagne and watch as Jonathan cooks. He chats about the planning meeting — he was in the public gallery as the councillors discussed various applications and he goes through the whys and wherefores of each decision, while my resolve to tell him about his father drains away.

He continues to talk shop. I pour myself a third glass of champagne.

Jonathan puts the salad bowl on the table and tips the rest of the bottle into his own glass. "Thirsty, are you?" he laughs. "Just as well I've got a rather nice Chablis for the fish."

I say nothing and smile. *For god's sake, Rachel — stop drinking and tell him.* The words are washed back down by another gulp of fizz.

With our meal in front of us, Jonathan returns to DSD. "I was thinking, you know, after our chat last night, what would work really well would be running some sort of archaeological consultancy within the company, then we'd be equals so I wouldn't be your boss. Nice steady income stream to cover the costs of my new right-hand woman — and some. I remember what I used to be charged for those reports — there's a great margin to be had, even undercutting the universities. We could set it up right now. Nothing to stop us, really."

I push a chip around my plate. "I suppose…"

"What shall we call it? Daubney Ward? Or Ward Daubney actually has a better ring, don't you think?"

I'm sweating. Panic rises in my throat and I put down my fork. "Jonathan — there's a major dig in Orkney this summer — I've emailed them — offered my services…"

He beams at me. "Our first client then?"

"No. You don't understand. This dig is of global significance. If they take me — and it's a big if — I'll be working for a pittance…"

He sits back and folds his arms. "So that's what you've decided to do, is it? You'd rather go to the ends of the earth to dig than to give our relationship a chance? Not too high up your priority list, am I? Is that your problem, Rachel? Everything's me, me, me?"

I lean over the table. "You can bloody talk! It's all about DSD, isn't it? It's all about what I can do for your precious business."

"Oh, so back to pots and kettles, are we? Accusing me of being work obsessed just because you are?"

"No! You're so bloody blinkered you can't even see there could be an us if I didn't work for you. You just want to replace Christopher, that's all you want."

He folds his arms. "You? Replace Christopher? Do yourself a favour, Rachel…"

"I am going to do myself a bloody favour. I'm out of here, Jonathan. Right now, and I'm not coming back."

I push my chair so hard it rattles to the floor then run down the hall, past the galleried staircase and out through the front door, slamming it behind me. I pelt through the darkness until I reach the safety of Bramble Cottage. It's only then I realise I left my coat at Jonathan's. My coat with my keys and my phone in the pocket. My hands fumble the key safe but I already know it's empty. Why the hell didn't I put the spare keys back? I sink onto the step and weep.

I don't hear Jonathan's footsteps. The first I know he's there is when my coat drops over my shoulders. I look up. His face is bathed in the yellow glow of the streetlights and his tired eyes gaze into my red rimmed ones for quite a while before he says, "I can't hack it when we do this to each other."

I nod. "Hurts, doesn't it?"

"You can say that again. And I've had enough of hurting — I'm worn down by it — Chris, now you…"

The words are out before I've even thought about them. "We can change that. I mean, not the Chris bit, but… Oh, god, Jonathan, I only wish we could rewind this evening and start again."

He shakes his head. "I'm struggling, Rachel. One minute you don't seem to give a toss and the next… Well the next I look at you and I know you feel the same as I do."

I try to smile. "What? Lost, confused and a little bit drunk?"

"Exactly that. I've been hitting the brandy I'm afraid."

"Then how long have I been here?"

"A good half hour. You must be freezing. I didn't realise … until your phone rang in your pocket. Have you been sitting here crying all this time?" I'm so choked I can only nod. He drops onto the step next to me and takes me in his arms. "Don't do this to yourself, Rachel. Let me make it better — let me love you."

I clutch his hand and our fingers intertwine. "It's not you, it's me."

"There you go again, the biggest lie."

I look at him. "No. It is me, but it's also you — or rather something to do with you…" I bite my lip. "There's something

I have to tell you, but it isn't a conversation we should have shivering on a doorstep. Let's go in and make a hot drink."

He hauls me up. "No. We'll go back to mine. At least the heating's on."

Jonathan makes us coffee while I sit on the sofa, hugging my knees but feeling strangely calm. All the same I'm wondering where to start. This has the potential to rock his world when it doesn't need rocking and Pat's words about him being more fragile than he lets on drift into my mind. Then it occurs to me — there's one way to make him feel more secure before I even start the story — one way I can make it easier for him. But it means putting my own feelings out there in a way I've never done before. Can I take the risk? Can I even do it? But on the other hand, everything's so raw anyway, what have I got to lose?

I watch as he crosses the room. His fair hair is spiked, as though he has been running his fingers through it, and the cleft in his chin seems more pronounced. Those things alone tell me more about the way he's feeling than I'd have thought possible and tears claw at the back of my throat. He puts the mugs on the table and sits down. As he turns to me, I take both his hands.

"Now listen, and don't say anything. Not until I've finished. Because the first thing I'm going to tell you is the hardest thing I've ever said, but OK, here I go." I take a deep breath. "I think this might be tough for you, but I'm here for you. I'm not going to Orkney — I'm not going anywhere. You see… I think the reason I'm so damned scared is that I'm falling in love with you."

His face relaxes into a broad smile. "Rachel…"

I put my finger over his lips. "Shut up, Jonathan."

"Sorry."

I shoot him a warning glance before carrying on. "Remember I told you Esther worked at Hemswell during the war? There's a reason she's never really talked about it, but, well, to cut a long story short, when I took her there for lunch she shared the whole sad tale." And so I tell Jonathan, while he watches me intently with those pale grey eyes. Esther called Teo's eyes 'pearl grey' and as I gaze back at Jonathan I can see why.

The end of the story is the hardest part. I'm keeping it simple; nothing about Freddie being in the room, or seeing Teo by the dig site, or the ring, or the tablecloth or the flying jacket. All that can come later. Maybe. What's important now is spitting the story out and not keeping Jonathan waiting.

As soon as I mention Freddie was pregnant, he gets it. "So the baby — that's what's to do with me?"

"Yes. Freddie died in childbirth and he was taken in by a local couple, but nothing was ever said about these things back then. He just became one of the family."

"My father was born in 1943. And his middle name was Frederick."

"Yes."

"So he wasn't really a Daubney?" He sits back on the sofa, closing his eyes. "He was very proud of being a Daubney, you know. Said it was a proper Lincolnshire name. Researched the family tree and everything. It would have broken his heart to know he wasn't."

"Then it's just as well he didn't. But I can tell you, Jonathan, whatever his parentage he was born from love. And brought up with just as much love by the sound of it — and that's what's most important. I've always thought ... you know, if I'd kept my baby, it wouldn't have been like that. And that's what makes it bearable I lost it."

He hugs me to him, squashing my face into his collar bone. "Oh, Rachel — it must have been so hard."

"Yes. But it was a long time ago. And anyway, this isn't about me — it's about you — I was just trying to explain." I settle myself more comfortably under his shoulder.

"Has Esther ever told anyone else about my father?"

"No. And she's pretty sure the few people who would have known are dead by now. She'd have carried her secret to the grave if ... well, if she hadn't told me most of it and I guessed the rest. You see, while I've been digging I've seen Teo. At first I thought it was you — it was when you were in New Zealand — I thought you'd come back and then I realised... You'll think I'm crazy," I finish lamely.

"I think you're the most amazing woman I've ever met. And I'm going to ask you to do something for me — keep my father's true parentage a secret. You were right to tell me, but I wouldn't want anyone else to know. Let him always be a Daubney in people's eyes — it's what he would have wanted."

"It isn't my secret to tell. And I'll make sure Esther does the same, although I suspect I don't really have to ask her." I look up at him. "But how do you feel about it?"

"That I'm one quarter brave Polish airman and one quarter a woman who was so kind to Esther? I think, when I get used to the idea, I'll quite like it. I already want to know so much more about them, although I have to say there's something else at the forefront of my mind right now."

"And what's that?"

"A little while ago you said you were falling in love with me. Were you just trying to sweeten the pill, or did you mean it?"

I close my eyes. "Of course I meant it. It was hard enough to say out loud."

"Because I'm so awful?"

"No." My voice is a whisper. "Because I've never said it to anyone before."

His finger traces the side of my face and along my jaw. "Me neither." Then his lips are on mine, coffee flavour kisses, gentle at first then more and more insistent, my insides melting into bubbling lava as his hands travel inside my shirt and over my back. This is it — this is the moment. My hand drops to his thigh then sweeps slowly upwards.

"I have one more question for you," I murmur.

There is fire in his eyes as he pulls away to look at me. "What now?"

"Here or in the bedroom?"

CHAPTER 50

Even half asleep I'm aware of Jonathan's breathing next to mine, the shared warmth under the duvet. We curled into each other for a while after making love but at some point drifted back into our own space, as though we've been doing this for years.

The pattering of the rain on the window is joined by the swoosh of tyres on the road. A car door slams, an engine starts, a blackbird chirps its solo dawn chorus. I have no desire to leave this warm cocoon and I turn to face Jonathan, only to find he is looking at me.

"I need to call Caroline — tell her I'm working from home this morning. I won't be long." His lips brush mine and he slides out of bed, pulling on a dark green towelling dressing gown.

As the door closes behind him I roll onto my back, the spell of togetherness broken. How do I feel? Out of kilter, certainly. Vulnerable. Scared. I'm not staring over the precipice any longer — I'm in free fall. What if he comes back and says he's changed his mind? A ball of duvet is twisted into my fist. Fight or flight?

But there is no indication whatsoever he's going to say that — remember last night? Not just his words — his actions. But maybe that's the kind of lover he is. Maybe he's like this with all his women? Will he really be different with me? *Oh, for god's sake...* With a huge effort I brush the devil off my shoulder.

When Jonathan returns he has a mug of coffee in one hand and an espresso cup in the other. Both are fine white china from the Villeroy & Boch set. They match, and yet they don't;

the same, but different. Is that us? He sits on my side of the bed and puts them down.

"Right, that's the morning freed up, but I'm afraid I can't get out of my lunch meeting."

"What did you tell her?"

"That there was something I needed to focus on completely and my phone would be off."

I wriggle up the bed. "Your phone's off? Wow, this must be serious."

"It is. I'm staring forty in the face, Rachel, and you're the first woman I've ever made love to. What have you done to me?"

I frown. "But surely you've… Denise thought…"

He laughs. "Oh, sex. It's a pretty sad indictment I stopped counting some years ago. And maybe that's why last night was so very special."

He's waiting to hear it was different for me too. "Just lying next to you, being so close. I've never felt comfortable like that with anyone," I tell him. "If I wasn't so terrified I'd tell you I thought it was where I belonged."

"It is. And there's no reason whatsoever to be scared. Although there's a part of me that's petrified too."

I look at the coffee cups. "I think we're alike in lots of ways. A lot of the ways that matter, anyway."

He touches my cheek. "We're late coming to love so perhaps we're overthinking it. We wouldn't even be having this conversation if we were twenty-one."

"At twenty-one, I'd have been out of here hours ago. I thought staying the night was tantamount to commitment. We'll have our problems I'm sure. And we'll fight. But as long as we're honest and open with each other…"

"And considerate…"

"And kind…" I stop and laugh. "All the things I never thought a man could be."

"I'm glad I changed your mind."

I slap him on the arm. "Don't take all the credit. It was Jem who started it, by being such a good friend."

"Yes, but I get to reap the benefits." He grins and slides up the bed, kissing me long and slowly as his fingers skim my breast.

I reach around him and pull the dressing gown from his shoulders. "No," I murmur, "we do."

Even after Jonathan leaves for his meeting it's another long wait for the plumber. I've had an email from the ballistics expert detailing what he needs before his site visit and attached is a factsheet about digging where there might be ordnance. I scan its dire warnings about the potential for explosions, but I don't suppose there'll be any risk at Hemswell. From my reading I know the crash site would have been made safe and the bodies removed almost immediately and from the scant evidence I'm finding it seems they did a pretty comprehensive job.

For the first time I wonder where the airmen who died were buried and I have a strong urge to find out so I can take Jonathan to visit his grandfather's grave. A quick google search reveals most Polish fighters were laid to rest at Newark so perhaps he's there. But what about Freddie? Maybe Esther knows. As soon as that damned plumber comes back to do his stuff I'll go to see her.

Thankfully when he does the part fits easily and the boiler springs to life, the radiators gurgling happily as I pull on my anorak and head down the village. It's still raining but the forecast is better for the end of the week, which is just as well because I need to get back to Hemswell.

Esther is in her room and to me looks frail, the lamp behind her chair making her features gaunt, but she tells me it's nothing and with a wink asks how Jonathan is.

I feel the smile spreading across my face. "He was fine this morning — quite chilled in fact."

She raises an eyebrow. "This morning? Or am I reading too much into your choice of words?"

"No, you're not. And it's wonderful but at the same time I'm so frightened I'll get it wrong."

"Wrong? How?"

"Oh, I don't know. It's just so completely new to me — and so very precious."

"So have you decided it's love, Rachel?"

Rather than shrug off her question I consider carefully before I answer. "I can't think of anything else that would be making me feel this way."

"And Jonathan? Was I right?"

I nod. "'He does seem … committed — determined, almost."

"Rachel, I have to warn you — when Jonathan really wants something he has a good track record of getting it." She's laughing as she says it.

"The problem is, so do I. And when we want different things the sparks are bound to fly."

"Love's about compromise, Rachel, compromise and small concessions. Without ever feeling the other one's riding roughshod over you — or you're walking a tightrope. It's not easy, but I promise you it's worth it."

I laugh but I'm far from sure I can do as she says and changing the subject seems the safest option. "I told Jonathan about Freddie and Teo."

She leans forwards. "And what did he say?"

"He wants it kept a secret. His dad was very proud of being a Daubney and he wants him remembered that way. But I have a feeling he might come to ask you about his real grandparents."

"Have you given him the jacket?"

"Is it time?"

"I think so, yes."

"Esther, will you do it? I could leave it with you and when he asks..."

She shakes her head. "No, Rachel my dear, that wouldn't be right."

"I don't understand…"

"Neither do I. But it's what Freddie wants, I can feel it."

A silence fills the room, as though we are waiting for some sort of answer, but nothing comes. I reach out and hold Esther's hand, her wedding ring loose around her bony fingers. In the end I tell her about the Polish graves at Newark and ask if Teo's buried there.

"I'm afraid I don't know, but I suspect so because he isn't in the graveyard at Hemswell."

"What about Freddie?"

"My mother told me a cousin took care of her funeral and she was laid to rest near her parents' grave in Coventry. It's funny, for years I tucked them away at the back of my mind, but now they're so vivid, so real. Perhaps that's what happens when you get really old," she laughs. Suddenly she clutches my hand. "Theirs was such a brief spark, Rachel. Make sure that doesn't happen with you and Jonathan. I know you can never guard against fate, but at least promise me you'll try."

"I will, Esther, I really will."

I feel a little as though I'm playing truant, but the rain is making any meaningful work at Hemswell impossible and the smell of beer and damp coats is so very welcoming as I step onto the wooden floor of the Tap. Jem is perched on a stool at the bar with a pint in front of him and Toast on his lap, but the little dog barks when he sees me and Jem puts him down to skid across the polished planks, his lead trailing behind him.

I crouch to tousle his ears. "Hello, boy. How's my favourite boy?" He puts his paws on my thigh and plunges his nose into my crotch.

"Pleased to see you, by the look of it. As am I."

"He knows I'll have a cheese sandwich and he knows he'll get some."

Jem laughs. "And he knows I'll have a ploughman's and he'll get some of that too. In fact, shall I order while you find us a table? What are you drinking?"

"Pint of the guest ale please. It's not as if I'm driving."

"You're not?"

I glance up at him. "No. I'm staying at Jonathan's flat tonight."

He folds his arms. "Oh yes? And in what capacity, might I ask?"

I stand and unzip my anorak. "Not in the guest room."

While we eat he updates me on his own news. He tells me he is getting on rather well with his lodger and admits he's toying with the idea of moving things up a gear. I discover she was widowed two years ago and has mentioned she feels ready for a new relationship, but he doesn't want to rock the boat. Or barge, he says with a grin. I put my hand over his.

"Don't hold back, Jem. We've only got one life, after all, and finding the right person to share it with is important."

He rocks back. "Wow, coming from you, Rachel... What the hell has that Jonathan done to you?"

"I won't let him take all the credit," I laugh. "You started it. You made me see that men could be as caring and kind and as much fun to be with as girlfriends. You helped me to understand the problem was me, not the other fifty percent of the human race."

"Ben wasn't the best example."

I look down into my beer. "No, but he was definitely part of a pattern."

"I saw him the other day, you know. He had the cheek to come in here when we were playing."

"Really?"

"Yes. He was with the woman who owns that big restaurant near the castle. Twenty years older than him if she's a day, but apparently he was spouting off she's going to pay for him to retake his final year so that's obviously the attraction. Nothing changes."

"No, Jem. Change is difficult and you have to want to make it happen. Trust me, I learnt the hard way."

CHAPTER 51

Jonathan's head is bent low over a plan spread out on the coffee table. His finger traces the boundaries of a squashed oblong of land which is marked in red as he consults the notes at his side. Classic FM burbles in the background, a piano concerto I don't recognise.

I can hardly take my eyes off him, or the sweeping elegance of his apartment in the old mill. There isn't a single wall in the place that isn't curved and a wrought iron staircase rises from the open plan living space to the bedrooms above. Downstairs the brickwork has been exposed, giving the whole room a rich red glow which is echoed by the leather on the sofa and pair of armchairs.

I tuck my feet more firmly under me on and return to the archaeological report I've found on the remains of a Spitfire shot down during the Battle of Britain. It was a different sort of plane, but I still need more evidence for the ballistics expert and it might tell me more about what to look for. The fragments of metal I've found so far at Hemswell are indicative, but not conclusive and he's advised I dig more pits. I'm fast running out of days so I need to get back there whatever the weather throws at me.

"What's up?"

Did I sigh out loud? "Hemswell. I need more for the ballistics guy or we're wasting his time — not to mention your money. And he wants to visit next week because he's going away over Easter. The forecast's filthy for tomorrow and I'm worried even if I do go up there, in all the rain I might miss something."

He sits back and takes off his glasses, twirling them around his fingers. "What's it like at the weekend?"

I consult my app. "Better. Maybe some showers on Sunday but Saturday looks all right."

"Could I perhaps help you?"

"That really is above and beyond the call of duty, Mr Daubney."

"I'd like to, you know. It means so much more to me now." He turns to me. "That place is in my blood — literally."

I untuck my feet and stretch my legs in front of me, before standing to cross the wooden floor and joining him on the sofa. "How do you feel about it now you've had a little time to think?"

"It's like a jacket that doesn't quite fit, but you can't work out what's wrong with it. I have only the vaguest of memories of my Daubney grandparents, but I keep thinking about Dad and his family tree. All that work and he doesn't belong on it." He shakes his head and I take hold of his hand. He pulls mine to his lips and kisses it. "Anyway, it's not the most pressing thing in the world right now. But spending time at Hemswell would be great. You can show me the room where Esther and Freddie worked."

I close my eyes and squeeze his fingers. "It's not an ordinary room."

"How so?"

"You know I said I thought I'd seen Teo at the dig site? Well I think I've seen Freddie in that room. And Esther ... she certainly sensed her when we visited together, even smelt her perfume. We both did, but then it could be that someone had spilt some lily-of-the-valley somewhere and…"

"I wouldn't be surprised if some echo of Freddie was still there. Charlotte says Christopher comes to read to her when

263

everyone else is in bed. It was what he missed most, when he split up with Ruby, that quiet time when they were alone and he could watch her as she fell asleep. It creeped me out when she first told me, but who am I to question it? Who am I to say I understand and know everything, because I certainly don't."

This is the moment. I can almost feel Esther's hand on my arm — or is it Freddie's? "Follow me," I grab Jonathan's hand and pull him upstairs to where the flying jacket is folded in the bottom of my suitcase. I fling open the lid and haul it out. "Try this on."

He takes the jacket from me and spreads it over the bed, fingering the leather. "Where did it come from?"

"That room at Hemswell. I'd seen it there before but when I went with Esther it was the only thing on the rail and she said we should take it. It felt like stealing it to me, but she insisted. She said it was for you."

"Could it have been Teo's?"

I shake my head. "It's possible but unlikely. He should have been wearing his when the plane crashed, you see."

He nods then picks up the jacket, putting his arms into the sleeves and shrugging it over his shoulders before shaking it down. Head bent, he joins the ends of the zip together and tries to work it upwards. "I won't force it — it could do with a bit of grease or something." He nestles his chin into the tawny fur collar. "It feels amazing — almost as good as a hug from you."

It fits perfectly as well. "Turn around and walk away from me a little." His footsteps echo across the floorboards. I look at him again; the back of his head, the bulk of the jacket, his long legs. I recognise them all.

I follow him and wrap my arms around his waist. The sheepskin is yielding, soft and press my face into it. A hint of lily-of-the-valley lingers in my nose.

The spring sunshine does little to take the chill off the wind scouring west from the wolds, none of its venom lost by the time it reaches Hemswell. As we get out of the car at the dig site, Jonathan turns up the collar of his flying jacket and I pull my beanie hat down more firmly over my ears. He's certainly the one winning prizes for sartorial elegance this morning, but when I say so he laughs, cups my face in his hands, and tells me I'm beautiful.

I take the finds tray from the boot and we walk across the field to where my little plastic flags are struggling to stay upright. Having read the ballistics instructions I fiddled a bit with the settings on my metal detector and taught Jonathan how to use it and yesterday he pinpointed quite a scatter of targets. The two I've already excavated revealed twisted scraps bearing traces of the camouflage paint used on Wellingtons in World War Two and as we walk between the markers we decide who's going to dig where.

For the first pit he watches me, and I explain about stripping the grass and how to hold the trowel to scrape. The fragments are tiny, but as they're all likely to be metal it's easy even for an untrained eye to hone in on what we're looking for.

Jonathan is strangely quiet, but this is very likely the plane his grandfather died in. The blood that runs in his veins percolated down into this very earth. And ran across the floor of the barrack room toilet in rivers. I close my eyes for a moment as I scrape. Feeling someone else's pain. Yes, love's about that too.

I stand back to watch as Jonathan begins to excavate his first pit. I'm losing time, but I can't not let him help. The sun warms my back through my fleece, but high above clouds scud across the endless Lincolnshire skies. I scan the remaining flags. I'll let him take the two targets at the northern tip of the field while I tackle the three in an arc nearest the hedge. I tell him to call me if he finds anything and we cross the grass to mark out his squares.

Because the find is different, Jonathan passes right over it and I spot it lying on top of his spoil when I come back an hour later to check his progress.

"Where did this come from?" I ask.

He looks up. "What?"

"This." I point at the piece of chain with my trowel.

"It's lumps of metal we're looking for, isn't it?"

I put my hands on my hips. "It's anything that could have come off that plane."

He shakes his head. "It's far too small."

It is a tiny scrap, no more than an inch long — too fine to be from the engine but too rugged to be from a St Christopher or anything like that. "Everything matters, Jonathan. Everything. I don't want any short cuts because you're worried something we dig up might take time and money to unravel."

He throws down his trowel. "Oh, don't be ridiculous. This isn't about money, for god's sake. Not to me. Not now."

I crouch next to him. "I'm sorry."

Jonathan gazes at me for a long moment before suggesting we go for a coffee.

We straighten together and I tuck my arm into his. "Come on — I'll buy you a chocolate brownie to cheer you up."

He kisses the top of my head. "I'm sorry too."

The café in the antiques' centre is gearing up for a busy Saturday but we find a seat near the window and take off our coats before Jonathan heads for the counter. I watch him as he stands in the queue — a tall, lonely figure this morning. I look away and find myself gazing at the flying jacket. Just above the maker's label, nestled into the fur where the collar joins the back, is a small chain for hanging it on a hook.

I am fingering it as Jonathan puts the tray on the table. I turn to him. "Recognise this?"

He frowns. "Yes, It's like the one I missed. Oh god, Rachel…"

I nod. "It's so poignant — such a personal thing. One moment touching a man's neck and the next…"

Jonathan sits down heavily next to me. "It makes life seem so very fragile, somehow. Teo and Freddie had so much to live for … like we do, Rachel."

I squeeze his hand. "I know. But we're in no danger and there isn't a war on. Unless we make one ourselves."

"Then we need to try very hard not to."

When we leave the café half an hour later the corridor down the middle of the antiques' centre is crowded with shoppers, people studying the glass cases full of jewellery and glass making it hard for others to pass.

"This place is a nightmare," Jonathan mutters.

"It's because it's the weekend. Come on, the old laundry room isn't far."

The space at the bottom of the stairs is quieter, an elderly gentleman browsing one bookcase while in front of another a mother with a child in a pushchair is trying to find something with pictures to distract her. I walk straight past the former toilet, and the room next to it where four people are crammed together, thumbing through the prints stacked against the walls. Then I stop and turn to Jonathan. "This is it."

Sunlight streams through the window, illuminating the blank walls. The scrubbed table has gone, as has the rail. There is a smell of new paint and there's a laminated sign pinned to the door post: *Available to rent — ask at reception.* Even so, Jonathan walks past me, his footsteps echoing on the boards.

"Freddie, where are you?" I whisper, but at the same time I know. I cross the room and gaze out of the window at the endless sky. She and Teo are up there somewhere and fragments of a wartime poem come back to me: ... *footless halls of air... delirious, burning blue... touched the face of God...* My skin floods with goosebumps. Gran would say there was someone walking over my grave and I shudder. It should feel peaceful but *touched the face of God* is more like a premonition. I close my eyes and see Jonathan emerge from the fog.

But this is now, not then, and his arm is around my shoulder. "Thank you for showing me. Thank you for giving me the jacket."

I look up but the sunlight has already darkened his glasses over his pearl grey eyes. I nod. "Come on, let's go."

By the time we return to the field, the wind is whipping the clouds along and there's a distinct chill to the air. I put on my anorak but all Jonathan has is the flying jacket. He looks down at it as he tries to tease the zip together.

"I don't really want to get it dirty," he grumbles.

"Well you can always leave me to it."

He shakes his head. "That's not why I'm here. And anyway, they'll probably clean it when I take it in to have the zip mended."

I watch as he disappears across the field, trowel swinging in his hand. "And call me if you find anything — anything at all." He turns and makes a thumbs up before carrying on.

In the lea of the hedge the wind is less bitter and I crouch to record the location of the chain on my plan before turning my attention to removing the turf from my next target. The sparrows are chirping close by, but scatter as some walkers troop along the path, their footsteps and chat fading into the distance. Eventually I have a square of bare earth in front of me and I stand to see what Jonathan is doing.

For a moment I'm surprised to see he's standing at the far side of the field, gazing out across where the runways would have been, but then my heart leaps into my mouth. I turn my head and confirm my suspicion; Jonathan is crouched over his test pit.

I want him to see Teo, but I don't know what to do. If I call out, or move, will he simply fade away like he has those other times? But then he does something — something he's never done before — he turns to face me. He's too far away for me to make out his features, but I know what he wants.

"Jonathan," I call, trying to stop my voice from shaking. "Jonathan."

He looks up and I point towards where Teo is standing. I hold my breath as Jonathan turns, then collapses back into his pit with a thump. Quickly, he gathers himself and stands to walk towards his grandfather. I am frozen to the spot, my heart thudding in my chest as one young man in a flying jacket walks towards the other. Same height, same shape, same…

The explosion rocks the ground with a cloud of white smoke, earth flung high into the air and in all directions. I throw myself onto the grass, covering my head as fragments of soil rain down for what seems like forever but must only be a few seconds. As soon as they stop, I look up to see Jonathan has done the same, but he doesn't move when I do and it takes me only a few seconds to see there's something wrong.

I race across the field but it feels as if I'm caught in the slow motion whirlpool of a nightmare, stumbling over the tussocks of grass, gasping to retain the air in my lungs. As I approach I see a shard of metal embedded in the sheepskin, its lining spewing out on either side like puss. And there's blood. Not much, but enough.

I drop to my knees just as Jonathan begins to turn his head but my relief is short lived. The metal is dangerously close to his spine. I put my hands on his shoulders.

"Don't move. It looks like you've hurt your back." How I'm stopping my voice from shaking I'll never know.

"I … touched the face of an angel … in the sky … I danced the skies with an angel." His voice is muffled, his mouth half in the grass. Jesus.

I am fumbling for my phone when I hear running footsteps and the walkers appear on the other side of the hedge.

"Is he hurt? Shall I call an ambulance?" one calls.

"Please."

I kneel close to Jonathan, holding his shoulders. His face is grey, but his breathing is steady and the blood seeping from his back seems to have stopped. It's an age before he speaks and thankfully this time he's coherent.

"What happened?"

"Some sort of explosion… I don't know…" Maybe there was ordnance left after all. If he'd been any nearer when it went off… I swallow the bile that's lurched into my throat.

The siren wails in the distance and the afternoon is split by blue flashing lights. Two paramedics run across the field and I move out of their way, but my legs are too weak to stand so I sit on the grass, the dampness seeping into my digging trousers and the chill into my bones.

One talks to Jonathan while the other inspects the wound on his back. I watch as he teases the metal shard away. It's small, but lethally pointed. More blood oozes through the jacket but with their help Jonathan sits up and they lift it from his shoulders. He's starting to shake and with a pad of some sort clamped against his back they help him to his feet. Somehow I manage to do the same and trail after them to the ambulance.

The police arrive as we walk across the field, radios crackling as they leap from their car. I tell them we're digging the site of a World War Two bomber and it was probably unexploded ordnance of some sort so they cordon off the area. Why didn't I make Jonathan read the guidance? Why did I pay such scant attention to it myself? *Oh god, I could have killed him.*

Inside the ambulance Jonathan is sitting up, unbuttoning his shirt for the paramedic. I sit down on the bench opposite and watch as he rather awkwardly lies on his front. There's quite a lot of blood but the gash in his back is less than a centimetre long. Jonathan winces as the wound's cleaned, his face grey. All the same he tries to smile as he turns his head towards me. "Hey, Rachel, it's fine. Just stings a bit."

The paramedic is focussed on his task but he says, "He's right. It won't even need stitching. His jacket bore the brunt of it, that's for sure. If that piece of shrapnel had gone much deeper it could have damaged his spine really badly."

"And I have you to thank that it didn't." Jonathan's eyes meet mine. His pearl grey eyes. Teo's eyes.

I sink my head into my hands and weep.

Fragments of the poem haunt my uneasy sleep. The painkillers the paramedics gave Jonathan have made him dead to the world so I slip out of bed and pull his dressing gown around me before padding into his conservatory living room. I bury my nose in the collar as I wait for my laptop to warm up. It smells of him, and that is strangely comforting.

Two words in the search engine are enough. *High Flight.* I read the poem carefully, line by line:

Oh! I have slipped the surly bonds of Earth
And danced the skies on laughter-silvered wings;
Sunward I've climbed, and joined the tumbling mirth
Of sun-split clouds, — and done a hundred things
You have not dreamed of— wheeled and soared and swung
High in the sunlit silence.
Hov'ring there, I've chased the shouting wind along, and flung
My eager craft through footless halls of air...
Up, up the long, delirious burning blue
I've topped the wind-swept heights with easy grace
Where never lark, or ever eagle flew —
And, while with silent, lifting mind I've trod
The high untrespassed sanctity of space,
Put out my hand, and touched the face of God.

Past and present. War and love. Yes, the poem's about flying, but it could very well be about love. The freedom of it, the elation, the danger. Yes, I've slipped my surly bonds too. Will I do a hundred things I have not dreamed of? Top new wind-swept heights? Or simply crash and burn on take-off, like poor Teo did?

The difference is, I have a choice.

EPILOGUE

I park my car at the northern tip of the field and Jonathan leaps out to help Esther from the front seat. A large gap has been cut in the hedge to allow construction traffic through and he takes her arm as we negotiate the rough surface. Ahead of us the earth is scarred with a zigzag of joined oblongs and at the far end a cement lorry is pouring concrete, its grind and slush reaching us across the warm, still air.

A little to our right a circle about forty metres across is pegged out in the earth. The crater left by the explosion has long been filled in. Jonathan remembered finding a loop of metal just before I called to him, and from that and the scatter of debris the ballistics expert reckoned he discovered a Mills Bomb. Unusual for a bomber but not unheard of. They weren't meant to carry them but many airmen did for fear of their lives if they crash landed in enemy territory. The Poles in particular had a reputation for going out fighting.

The pegged circle marks where the crew will have their memorial. A memorial garden, to be precise. Somewhere for the people working in the starter units DSD is building to take their lunch, or their coffee, or just sit in quiet contemplation. Jonathan organised a competition for would-be architects and we're here on the seventy-fifth anniversary of the crash to choose the final design. And the prize? The very first Christopher Sinclair Scholarship.

I'm used to coming to the field but I'm still grateful it's changing. Now the building has started I won't ever be able to stand at the spot by the hedge and watch the explosion rip the air, turn to see Jonathan prone on the earth. Teo's gone too. I can feel it. And I'm glad.

"Rachel, are you coming?"

"Sorry." Jonathan and Esther are yards ahead of me and I lock the car and follow them.

He gives my arm a squeeze. "OK?"

I nod. "Fine. Perfectly fine. What do you think, Esther?"

"Well there's a great sense of busyness about the place, isn't there? I can hear the building work's making progress. How many units will there be, Jonathan?"

"Twelve, with communal meeting rooms and a chill out zone. For when it's too wet to come to the garden."

She smiles. "The garden is such a wonderful idea. From the tape I can see it looks like quite a large area."

"Well, it's part of my story, isn't it? Although only the three of us will ever know."

"So what do you say when people ask why you're doing it?"

He laughs. "Planning gain."

"What?"

"Planning gain. It's what developers do to make the council look more favourably on their plans, isn't it, Rachel?" he winks.

I don't answer him, just roll my eyes.

We walk Esther around the taped area then go to the café at the antiques' centre for tea. We choose a large table so we can arrange the shortlisted drawings side by side. Esther pulls out her magnifying glass to study them. The first has majestic swirls of raked white gravel, the centrepiece of which is a piece of roughhewn stone which would form the memorial. It's neat and beautiful, with cloud pruned shrubs alternating with stone benches around its edge. It has a timeless calm about it which I love, but Jonathan fears it would be too high maintenance.

The second is apparently in the style of a Polish formal garden. The young architect has credited a garden designer in his notes, so Jonathan worries much of the work isn't actually his. The effect would be stunning though, with bright blocks of colour surrounding a precision cut white marble obelisk. Two thirds of the circle is edged with a dry stone wall, which curves up from entrance path to a height of four feet and provides an impressive boundary to the space.

The final design is the one Jonathan has found least fault with, although we agree the decision has to be Esther's. I know why he likes it — in this one an architect's skill shines through the design of a wooden shelter which echoes the shape of the aircraft hangars and Jonathan's own building. The garden is bordered by a thick hedge of copper beech to keep out the wind and the memorial is a simple fountain with the names of the aircrew — and Freddie — carved around its circular base.

Esther is taking her task seriously, asking questions about each design, which Jonathan answers. I sit back and sip my tea, watching them, two of the people I love most in the world. Who'd have thought I'd be saying that? Six months ago Jonathan and I weren't even speaking. Six months ago men were no more than sex toys in my eyes. And then my past reached out and grabbed me by the throat and something — no, everything — had to change. Honestly, I feel quite proud of how far I've come.

Not that it's all a bed of roses. It can be blue murder working with Jonathan and more than once Caroline's had to play peacemaker when it comes to the shaping of Ward Daubney. The reality is we probably shouldn't be doing it at all, but professionally my future is so uncertain and I won't live off Jonathan's money, however wealthy he is. We argue about that too. But making up is glorious. And when we escape to Winteringham at weekends everything's different anyway.

"Really, Rachel — you're miles away today." Esther sounds quite sharp.

"Sorry." I put down my cup. "I'm listening."

"Well I hope so, because I think I know which one I like best, but we should decide together."

Jonathan shrugs. "No, it's up to you. Any one of the designs is fine by me." I mouth *liar* at him over Esther's bent head.

"I think it should be the one with the copper beech. The architect's clearly been here and thought about protecting the people using the garden from the elements. And I love the way the names go round and round at the bottom of fountain too, but there's just one thing I'd like changed. Do you think Freddie and Teo's names could be next to each other? Then I could imagine they're holding hands."

Jonathan grins at her. "Of course."

Esther stands. "Then shall we go and tell her?"

Together we make slow progress down the corridor, Esther leaning heavily on her stick. Past the glass cabinets, past the bookcases.

"I wonder if they've let the space yet?" I ask.

It seems that they have. A clothes rail has returned, but this time it's full of vintage wedding dresses. Four more are displayed on tailors' dummies around the room. My hand flies to my mouth. "Oh, lord. Do you think she'd mind?"

"Of course not," Esther replies. "Don't you like them?"

"I do — they're lovely — especially that 1920s one with all the beadwork."

"Do you want it?" Jonathan is leaning against the door jamb, a slow smile creeping across his face.

"Of course not — it's a wedding dress. When would I wear it?"

"My question still stands."

I look at him for a moment, then at Esther. "No, no way." I back away from him across the room. "No, no, no. Definitely — no."

He raises an eyebrow. "Really? You mean I'm wasting my time?" But he's still smiling.

I'm still shaking my head. Esther looks from one of us to the other, then takes Jonathan's arm.

"What I think Rachel really means is not yet. You mustn't pressurise her in this way — it's not fair. Whatever would your grandparents say?"

I look out of the window, at the endless blue of the sky. I know what they'd say — grab happiness while you can. And maybe I will. Not quite yet, but very, very soon.

"Thank you, Esther," I whisper. "Thank you, Freddie. Thank you, Teo."

HISTORICAL NOTES

The World War Two aspect of *Endless Skies*, like the book itself, was inspired by a place. The former RAF station at Hemswell now has many uses; part industrial estate, part residential, but it's most famous for its antiques' centres and Sunday markets. The most fascinating thing about it is that the layout of the base is still much in evidence, with buildings and hangars repurposed rather than torn down and the parade ground becoming the central car park.

A walk around Hemswell Antique Centres is a step back in time. Not just because of the contents, but the way their buildings' characters have been retained. Three of them were barrack blocks and you can sense the history as you walk around them. Close your eyes and you really can hear the airmen's footsteps in the corridors — or at least, I thought I could.

Hemswell was an RAF base before the war and on 3rd September 1939 it was the only airfield in North Lincolnshire ready to take part, so their bombers were amongst the first to be used in anger. But the period I was interested in came a little later, because from July 1941 until June 1943 the station was given over to three Polish squadrons. They were equipped with Wellingtons and had a reputation for being brave, if a little reckless. In the spring and early summer of 1942 they suffered enormous losses, following which the remaining crews were put on much safer minelaying duties. It didn't take a great deal of research to discover that Hemswell reputedly has its ghosts — including objects being moved and the sound of bombers overhead — but it goes without saying Freddie and Teo, both now and then, are completely fictional.

A NOTE TO THE READER

Thank you for investing your precious time and money in *Endless Skies*, and if you have reached the end I sincerely hope you enjoyed it. If you feel so inclined, reviews on Amazon and Goodreads are important to authors. It's not about basking in five star glory (although that is rather nice), it's about learning how to improve our work. Reviews don't have to be lengthy or erudite — a few words will do — but rest assured they are all appreciated.

Endless Skies came about because my husband Jim and I are avid fans of *The Great British Menu*. But the book has nothing to do with food, I hear you cry. Quite so, but all the same it's true. Back in 2014 a chef called Colin McGurran earned a place to cook in the final banquet for the second time, and to celebrate ran a Facebook competition to win a stay at his Lincolnshire restaurant, Winteringham Fields. Jim entered — as did very many other people — and we were both delighted and surprised when he won. As soon as we arrived, we know we were in a magical place. Not just the restaurant, but the village of Winteringham itself, a peaceful enclave close to the River Humber, under the widest skies we had ever seen. It was a roasting hot afternoon and we went for a walk, but the weather broke as we crossed a field of stubble, the rain sounding just like footsteps chasing us. I was inspired.

Endless Skies was not an easy book to write. There were three of four different versions along the way, but in each one the relationship between Rachel and Jonathan became richer and better defined. They fell in love, and I fell in love with their story, but it needed something more and I struggled this way and that, increasingly desperate to find it. We've visited

Winteringham Fields several times, including for our twentieth wedding anniversary and for Jim's fiftieth birthday. It was during this last trip the jigsaw fell into place. My present to Jim was to spend a day in the kitchen with Colin and his team and I made myself scarce to browse the antiques' centres at Hemswell. I was intrigued it was a former RAF base and as I was walking around I just knew it was where Esther had spent her war. Sapere were already in the process of acquiring *Another You* and wanted a second book, and suddenly it felt entirely logical that this one would look back to World War Two as well. The poem *High Flight* by wartime pilot John Gillespie Magee is well known and much used in literature, but has an extra poignancy for me because Magee was killed in a mid-air collision over Lincolnshire. There is a theory that some of the imagery in the poem comes from high altitude hypoxia, when lack of oxygen can cause hallucinations, an idea I used in the prologue.

The character of Esther is based entirely on my mother. I lost her in February 2015 and on the morning she died she asked what my next book would be. I told her it was a story about an archaeologist — and she approved. Mum was bright, and brave, with a huge interest in other people, and while ageing gracefully she never sought to come to terms with being old and I wanted to pay tribute to her. The book is also dedicated to Jim's uncle, John Reeve, an artist and farmer who had a lifelong passion for wartime aircraft and who died as I was working on the final edits.

If you have any questions about *Endless Skies* or would like to consider it for your book club, please contact me via **Twitter: @JaneCable**, **Facebook: Jane Cable, Author**, or my website **janecable.com**.

Jane Cable

Sapere Books is an exciting new publisher of brilliant fiction and popular history.

To find out more about our latest releases and our monthly bargain books visit our website:
saperebooks.com

Printed in Great Britain
by Amazon